"A sparkling fantasy."

— KIRKUS REVIEWS (FOR THE WITCH'S TOWER)

"Grantham is prepared to make her mark in the urban fantasy scene with this one."

— READERS' FAVORITE REVIEWS (FOR DREAMTHIEF)

"Springs to life from the very first sentence."

— IND'TALE MAGAZINE (FOR SILVERWITCH)

PRAISE FOR THE END OF NEVER AND TAMARA GRANTHAM

"*The End of Never* is filled with well-written characters on an incredible journey, unpredictable twists and turns that keep you guessing, and brilliant, detailed descriptions that leave you with a happy ending."

— VICTORIA ZUMBRUM, *PEN BOOKS REVIEWS*

"*The End of Never* is an incredible journey. The amazing worldbuilding is full of wonderful twists and turns. This fun adventure was so full of fantastic detail I felt I was there at times."

— ANGELA FIRUCCIA, *BOOKBUB*

"*The 7th Lie* is a surprising combination of fantasy and science fiction. The imaginative characters and settings are fantastic, and the answers to the mystery of the domed city were definitely not expected."

— WCJ, *GOODREADS*

"Part *Twilight*, part *Beauty and the Beast*, readers will eat up the lush settings, mystery, and romance of *Never Call Me Vampire*. Tamara Grantham has created a high-stakes story rich with history, myth, and legend."

— ANGELA LARKIN, CO-AUTHOR OF THE *BEYOND SERIES*

"[T]he plot is suspense-laden, delivering the perfect adrenaline-filled cocktail for an entertaining and exciting read. The characters display a near-perfect balance between normal and paranormal traits….Readers will love the delightful ending…"

— JM LAREEN, *IND'TALE MAGAZINE* (FOR *NEVER CALL ME VAMPIRE*)

"I found *Never Call Me Vampire* mesmerizing and worth reading in one sitting. Tamara Grantham takes the enchanting theme of vampires and builds on their reputation and thrilling mystique to create a novel that will haunt you until it is finished…I could not put this book down and look forward to seeing what could happen next at Crimson Hollow."

— PEGGY JO WIPF, *READERS FAVORITE*

"*Never Call Me Vampire*…is the amazing start of a promising paranormal series. If you've been longing for a good vampire novel with a new spin, your search ends here….Grantham throws off the shackles of traditional vampire stories and gives us one that we can sink our teeth into….This author is exceptionally skilled at building a world we can believe in…"

— TAMMY RUGGLES

"[T]his story works well because of the value that Tamara Grantham adds to the theme, which makes it hard to put down once you start reading."

— VINCENT DUBLADO (FOR *NEVER CALL ME VAMPIRE*)

THE END OF NEVER

THE END OF NEVER

THE CHRONICLES OF ITHICAL
BOOK TWO

TAMARA GRANTHAM

For my sister, Andrea Daws

All we have to decide is what to do with the time that is given to us.

— J.R.R. TOLKEIN

1

The metal cable burned my palms as I dangled from the two-hundred-foot drop. Long strands of dark hair stuck to my sweat-dampened face, but I refused to loosen my hold on the cord.

"Sabine." Cade's voice cut through the static of my headset. "Fifty feet to go."

"Understood." I slid down an inch, then another. The lights on my helmet didn't illuminate the cave's floor. I could've been descending into the abyss of Hades for all I knew. There was a reason thieves had picked this place to mine cerecite—it was nearly impossible to access, which made me wonder how they planned to get their stolen ore topside.

"Almost there," Cade said. "What do you see?"

"Rocks," I answered.

I couldn't find it in my heart to be polite to Cade MacDougall, who'd nearly killed me six months earlier. Though it turned out he'd had his reasons, I found it hard to trust him. And I wasn't sure I'd ever get to that point.

My light shone on the granite stones enclosing me in their tomb. I breathed through the panic of claustrophobia tightening in my chest. My hands slipped on the cord, and I dropped a foot. My stomach bottomed out, and I cursed as I caught myself. The harness tightened around my ribs.

"You okay?" Cade asked.

I ground my teeth. "Fine. Lost my grip. Next time we do this, remind me to wear gloves."

"Next time? This is the last time I'm doing anything like this. Sorry, but I've got better things to do than chase criminals."

"Like plant flowers?" I asked.

"Exactly." His voice held a hint of humor. "You know me too well."

I couldn't help but smile. He'd been the charming, unassuming palace gardener before I learned he'd been born in the future and worked as a miner on Ceres; he'd tried to sabotage the gateway; and he worked to keep Ithical a secret from Earth by murdering anyone who would expose his world. Despite it all, he managed to redeem himself and was now working to stop the thieves stealing cerecite.

Goose bumps formed on my arms, and I found myself trembling as the air chilled around me. The squeak of the cable running through pulleys echoed through the empty shaft running deep into the center of the dwarf planet Ceres.

Ceres.

Though I still had trouble believing I was somewhere other than Earth, coming back had filled a hole in my heart, and I couldn't help but think I belonged. Ceres had become a part of me, and protecting it kept me moving downward into the abyss.

My feet touched bottom. Breathing a sigh of relief, I unhooked the carabiner from the cable, then I smoothed my sweaty palms over my nylon vest.

"Made it."

"Good. There should be a pathway directly behind you. Do you see it?"

I turned to face the wall, my light's beam shining on a

narrow sliver of a tunnel cutting through the rock. My combat boots splashed through puddles, and dripping water echoed as I approached the shaft and entered the passage.

Darkness closed in around me. I pressed my hands to the stone, its coldness helping to ground me. I ducked as the ceiling dropped. My shoulders brushed the walls. How had anyone fit through here? If they were planning to steal cerecite, how would they manage to smuggle it out? That was a question Vortech wanted answered, and somehow, I was supposed to find out.

"We're sure this is the right cave?" I asked.

"Yes," Cade answered. "Keep going. The tunnel will widen soon. Once you enter the main chamber, use extreme caution. That's where the majority of the cerecite ore is located. If they're here, that's where they'll be."

"Got it."

"Remember. Don't confront them. This is an information mission only. We need to know how they got in here, who they are, and who they're working for."

"No need to remind me. I'm not fond of confronting angry miners. One too many bad experiences with it, you know."

"I remember," he said, and I thought I could hear a trace of remorse through the headset.

As I turned sideways to pass through the tunnel, an image of Cade standing over me with his yellow cerecite blade flashed through my memory. Shuddering, I did my best to push away the thought.

"I had my reasons, you know," he said. "Plus, I've apologized. A million times now."

"I know." I bit my lip to keep from saying anything else. This was a topic I'd rather not discuss.

The tunnel widened. Soft gray light came from up ahead. "I'm in," I whispered.

"Good. You've got the camera?"

I reached inside my vest pocket and pulled out the slim metal case. A rock outcropping blocked my path, and I crept toward it. Voices and the clanking of machinery drifted from below. I peeked over the stones and peered down into a concave bowl at the bottom of the cave.

Floodlights illuminated the trucks running on track wheels. Yellow crystals glittered from the bed of a truck. Half-a-dozen men with shovels and pickaxes crowded around the cave. Clanging metal echoed through the naturally carved amphitheater. The air held the acrid scent of engine grease.

"I see them," I whispered through my headset. "I count six men. Three trucks. One is fully loaded with cerecite. Cade, it's yellow cerecite."

Cade cursed. "They've managed to fill a whole truckload?"

"Yes."

"This isn't good. That's enough to wipe out half the capital."

"Agreed."

"Do you see any other access points?"

I scanned the cavern, focusing on the smallest details, allowing my ability to help in my search. Doctors said I had something called ECP. Extra Cognitive Perception. It helped me look for details others overlooked. It also made me obsessive, but I'd learned to live with it. My focus snagged on every detail, from the yellow crystals glinting from granite walls to the minute details of the pockmarks in the rocks, forcing me to count every pillar. I had to stop myself before it became an obsession, so I turned my focus to the thick walls of stone. There weren't any openings except the one I'd entered through.

"I don't see any. But I barely managed to fit through the tunnel in here. How did *they* get in?"

"That's what we're trying to find out. You've got to get a photo of every person in there. We need to be able to identify them and hopefully find out how they got inside in the process."

"Agreed, but I won't be able to get any detailed pictures from up here. I'll have to climb down."

"Fine. Just be careful. Get in and get out quietly. If they see you, this mission is blown."

"Got it." I snuck down a path leading through the boulders. Crystalline pillars towered over me, casting their soft light on the rocky ground. I placed one foot in front of the other, staying close to the inside wall to block the miners from seeing me, which also meant I couldn't get a good view of them.

The path trailed away from the wall. I pressed my body against the protruding stones and peeked around the edge. Some of the men shouted at each other in a foreign language. I didn't recognize any of the words, but I paid attention to their inflections. An Arabic tone carried through their accents.

I didn't know of anyone on Ithical speaking Arabic, which meant these men were most likely from Earth. Vortech had suspected the same thing, and now I'd be able to confirm which world they came from. Still, I had no way of identifying them or who they worked for.

Grasping the old-fashioned instamatic camera, I snuck around the wall and crept along the floor. I knelt on the stony ground and held the camera to my eyes, focusing through the lens, though I still couldn't distinguish their facial features.

Gritty sand stuck to my palms as I continued down toward the cave's bottom. Boulders rose around me, hiding me—at least partially—from view. I made it halfway to the bottom when I stopped again.

The ground sloped, and I propped against a rock to keep my balance as I focused the lens on the workers. My camera clicked every time I pressed the button, and shiny slips of polaroid paper reeled out like receipts from a cash register.

Vortech didn't want anything digital. They'd had a

massive data breach two months earlier, and hackers had taken maps of Ceres and mining locations. Vortech learned anything sent digitally through the wormhole portal was completely vulnerable to cyber-attack. Not even their top tech whizzes could create an encryption system that withstood the wormhole. Consequently, Vortech now demanded all information be on paper and hand delivered back to their headquarters in L.A.

Technologically speaking, it felt like stepping back half a century. But there was nothing I could do about my employer's methods. I'd learned long ago I had to play by their rules if I wanted a paycheck, so I went along. For now.

"Getting anything?" Cade asked quietly through my headset.

"Pictures of four of the miners. Pretty sure they're from Earth. They're speaking what sounded like an Arabic language. Two are headed to the other side of the cave."

I followed the movements of the two who walked toward a rocky outcropping hidden in shadows from the glare of the floodlights. I held the camera up, zooming in, but only got a view of their backs as their forms grew smaller.

"I'll have to move in closer," I said.

"Just stay invisible," Cade said.

"I will."

The path sloped to a near-vertical angle, and I held to the rocks to keep from falling. Stones slipped under my feet. Rocks clattered to the cave's floor. I froze.

The men below me didn't look up. The roar of their truck's engines overpowered any other sounds.

"What was that?" Cade asked.

"A few stones fell. I'm fine." My already blistered hands burned as I climbed down to the bottom. I stopped when I reached a boulder. Hiding behind it, I peeked over. The four men gathered around the track vehicles. They held shovels and piled yellow crystals into the back.

Discarded laptops lay on the ground near me.

My heart pounded with unexpected anxiety.

"Cade." I spoke quietly into the headset.

"Yes?"

"They've got laptops. I think I can grab one."

"I don't know. What if they see you?"

"They won't."

"They will if you stay too long."

I hesitated behind the boulder, my gaze fixed on the laptop nearest me—a thick metal construction with lights blinking at the edges, tempting me to grab it. "What if I grab it and put it in my backpack? We can access it later. They'll never know I took it. Plus, there's a good chance it'll have information on how they got in here. Don't you think it's worth a shot?"

"Fine." He sighed. "But you're taking the heat if this goes south."

"All right. But you've got nothing to worry about." I crept away from the boulder, making sure the men kept their backs turned as they shoveled yellow crystals. *Five feet to the laptop, four, three...*

The roar of engines quieted.

I held my breath, frozen to the spot.

"Sabine?" Cade's voice whispered through my headset.

I didn't answer, clenching my jaw as a man exited the cab of the loaded truck. Seconds ticked past before one of the empty trucks moved to take the place of the first.

The men continued shoveling as if automatons. None looked in my direction. I grabbed the laptop before over-thinking it, the metal casing warm, then escaped back to the shelter of the boulder.

I unzipped my bag and stuffed the laptop inside. "I got it," I breathed.

"Good. They didn't see you?"

I zipped up my bag. "I told you. Nothing to worry about."

He grumbled under his breath. "Just get the rest of those photos and get out of there."

"On it." A coating of sandy grit stuck to my fingers as I held my camera and took several more pictures. Photos spat quietly from the camera. After placing the metal device in my pocket, I edged along behind the rocks, heading toward the fissure where the two men had disappeared.

As I skulked behind the larger boulders, the roar of the engines faded again. A level field of smooth stones spanned toward the outcropping where two men stood talking. Their voices carried, and they spoke in English. Without the shelter of the boulders, I would have a hard time hiding. I scanned the place.

My only option was to edge along the back wall until I made it near the outer edge of the outcropping. I wouldn't get a good view of the men from that angle, but what other choice did I have?

My heart quickened as I crept along the wall, pressing my back to the plane of cold stone until I neared the entrance. I stood in an alcove sheltering me from view of the two men, but also making it impossible to get any pictures, so I focused on their conversation instead.

"…back to Russia for processing."

"That takes too long."

"We're patient."

"Of course, you can afford to be. You're not the one depending on this."

Their voices lowered to whispers, and I couldn't make out the words. One of the men spoke with an accent. Not Arabic. Asian. Japanese, maybe? He also spoke quietly, though his words had a commanding presence.

"…if you didn't return."

"Why do you say that?"

"Too much knowledge is a dangerous thing."

The *smack* of a slamming fist echoed. Screaming pierced

the air for half a second, then abruptly cut off, replaced with gurgling.

"…*traitor.*"

I peeked around the edge. An older man with a hardened, leathery face pulled a knife from a sheath at his belt. He thrust it at the other miner—one with a braided goatee, who jumped back with the grace of a panther, light on his feet, as if he were a trained fighter.

The older man's blade cut at the younger miner's neck, nicking flesh, severing the necklace the man wore. Something gleamed and scattered across the floor, coming to rest near my feet.

A pyramid-shaped pendant glinted with facets of gold and black.

Cade wore an exact match to this pendant. He said he'd found it in a cave. I'd never found out its significance, if there was any. But this…. Didn't this mean it was important?

I snatched up the pendant and stuffed it in my pocket.

The men fell to the ground, fighting and growling as they clawed relentlessly at one another.

I snapped three pictures before backing away.

The brawl had drawn the attention of the others, who raced toward the fighters. As they did, I searched for an escape. I couldn't go back the way I came; they'd see me. Panicked, I spun around and peered up at the wall. Solid rock. A few handholds. Were there enough?

I didn't have time to decide. Frantic shouts echoed, and several miners charged toward me. I sprinted, grasping at any handholds I could find. Muscles burned as I climbed up, one inch after another. My sweat-slicked palms slipped on rocks, yet I managed to dig my nails into stone and plant my feet firmly.

"They spotted me," I hissed to Cade.

"Get out of there!"

My breath came in short bursts. My knees and shins bumped the unyielding rock, cutting and bruising my flesh.

A gunshot rang out. Stone chipped from the wall near my head.

Focus. Just keep climbing.

"Was that a gunshot?" Cade asked.

I ignored him, concentrating on climbing. Adrenaline pulsed through my blood. The top ridge of the wall appeared above me. Another shot blasted below me.

Shouts echoed over the chaos of the rumbling engines, though I barely heard any of it over the pounding of my heart.

Keep going.

I reached for the top, though my fingers were a few inches too short, and I was forced to find another handhold and maneuver upward.

Rocks crumbled as I grabbed the ledge and pulled my body over the top. I rolled away from the drop. Breathing heavily, I laid on my back, my pack pressing into my shoulder blades.

It only took a second before I got to my feet. Racing to the tunnel, I watched the cavern blur past. Voices echoed, and more gunshots fired, but I ignored everything to focus only on escape.

When I reached the narrow crevasse, I edged inside, my bag bulkier than it had been earlier. I took it off and held it with an iron grip.

Chancing a glance over my shoulder, I spotted several men's heads peeking over the ledge.

I didn't look back again. A bullet punched through the rocks above me, sending pebbles and sand raining down. Sharp stones pelted my head and shoulders, but the pain didn't register.

"Sabine, what's happening? Where are you?"

"Almost… back to the cable," I breathed heavily, my windpipe choked by clouds of sand. I burst free of the tunnel. The metal cable glinted in my helmet's light—a shining thread to freedom.

My heart thudded so fast I feared it would burst by the time I reached the dangling cord. My hands shook as I grabbed the carabiner. It took three tries before I got the harness connected.

"*Stop!*" a man's voice yelled behind me.

"Cade! Pull me up," I yelled.

The ground fell away as the cable yanked me up, so fast my breath stuttered. More shots exploded. I held the backpack tight to my chest, feeling the weight of the miner's laptop inside.

The gunshots ceased abruptly, leaving my ears ringing.

I chanced a glimpse below me.

One miner stood looking up—the man with the braided goatee. I only got a moment to look at him, but the intensity of his gaze held mine. His angular face and dark, slanted eyes hinted at Asian ancestry. His gaze lingered on mine, and I felt a furious promise in his knowing glance.

"I'll find out who you are." His deep voice was calm, and he spoke with certainty.

I didn't bother to reply. Any information I gave him would be too much.

He clenched his fists. "You'll regret meeting me."

2

Cade swabbed the alcohol wipe over my shoulder.

"Ouch." I winced.

He gave me a tight-lipped smile. "Almost done."

I bit my lip, then focused on the view out the palace window to stay distracted. The towering ornate buildings of Ithical city rose against the purple sky. Light rails wrapped the city in a complicated web as trains ran along the lighted tracks. The engines rumbled faintly through the glass.

We'd made it out of the cave without detection, but a lingering fear had needled in the back of my mind, and the stare of the miner with the braided goatee stayed with me. The ride back the palace had gone by in a blur, although I still marveled as we'd passed by barren landscapes that could have been stolen from the surface of the moon, and back to civilization, where the residents of Ithical lived secluded under their dome.

After making it back to the palace, we sat in the comfort of the healer's room. The sharp scent of antiseptic mingled with the sage-smelling aroma of healing herbs. Gray stone walls were softened by sconces burning blue cerecite. Bottles and jars sat on shelves lining the walls. Most were filled with a solution of green cerecite, which the people of Ithical used for healing.

I still marveled at how quickly the palace had been rebuilt after the miner's revolution. The building blocks of cerecite had sped up that process, and it made me realize how valuable a commodity cerecite could be—and why there were those determined to steal it.

"You were reckless back there, Sabine." Cade placed the wipe aside to give me a stern glare. I couldn't meet his penetrating gaze, so I turned to stare at the floor instead. His eyes had always unnerved me anyway. Turquoise blue sparkled too brightly in an unnatural way, almost as if he weren't human. Since I'd learned he could transform into a cerecite dragon at will, I supposed that made sense.

"I got the photos, didn't I? Plus… I got that." I pointed to the metal case sitting on the table.

"Yes, but at what cost? They saw you. They'll find out who you are and come after you."

"Then let's find out who they are first."

Cade sighed, running his hand through his sandy blond hair, leaving it mussed and sticking up at odd angles. "Why did I agree to this again?"

"Because you're trying to protect Ceres. It's what you've always done, although I don't agree with some of the methods you've implemented."

"For the millionth time, I apologized for that." His eyes didn't meet mine as he gathered the soiled wipes and gauze.

"Are you mad at me?"

His sigh told me I was wearing down his patience. "No."

"Then what's the matter?"

"You've put yourself in danger and I don't know how we're supposed to fix this. They nearly shot you. You could've been killed."

"But I wasn't, so let's not worry about it."

He shook his head. "It's not that simple."

His worrying annoyed me. I much preferred having conversations with Morven, who knew better than to dwell on the past, who made me laugh in situations like these. But he'd been spending more time on Earth, and when he was here, he practically lived in the library. He had promised to meet me for dinner tonight, and I fully intended to enjoy every second with him.

Cade's gaze went to the window, and his brows furrowed as if deep in thought. His expression brought back memories of the fierce intensity I'd seen in his eyes when he'd trapped me in his home and nearly killed me. A tingle of fear shot down my spine. I knew that look. He would do whatever it took to protect his world.

"I understand how you feel," I said, attempting to pull him away from that place he went whenever he thought about Ceres.

"Do you?" he asked sharply.

"Of course, I do. This is your home."

He sighed. "It's more than that." He stood and walked to the window, his face reflected in the glass. The city spanned, and beyond it, the sloping mountains of Ceres, hills turned blue against a hazy sky.

"This is a special place, Sabine." He spoke softly, wistful. "There's a reason I work with cerecite to cultivate seeds and grow the plants. This place was once a wasteland, and now it's a utopia. There's nowhere else in the universe like it. It's unique and beautiful, and the people here don't even realize how special it is—don't even know they're somewhere other than Earth. We have to keep it that way." He turned to look at me, and the fire in his gaze caught me off guard. "I've worked my entire life to protect this place, and as you know, that's been a while."

"Yeah, hundreds of years. I get it."

He shook his head. "I don't think you do. No one does. But that's okay. I've already killed too many to protect this place. I won't do that anymore, but I also won't allow my home to be mined into oblivion. I hope you understand that."

"I do, Cade."

"I hope so. When the time comes, I hope you do."

His words held a pleading tone—a warning. I stood and crossed to him, then took his hand and squeezed it. I'd never felt anything romantic for him. He was more like a brother to me. But I had to show him that I meant what I said.

"Cade, I realize I don't understand Ceres as well as you. I don't share the same connection you have. I've only been here six months; you've lived hundreds of years here. But I give you my word, I'll do what it takes to keep it and the people safe."

His forehead creased. "Do you mean that?"

"Every word," I said solemnly.

He glanced away, and I couldn't be sure if he believed me. But I knew, deep in my heart, what a special world this was. I'd only been here a little while, but that didn't mean I hadn't created a bond with it. Time didn't make a difference on Ceres. It had become my home, and I wouldn't rest until it was safe.

How could I convince Cade that I meant what I said? Maybe I couldn't. Not with words, anyway.

I stood and turned toward the door. "I'll go now."

"Yeah. Okay." He didn't turn to look at me.

I reached down for the laptop when the pyramid pendant I'd taken from the miner dangled from my neck.

Cade caught the motion, and his forehead scrunched in a gesture of curiosity. "What's that?"

I grasped the necklace. "It belonged to one of the miners. It looks like yours."

He walked guardedly to me, his eyes wide with surprise. "You took it from a miner?"

"Yes. They were fighting. The cord broke."

"Why'd you take it?"

I removed the necklace, the leather tied where it had been

severed. "Because it was odd that he wore one the same as yours." I glanced up at him. "What do you make of it? What's the significance?"

I handed it to him, and he inspected the pyramid. Golden bands of glittering light spiraled through obsidian. Like Cade's, the bands of gold moved fluidly as if by magic.

Cade shook his head. "I never found out anything about it."

"You said your da found it in the mines."

"Yeah…" He gave a nonchalant shrug. "I lied about that. Never had a dad. Not on this world, anyway."

I shot him a suspicious glare, although his admission didn't surprise. He'd told more than his fair share of lies since I'd met him. His entire past had been a lie until I'd learned the truth—that he'd been a miner from Earth, born in the future until he'd enlisted to work for Project Ceres. He'd come here, working to mine raw cerecite ore, when an explosion had sent him back in time.

He handed it back to me, then pulled at the chain around his neck, revealing his own pyramid pendant. "I found it in the mines when I worked for NASA. I never knew if it had any significance. It's just a trinket, really."

I eyed him. "A trinket?" Did he really expect me to believe it was a worthless knickknack? "Yours came from the future. Don't you think this one might have, too?"

"Yeah, but Morven and I were the only ones to survive the explosion that sent us into the past. More likely he found it while mining."

"You don't think it's remotely possible the miner is from the future?"

His shoulders stiffened. "Not possible, Sabine. Time travel happened only once, through a major fluke—and only two of us survived. If the miner came from the future, don't you think I would know about him?"

"Then how did that miner get this?" I asked.

"The same way I did. He found it. End of story."

I bit my lip to keep from snapping at him. "It's not the end of the story. You're hiding something."

He frowned. "Hiding something?"

"Yes." I put the leather cord back around my neck and tucked the pendant under my shirt.

Cade crossed his arms defensively. "I'm being honest with you. I don't know anything about that pendant. About either of them."

"We'll see." I grabbed the miner's laptop and headed for the door. The metal case had grown cold in the air of the healer's room. I left without giving him another glance.

3

L ight shone from blue cerecite stones tucked inside glass sconces. Their glow encompassed the hallway as I passed by closed doorways. Walking to the library, I hoped to catch Morven before dinner, get his thoughts on the pendants, and hopefully get some insight on why Cade would lie about them.

My heart gave the tiniest of flutters as I approached the passage leading to the library. I hadn't spent much time with Morven since our last trip back to Earth. He'd admitted he had feelings for me, and I'd said the same, but we'd been too busy for any sort of relationship.

Heavy bronze doors stood ajar at the end of the antechamber. When I stepped into the quiet space, the scents of oiled leather and old paper greeted me. Scrolls were stacked neatly on the shelves.

A globe caught my eye. It sat on an ornate table in a corner, and I went closer to it. The sphere was made of cerecite—blue cerecite for the oceans, and green for land. At the globe's top, on an island above Russia, was a white opal representing Champ Island. I ran my fingers over the smooth stone, focused on the pearlescent sheen of the semi-precious stone.

When I'd arrived on Champ Island to start my training, I'd hardly expected to be transported all the way from Champ Island on Earth to the dwarf planet Ceres in the asteroid belt, or to find a hidden civilization under a dome. The Scottish ship that had crashed on Champ over two-centuries ago remained frozen at the top of the world, its inhabitants unknowingly sucked into a portal millions of miles away, where they'd remained here, tucked away inside the asteroid belt, never knowing their true home.

Above the globe, a painting took up most of the wall. It was a depiction of the original ship that had crashed on Champ Island. The image was so lifelike, I could almost feel the freezing ocean spray on my face, the snow beneath my feet, as a scraggly group of survivors filed off the ship and onto the shore of an island that would become their home.

I shook my head and stepped away from the globe and the painting. I had a mission to complete, and I wondered if I'd ever have time to explore Ithical without the threat of annihilation hanging over my head.

Light filtered through two-story windows at the back of the room. Through their panes, I could see a purple-tinged sky, one that never looked quite the same shade as the real sky back on Earth. Beneath the window, overstuffed leather chairs had been arranged. A few select shelves sat along the wall. They held a scanty row of ancient books with tattered binding. Could they be original books brought from Scotland?

I gazed at the embossed titles. *Scotland through the Middle Ages. The House of Tremayne. The Mystery of Cerecite.*

After wandering away from the shelves, I found Morven hunched over a table strewn with scrolls and open books. His black-clad frame was still thin, though more filled out than when he'd been in the wheelchair. Pale white skin contrasted with dark eyes and hair.

When his hooded gaze met mine, I reminded myself to breathe.

He's human.

Still, the intensity in his eyes spoke of *more*. More intelligence, more intuition, more seductive than I cared to admit. Although I'd gotten to know him, there was still an air of mystery that intrigued me.

"Sabine?" His deep, velvety voice made a shiver dance down my spine.

"He-ey." I attempted casualness, but my voice cracked, and I cleared my throat. "Um, hey."

He arched an eyebrow. "You okay?"

"Fine." I sat in the chair beside the desk. The laptop's metal case rattled as I placed it on the tabletop.

"What's that?" he asked.

"It belongs to miners illegally stealing cerecite." I motioned to the laptop. "I may have… borrowed it… from them."

He lifted an eyebrow, a bemused grin tugging at his full lips. "Borrowed it, huh?"

"Yeah." I scratched my cheek. "I'm hoping to find out who they are and how to stop them."

"Is it encrypted?"

"I don't know yet."

I pried the lid open—heavier than it looked, to reveal a blank blue screen. The boxy construction seemed to be made of solid iron, not a plastic device like the ones back home. "Odd computer. I've never seen one like this on Earth."

"I've never seen one like it on Ithical," Morven said.

"Maybe it's especially for mining operations?"

"Maybe."

Words appeared on the screen.

Initiate operations…

The words disappeared, followed with scrolling code.

Morven waited beside me. "How long does this take?" he asked.

"I don't know." I pressed a key, then hit ENTER, but the

code continued scrolling at a dizzying rate. I tried a few more buttons, but nothing registered.

"What's that say?" Morven pointed at the screen.

"It's computer code. HTML. You'd need a serious computer geek to translate it."

"Ah. Got it. We're fresh out of those on Ithical. Little behind the times, you know."

"If you're referring to computer tech, then yes, I agree. But your people are way ahead of ours in cerecite technology."

"We're still behind. Especially this ridiculous monarchy system." He sighed and sat back in his chair, arms crossed, dark eyebrows knit in a pensive expression. "Did you know that none of the modern countries on Earth still use a true monarchy? They all have a system of parliament and judges of some sort. Even if they have a king or queen, those rulers have little true power. It's the people who rule, not some snooty noble class. Plus, we still believe in betrothals and arranged marriages, for goodness' sake. How much more antiquated can we get?"

I studied him. Was he hinting at something when he mentioned arranged marriages? Surely not. But I didn't have the heart to question him further, so I eyed the stacks of books and scrolls on the table. "Is that what you've been researching?"

"Yes. I brought a few books back from Earth to compare them to Ithical's government. We're so behind, it's laughable."

"So." I gave a slight smile. "You're wanting revolution."

"It'll never happen. Not with my aunt in power. But yeah. If I could, I would change it this minute."

The code stopped. The screen shifted to black. Bold white letters appeared.

MAP?

TAB Y/N

"Map?" Morven asked.

"Let's see what happens." I hit Y. The screen morphed to a 3-D map of Ithical island. Blue lines connected to form mountains and plains. White lines contrasted, representing lakes and rivers.

Red dots appeared over four places. One over the north-western half of the island near the mountains—the cave I'd been in earlier. Southern plains near the fishing village. Western peninsula, past the canyons. Eastern village near a large lake. My eidetic memory absorbed each location.

"They're caves," Morven said.

"How do you know?"

"I've studied all the maps of Ithical. Each spot is located where cerecite mines are, though most of them have been abandoned."

"Then they're most likely places they've hit, or plan to hit next," I added.

Morven narrowed his eyes. "If so, then they're idiots. Those mines were closed because they were unstable."

"I don't think they care."

The screen went blank, and a red button pulsed twice from the bottom edge before it also went dark.

"Battery problems?" Morven asked.

"Yeah." I picked up the computer and eyed the charging port. "Must not be powered by cerecite."

"Is there any other way to power it?"

I shut the lid with a click. "Maybe if I grab a charger when I get back to Earth."

He shot me a quizzical glance. "Back to Earth?"

"Yeah. I'm supposed to go back and deliver information to Vortech."

"When?"

"First thing in the morning, I guess." I stared around the library, the comfort of the blue cerecite lights lending a cheerful glow to the tables and stacks of scrolls. "I'll miss this place."

"You'll miss this place?" He leaned forward. His eyes glinted with mischievousness. "Or you'll miss me?"

I laughed. "Fine. I'll miss both." I playfully jabbed his shoulder. "What will you do while I'm gone?"

A dark look flashed in his eyes. It happened so quickly, I almost missed it. Shaking his head, he motioned to his stack of books. "Stay locked in here, hopefully."

"Why do you say that?" I questioned. "It seems like you're trying to avoid everyone."

"Maybe I am." He took a deep breath. "But I need to keep reading. I plan to approach my aunt at some point with my genius plan to dissolve the monarchy. I'm sure she'll have no problem with it."

"Yeah. I'm sure she'll completely agree." I eyed him with a feeling there was something he wasn't telling me.

He sighed and tapped his fingers on the cover of a leatherbound volume. "I've got to make her see how backward this whole system is—how backward our society is. We need a university. We need to expand our knowledge of the world and of the universe."

"Do you plan to tell the people that they're not on Earth?" I asked.

"I wish." He rubbed his neck. "But no. Now isn't the time. Eventually, though, I hope things will change."

"Then I'll help you."

Surprise lit his face. "You will?"

"Sure. After I'm done with all this Vortech nonsense and we stop the miners, I say we usher in a new era."

"You sound like a revolutionary."

"Maybe I am, but you started it."

He smiled, though it was strained. "I don't know if it's possible, Sabine. The people here are so set in their ways, I don't think they want to change."

"But wouldn't you want to know the truth?"

"Of course *I* would, but them? Their way of life is so

engrained, changing things up would tear them apart." He pulled his pocket watch from his vest and checked it. "Nearly time for dinner. I'd better get changed."

"Me too." I tugged at my shirt stained with blood and crusted with dirt from the mine. "I don't think your aunt would like it if I showed up in this."

"True." He clicked the lid shut and replaced it in his suit's pocket, and I had to suppress a smile at the little round watch made of white cerecite I'd once stolen from him.

But my mission was different now, and a shiver of fear skittered down my spine as I thought of the miner who'd chased me through the cave. There was something unusual about him, though I couldn't figure out what.

I tucked the computer under my arm and followed Morven out of the library, then we parted ways. When I reached the small wooden door at the end of a second-tier hallway, I opened the bronze knob to enter my room. I'd left the window open, and the breeze ruffled the gauzy chevron-patterned curtains.

Evening sunlight shone over the single bed with the patched duvet cover, the scuffed armoire made of a dark wood, and the desk arranged by my bed, a black-and-white photo of my mima on top. The place was an upgrade from the closet I'd had last time. The bed was comfortable; the armoire had room to spare. I had a few palace uniforms to my name—black shirts and pants, and a green plaid tartan that I wore around one shoulder.

In addition to the uniforms, a row of gowns made by the palace seamstress, Mrs. Jennings, hung inside. Most were made of soft satin or crushed velvet, although I only ever wore them to dinner or formal occasions. Morven's aunt demanded I dress more formally since I was no longer the prince's care-taker. Although the gowns weren't the most comfortable, it was freeing to know I was no longer a pretend servant.

A sheepskin rug cushioned my footfalls as I paced to the

bedside table. After opening its single drawer, I placed the computer and the camera case with the pictures inside.

I made quick work of washing up and changing into a pale ivory-green gown. The satin hugged my waist and high neckline, although the long sleeves hung loosely around my arms, and the silky fabric fell to the floor in a waterfall of rustling fabric.

After grabbing a brush from my drawer, I set to work combing the tangles out of my hair, which had grown so long, it took an act of God to get all the knots out.

A knock came at the door, and I opened it to reveal Morven. My breath stuttered at the sight of him. He wore a charcoal gray suit jacket and pants, and a dark green plaid tartan that was fastened over his shoulder with a golden dragon brooch. Although he'd combed his hair, a chunk fell over one eye, and I playfully brushed it away, my fingers tingling as my skin touched his.

He grabbed my hand and gave it a kiss, and I led him into my room.

"You look beautiful," he said.

"Thanks," was all I could manage.

His gaze snagged on the black-and-white picture of my mima that was sitting on my bedside table. She was seventeen, maybe? With a willowy frame and long raven hair that fell to her waist, beautiful dark eyes shuttered in long lashes, and a coy, playful grin on her lips.

Morven nodded toward it. "That's your grand?"

"My mima. Yes." I sat on my bed and continued working the tangles out of my hair.

A crooked smile tugged at his lips. "You look just like her."

I laughed quietly. "Yeah, I get that a lot."

Through the window, soft lights sparkled from the skyline of Ithical city. The buildings glistened with bits of turquoise cerecite worked into their stone facades. Spires rose like pyramids into the sky, and it didn't take a wild imagination to realize I was somewhere other than Earth. Ithical had evolved into a world of its own.

Morven sat beside me as I continued tugging the brush through my hair.

"May I help?" he asked, nodding at the brush.

"Sure," I answered. "Although it's a useless cause. I'll never get all these tangles out."

He only smiled as he took the brush from me, then gently combed through the unruly strands. My pulse quickened, and I had to catch my breath at the feel of his feather soft touch. Morven awoke emotions in me that were too powerful to describe, except I knew I'd never felt this way toward anyone before. Yet a piece of me resisted becoming too close to him. Knowing I would one day return to my life in Kansas meant our relationship couldn't be anything more than temporary.

"There," he said quietly. "All done."

"No, you're joking, right?" I tentatively reached up and combed my fingers through my hair, shocked to find the strands silky and smooth without a single tangle. "How did you—?"

He brushed my hair away from my neck and kissed my collar bone, silencing me, and driving every rational thought from my head. I didn't know how long I could last with him so near me—didn't know how to sort out my feelings. Part of me felt terrified to let him too close. There was still so much I didn't understand about him.

When I finally found my voice again, I settled on a generalized topic, hoping to steer his attention from me. "The city is so beautiful."

"Yes, it is," he answered softly, a hint of seduction in his voice. He brushed my hair with his fingers trailing along my neck. Tingles erupted over my skin. He touched his lips to my forehead and kissed me gently, so lightly I barely felt him.

"Sabine, will you look at me?"

I swallowed the knot in my throat and turned to him, his eyes lingering on my lips.

"I've missed you," he said.

"I've missed you, too."

His arms surrounded me, and the bulge of his muscles pressed against me. I pressed my head to the firmness of his chest and inhaled the woodsy scent of his clothing. An emotion stirred within me—one that made me feel I could never live without him. Its intensity terrified me. Since I'd lost Mom and Mima, I hadn't let anyone get close to me. Not even my dad. Even he'd grown distant since I'd left for Ceres.

He kissed the top of my head. "I guess we should get to dinner."

"I guess," I answered without much enthusiasm. I chanced a look up at him. Dark eyelashes hooded his eyes. I had the urge to reach up and cup his face, to tell him how I really felt —how I wanted to be with him, to have him always near me, how I felt I could never live without him—but fear kept me saying any of those things.

He stood, and I followed. We didn't speak until we reached the dining hall.

"Salmon," he said as we approached the long table laden with food. "Must be an import from Fablemarch."

"Yeah," I answered.

People crowded around the table—more than I'd seen at any previous meal I'd eaten the last time I'd been here. I'd heard the queen was working on extending the olive branch to the noble families after the miners had revolted.

A man with a booming voice, broad shoulders, and a neatly trimmed, red beard sat at one end of the table. He motioned wildly as he spoke, his face animated. He had the air of a genuine Scot, though his voice was cultured, and his dark blue doublet trimmed in gold, his brown pants without creases or wrinkles.

Queen Tremayne sat at the opposite end of the table. She

smiled as she sipped a goblet of wine. Her frame appeared thinner now than the last time I'd seen her, her cheeks gaunter and paler. The haughtiness I'd once found in her eyes was gone.

Morven and I sat to her left. She gave us a curt nod as her gaze remained fixed on the Scot at the end of the table.

"…told them to leave my lands or I'd treat them with the same courtesy our ancestors once did in the Highlands. Am I right?" The man bellowed with laughter, and others at the table joined in.

"Who is that?" I whispered.

"George MacKinnon," Morven answered quietly as the conversation continued around us. "Chieftain of the MacKinnon clan. They're one of the most influential families on the island. My aunt had offended him at some point in the past, but after the ordeal with the miners, he stepped in and smoothed things over. Aunt Tremayne has been acting tolerably toward him since then. In my opinion, I think she's terrified the miners will revolt again, so she wants him close in case that happens."

"I see." I took a sip of my water, then speared a small potato and ate it while glancing at the Scottish chieftain.

A girl about my age sat near the man. Her fiery red hair matched the shade of his beard. She sat with a straight back, her dark green eyes roaming the room as if she were searching for threats. Freckles dotted the bridge of her nose and high cheekbones. Her lips were pink and bow-shaped, and they complemented the rosiness in her cheeks. She gave me a quick nod as she saw me looking at her, and I dipped my head in return.

"Is that his daughter?" I asked Morven.

"Yes." He heaved a sigh. "Vevina."

I detected a hint of emotion in his voice, one that I couldn't quite determine.

"Do you know her?"

"I suppose you could say that."

I glanced at Morven, though he didn't look at me. The straight line of his profile stood out against the backdrop of gray stone walls.

"Are you friends with her?"

He shrugged. "Except for you, Sabine, I'm not friends with anyone. You know that."

I forced a smile. "You haven't changed much."

A sly grin crept around his lips. "You're lucky I haven't." He took my hand and held it under the table, gently squeezing my fingers. My face heated until I felt my cheeks would catch fire.

Morven leaned close. "You haven't changed either. You still blush when I touch you."

"Stop it," I teased. "You're embarrassing me."

"Am I?" He kissed my cheek. "How about now?"

"Prince Morven," his aunt said loudly, her voice robust for someone so fragile. "I'm glad you and Miss Sabine have joined us. We were just speaking to Mr. MacKinnon about the reparations being made to the mines. Do you think they're sufficient?"

"Yes, actually." He straightened. "I was at the northern mines just last week. The improvements to the ventilation system were impressive. As were the upgrades to the rail trolleys. We even managed to put in an order to build two new sky transports. Should be ready in the next year. Not an easy thing to do to get them commissioned so quickly, but those transports are desperately needed. The miners I spoke with had no complaints, other than their long hours, which I assured them would become shorter once we introduce the new transports and pulley systems."

"Aye." Mr. MacKinnon took a drink from his tankard. "They'll have all the necessary advancements soon enough. I've promised them that and I mean to stay true to my word."

He spoke with a Scottish brogue, though his accent wasn't thick enough to make him unintelligible.

Vevina leaned forward, her deep plum-colored gown rustling as she rested her chin in her hands. "And what have you been up to, Prince Morven? Hiding away in the library?"

Morven sat stiffly, his back rigid as he eyed the girl. "What I do in the library is my own business, but if you must know, I'm studying. There are more ways to improve our island than in the mines."

"You mean to improve the island?"

"Eventually, yes."

A crease formed between her eyes. "How interesting. There are some who might argue our island doesn't need improvement."

"Yes. And that's why we'll never move forward."

Her eyes remained narrowed, but she didn't press the issue.

A man sitting across from me placed his tankard on the table with the clank of pewter on wood. "You've done a commendable job, Mr. Mackinnon. Let's hope this stability with the miners continues. We wouldn't want a repeat of what happened six months ago."

"Agreed." Mr. MacKinnon squared his shoulders.

I took a sip from my goblet as the conversation continued. After dinner ended, I made it back to my room and changed out of the dress and back into my standard palace uniform—black shirt and pants, then I glanced longingly at the soft covers on my bed. My shoulder ached where I'd been cut, my bruises throbbed, and my eyes wouldn't seem to stay open. But I'd promised to meet Morven for a walk after dinner, and since I'd spent so little time with him lately, I didn't want to miss the chance.

After leaving my room, I caught up with Morven in a hallway near the dining hall.

"You okay?" Morven held out his hand and I took it.

"Just tired." I ran my free hand down my black shirt and plaid tartan. "Today was exhausting."

I followed Morven through the expansive foyer, our footsteps echoing over the marble floor. Pillars rose over us as they supported the domed roof. Morven kept my hand in his as he guided me into a hallway.

"Will Vortech ever leave you alone?" he asked.

"I doubt it," I answered with a sigh. "They need me."

"Can't they get someone else to do your job?"

"They keep me because I know the truth about Ceres that they don't want anyone else knowing. They're possessive about information. Right now, they're telling the world they've been mining on Champ Island north of Russia. Said they discovered cerecite there. They saved the world from another solar flare, so no one argues."

"And they think you can keep their secret?"

"I suppose. They also think my abilities come in handy. I'm a great resource."

"You make it sound as if you're also a great servant."

I shrugged. "I wouldn't get better pay anywhere else. Plus, I got to meet you, didn't I?"

His teasing grin lit up his face. "Completely worth it."

We took the stairs leading to the second tier, and I marveled that Morven walked beside me with such confidence, as if he'd never been confined to a chair. Getting the poisonous yellow cerecite out of his system helped, but the healing properties of green cerecite had ensured he made a full recovery. A prick of sadness tugged at me. Earth knew nothing about the uses of cerecite. So far, Vortech's only interest was in mining yellow cerecite to use for a fuel alternative.

Was it wrong of me to hope green cerecite could be introduced to Earth as well? How many people could be helped because of it?

But Cade's warning came back to me, and I knew there

could never be enough cerecite to fit Earth's needs. Ithical Island would die if Earth took too much, and so it would have to remain a secret.

We neared a hall that ended at a balcony. A row of windows displayed a view of the city. I followed Morven through a doorway and onto the open-air platform. A breeze tugged strands of my hair across my face.

The air hadn't changed. A hint of a mechanical smell wafted—one that I now realized was caused by the shield generators as they created a man-made atmosphere encompassing the dwarf planet.

Gripping the iron railing, I glanced up at the palace. Three tiers rose into the sky. The structure looked impossibly tall from this perspective. A waterfall flowed down from the top level to the tiers beneath. Flowers and ivy vines grew along the rooftops. The place reminded me of something from pictures I'd seen of the hanging gardens of Babylon.

Morven pointed to a window a few floors above us. "Your room is up there."

I eyed the glass. Even with my ability to spot minute details, I couldn't tell any differences between it and the other windows. "How do you know?"

"Because I've been stuck here my whole life. Your room is located on the second tier, third level, and it faces south."

I glanced up at the window again. "Are you spying on me?"

"Spying?" Laughter danced in his eyes. "I have no need to spy on you, Sabine. You're like an open book, and you're terrible at lying."

"Is that so?" I asked.

"It is."

"So." I rested my elbows on the railing. "Even when I was here pretending to be a fisherman's daughter, you never bought it?"

He shook his head, lips pursed, eyes glittering with mischief. "Not even for a second."

I poked his shoulder. "Then you're terrible at lying, too."

We laughed, and it felt good to hear the playfulness in his voice. When I'd first met him, I didn't know he was capable of laughter. It was good to see this side of him—someone who could laugh and have fun without the taint of his past cynicism.

My gaze wandered out to the city where the darkening sky loomed beyond the palace.

I pointed to a cluster of twinkling stars. "Are those real?"

"Some of them. I wouldn't know for sure without my telescope."

The pinpoint lights twinkled in shades of periwinkle blue, so lifelike it was impossible to tell what was real and was merely a construction of pigments glowing from the dome. The creators of Ithical Island—who I'd recently learned were time travelers from the future—had made the dome to appear as if the inhabitants were on Earth. Morven had been the one to discover the truth that only the actual stars could reveal— their true location in the universe.

"Does it bother you that the people here still don't know they're fake?" I asked, gesturing widely at the sky.

He shrugged. "Sometimes…" His voice trailed as he stood transfixed by the stars. He'd always had a fascination with astronomy, which had led him to finding the truth. He seemed so different from the other people of Ithical Island, and some- times I wondered who he really was at heart. He'd admitted the cerecite had transformed him. He was a cu sith. A shape changer.

The wind picked up, carrying a chill.

Dark clouds gathered, hiding the real and false stars alike. I ran my hands over my arms where goose bumps formed. A fragile stillness hung in the air as the wind died down. The soupy clouds highlighted the glow of the city, and I imagined the dome beyond, and past that, the emptiness of space.

Ceres was so far from home, I had trouble fathoming the expanse. Without the gateway linking the two worlds, I would've been stranded here.

I tried not to ponder it too much.

Something glinted in the sky. I tracked the movements of a long, oblong-shaped craft gliding through the clouds.

I pointed to it. "Do you see that?"

"Yeah," Morven answered.

"I didn't realize Ithical had airplanes."

Morven's eyes narrowed. "That's no airplane."

"Then what is it?"

"I don't know."

"A UFO?"

He knitted his brows. "A what?"

"Unidentified flying object. That's what we call them on Earth."

"It must be an aerial transport. We use them for shipping cerecite from the mines to the cerecite stations outside the city. But they rarely come into the city. I wonder what that one's doing."

The ship flew so close, the rumble of its engines made the floor shake. A burst of light pulsed with a deafening roar. The bolt hit a window above us.

Was that my room?

An explosion rocked the palace. A blast of stones and broken glass rained down on us.

Shock tore through me as I fell to the ground, covering my head.

Morven cursed as he landed beside me. He grabbed my hand and we crawled off the balcony and back into the palace as a second blast buckled the ground.

"That hit your room," he shouted over the roar.

"Are you sure?"

"Yes!"

We scrambled until we were able to climb to our feet. At the end of the passage, a staircase loomed ahead.

"Up there," he shouted.

I followed him as we raced to the stairs.

If the blast had hit my room, I knew why—and I also knew what they were after. The miners had returned for what I'd taken, and they were willing to blow up the palace to get it.

4

"What was that?" Cade appeared in the stairwell as Morven and I raced up to the next floor.

"The miners," I shouted.

Cade's face blanched as his mouth fell open. "How do you know?"

"Because they bombed my room!"

I didn't argue as he followed us up. Adrenaline flooded my blood when we reached the third floor and I dashed down the hallway to my room. The scent of smoke pervaded the air.

Thick, yellowish clouds obscured the passage as I neared the doorway. The remains of my room stood out, skeletal wooden bones charred and blackened. The night sky appeared through the gaping hole where the wall had once been. A breeze wafted from outside, throwing the smoke into whirlpools.

A hulking form moved toward us through the smoke. Someone was there.

Morven pulled a knife from his boot. Cade yanked a gun from a holster beneath his jacket.

The man rounded on us. Surprise lit his face. In his arms, he clutched the laptop I had taken.

"Stay back," he yelled, his accent thick. He backed toward the gaping hole in the wall.

"Drop the computer," Cade bit out. "You're mining illegally on our planet. You have no right to be here and strip our resources."

"Also no right to blow a bloody hole through our palace!" Morven added.

"I warned you." The man pulled a wicked-looking weapon from his pocket. Metal glinted from gears and a slender barrel.

Morven cursed and shoved us back. A shot pulsed from the gun. I hit the ground hard as the wall behind us shattered into wooden splinters, my elbow and backside digging into the unyielding floor. Pain shot through my spine, but it barely registered.

The roar of an engine filled the room.

Through the open wall, a flying vehicle hovered, its engine humming with an unnatural grating sound. A metal hatch door slowly slid open, and the man backed toward the ship.

The wind picked up, howling loud enough to overpower the engine's roar.

Shouts came from the hallway. Vevina rushed into the room clutching twin daggers. The wind caught her hair and rustled her plum-colored dress. Red strands fanned around her face.

"What's going on?" she yelled.

Cade climbed to his feet. "Stop him!"

Morven and I stood. The mechanical roar grew louder as the ship's hatchway lowered, the wide metal door creating a bridge between the palace and the aircraft. The miner turned around to face the ship, and I saw my camera swing around his neck, reflecting the lights from the ship.

"He's got my camera with the photos still in the case, too," I shouted.

We charged toward the man as he leaped into the ship.

Cade did not hesitate before jumping the distance to the open hatch. A low roar trilled as the aircraft steered away.

Morven grabbed my hand, and we sprinted to the airship's opening. My stomach went to my throat as I took the leap, the air ripping past, and landed with Morven on the metal plating.

We fell forward as the hatch began to close, tipping up inside the room.

"I'm coming!" Vevina yelled behind us.

Twin blades flew through the opening as Vevina jumped with the grace of a cat. Her feet barely made a sound as she landed beside us and snatched her knives in the same motion.

"You couldn't have waited for me?" she exclaimed.

Before we could reply, a crash and scream came from the ship's interior. We spun around to find the miner flailing on the ground, blood spurting from his nose. Cade stood over him with clenched fists, his chest rising and falling with breath. He reached down and plucked the computer and camera from the floor. "Got it," he stated matter-of-factly.

I shared a glance with Morven as the hatch sealed shut with a hiss behind us, trapping us inside the bowels of the dark ship. The air smelled of grease. Rusty metal gears and engine parts lay like discarded corpses around us. Dim blue lights glowed around a sealed metal doorway, which I hoped led out of the room.

Vevina placed her hands on her hips, still gripping her knives. "Would someone please tell me what's going on? I was on my way out when I heard a massive explosion, then I came up here to find the three of you leaping onto a flying machine. What is going on?"

Cade tucked the computer under his arm and grabbed the camera off the ground. "We're trying to save the planet."

"Hmm, and do you heroes know where we're going?"

"You shouldn't complain, Vee," Morven said, and his use

of the nickname *Vee* didn't escape my notice. "No one asked you to come along."

"Well, I couldn't let you three go without me, could I?" She pointed a knife at the miner on the floor. "Not when you let the miners nearly destroy the planet last time."

Morven sighed and rubbed his head. "We followed the miner because he and some others have been stealing cerecite. Sabine took a computer from him that has sensitive information. He tried to steal it back. Now we're re-stealing it."

"*Re*-stealing?"

I looked at Cade who held the computer. "We have to get it back to the palace."

The ship lurched, and the miner on the ground moaned. Cade kicked him in the head.

"Well, that's one way to do it," I mumbled under my breath. I stood, my muscles stiff and protesting, and Morven also got to his feet. "We need to find a way off this transport."

"Agreed," said Morven. "But where do we go from here?"

Cade nodded toward the door. "I worked on a ship like this once. There should be an emergency landing panel near the rear turbines. We'll have to find it quickly before the others find us."

"Do you think they know we're here?" I asked.

"Maybe. But a ship like this is clunky and only has one viewport. It's doubtful the pilot even saw us get on. Still, be ready to fight."

Cade inspected our weapons. He frowned when he looked at my empty hands.

"Here." He picked up the miner's gun that had fallen to the floor, then he tossed it to me. "Use that."

Metal warmed my hands as I inspected the weapon.

"I've never used anything like this," I said.

"Phage weapon." Morven pointed to a gear on the barrel. "Turn that ninety degrees to stun. One-eighty to kill. Be sure to release the pin first. It's powered by yellow cerecite, so you'll never have to reload. Careful. That thing can blast a room apart—which you might've caught on to."

"Yeah." I stuck the thing in my belt. "Kinda got it when the miner blasted my bedroom apart."

"Let's go." Cade paced to the door outlined in blue lights.

Morven stayed near my side, Vevina ahead of us. She gave us a smug glare, but she didn't speak as we crowded by the doorway. Cade pressed his ear to the metal, his brows knit as he listened.

"Hear anything?" I whispered.

"Nothing," he whispered back. "We'll still have to be careful." He reached for a button beside the door and pressed it. The panel slid up with a quiet hiss, revealing a dimly lit hallway lined in metal panels.

We crept into the passage, the walls pressing in, the ceiling so low I could've reached up and touched it. Lights blinked in reds and blues from control panels as we made our way to an adjoining hallway.

"Which way?" Morven asked quietly.

"Not sure," Cade answered. "This layout is different from the ship I served on. Keep moving. We've got to find the rear turbines."

Gripping the gun, I followed alongside the others. Smooth metal pressed into my palms. The weapon felt completely alien, and I had the urge to trade it for Morven's knife. If it came to it, would I be able to kill a person? If I wanted to live, I'd have no choice, although that thought unsettled me.

How had my life come to this point? I'd gone to work for Vortech to prevent another solar flare. Here I was on an alien world, sneaking through a spacecraft, talking myself into being okay with killing someone.

We made it to another hallway when the ship lurched upward. My ears popped at the change in pressure.

"We're gaining altitude," Cade said.

"What does that mean?" Vevina asked.

"We're leaving the city." He shook his head. "Could be going to another mine."

Morven pressed forward. "We've got to get off. This thing could take us anywhere."

Our footsteps echoed through the metal-lined corridors until we reached an open room, at the far end of which two men hunched over a computer board. The roar of engines drowned out any other sounds, and the men didn't react as we glanced inside.

Cade pressed his finger to his lips and motioned for us to stay in the hallway. We pressed our backs to the wall. I caught a glimpse of the two men from my vantagepoint.

Cade checked his gun, then glanced at me. "Sabine, take them out from here. You've got the best shot."

I felt the blood drain from my face. "Me?"

Cade sighed. "Yes. You've got the best weapon for it."

"But I…" I inspected the gun—its metal cold and unyielding. "I don't know."

"Oh, for heaven's sake." Vevina snatched the gun from me, turned the gear, and pulled the trigger twice. Twin orbs of light pulsed from the barrel, hitting each man squarely in the back.

They fell without a sound.

"You're welcome," Vevina said smugly, handing the gun back to me.

I stood motionless as Cade and Vevina marched into the room. Morven stood by me as I held the weapon in shaking hands.

"You okay?" He placed his hand on my shoulder.

"I-I'm…" How was I supposed to answer?

"You aren't trained to be a killer, Sabine. Don't take it too hard."

My eyes met his. "Is Vevina?"

"Have you met her father? She's trained to be a Highland soldier."

"But." I swallowed my nervousness rising up to choke me. "What am I doing here, Morven?"

"Same thing as the rest of us. Trying to get off this ship. Now, let's go." He held out his hand, and I took it.

He hadn't answered my question. Not really. What was I doing here? Stealing information for Vortech should've been handled by someone more adept at survival than me. But Vortech cared too much about keeping their secrets, and so I remained, qualified or not.

I followed Morven into the room—the largest one we'd been inside yet. The rear hatch took up the entirety of the back wall, with blinding white lights rimming its square-shaped outline.

"This one." Cade pointed to a lever on the circuit board.

"You're sure?" Vevina asked.

"Has to be."

She waved her hand. "Open it."

Cade glanced at us. "Might want to find something to hang onto. Once I initiate the emergency landing, the hatch will open. You'll get sucked out unless you're hanging on tight. We'll have to wait until the ship lands, then make our escape."

I searched the room, then grabbed a pole wrapped in wires. "Sounds simple enough."

Cade frowned. "I wouldn't use those words exactly."

"Any idea where we're at?" Morven asked.

Cade shook his head. "At the speed we're going, I doubt we're inside the city. Could be halfway across Ithical for all I know."

Vevina grabbed the edge of a bulkhead. "We'll find out soon enough."

"Good point." Cade nodded. "Ready?"

Morven grabbed onto the same beam as me, his fingers brushing mine. "Ready."

"All right. Hold on." The lever clicked into position as

Cade pushed it down. White lights turned red and flashing. An alarm blared.

Cade raced to the bulkhead where Vevina stood and held it tight.

The hatchway slowly lowered, revealing a blinding strip of sunlight.

"They're sure to know we're here now," Cade yelled over the roar of wind and turbines.

The pressure built until the wind tugged on me so hard, my hands burned as I held to the bulkhead. Open desert appeared beneath us as the hatch opened wider.

On the far side of the room, the door slid open, and a man stepped inside. He hit a button on the wall, and the hatch stopped mid-way.

As the man took a step inside, I recognized his braided goatee and severe eyes that spoke of violence.

He pulled a saber from his back before rushing toward me.

"Run," I heard Cade yell as I jumped back seconds before the man's blade sliced into the bulkhead. Morven grabbed my hand, and we raced toward the half-open hatchway, Vevina and Cade in front of us.

The ship dove downward, pitching me on my knees. My fingernails bent as I clawed at the floor. The man with the sword stood over me, balancing to stay upright. He grabbed my jacket and dug through my pockets, then—almost mechanically—his gaze shot to Cade's, zeroing in on the camera case and computer.

"I'll need those," he said to Cade, his tone casual through an undercurrent of warning.

Cade backed to the hatch. Through the opening, the desert ground looked a hundred feet below us. Too far to jump. Vevina stepped in front of him, twin knives ready. "You have to get through me."

"I don't want to hurt you." He sliced his sword in a warning. "But I'll do what I must."

She charged. He batted away one knife before she dodged back. Her blade skittered down through the open hatch and out into the desert.

She pressed her bloody hand to her skirt, her other clasping her knife, as she attacked again. The man dodged back on lithe feet and spun around with the movements of a trained martial artist. His body became a blur as he kicked the knife from her hand. Screaming, she clutched both her empty hands to her chest.

Morven grabbed my arm and backed me to the wall.

"What—?" I asked when he pointed to a lever marked EMERGENCY LANDING ONLY.

"Hold on," he mouthed.

I grabbed the edge of a metal desk a second before Morven pulled the lever, and the ship pitched, gaining speed as it sped downward.

Everyone hit the ground. A tornadic wind and blaring alarm deafened me. The world spun. I focused on the strip of sunlight shining from the open hatchway.

Morven gripped my hand, and together, we crawled toward it.

Wind tore at my skin, and blowing sand stung my eyes when we made it to the opening. The ship spiraled. Metal panels and computer parts ripped from the walls and lurched toward us. We ducked and ran for the outside.

Cade screamed behind us. I rounded to see the sword warrior standing over him. Blood spread from Cade's torso. The man held the computer, then ripped the camera case from Cade's hands. Blood stained the device and dark red drops got caught on the wind.

Vevina dashed toward the sword warrior, then kicked behind his knees. He grunted as he pitched forward. He spun on her, knocking her backward. Her body flew through the air and got sucked outside.

The sword warrior lifted Cade by his collar and tossed him at us. His body hit Morven and me. The breath left my lungs as I flew from the open hatchway. A current of air whipped past moments before I landed in the sand.

Pain enveloped me. Searing heat spread from my neck down my spine. Sunlight blinded me.

My consciousness ebbed. My next memory was of looking into the sky, strange and purple, a reminder I wasn't on Earth.

"…awake?" a voice asked.

I focused on the sound. Morven.

"Sabine, are you awake?"

"Yes," I managed.

He grasped my shoulder. "Can you sit up?"

I attempted to move, but my neck was too stiff, and I was forced to stay in the sand. "My neck," I breathed.

"Just stay still," he said, squeezing my shoulder.

I blinked, hoping to stay conscious as the world spun around me. "What about… the others?"

"Vevina's in bad shape but I think she'll make it. Cade's fine. But he's got an advantage. He's mixing some green cerecite in his canteen. Should help you. Just rest for now."

I tilted my head, but even that movement sent a wave of pain radiating through my neck and down my back.

"Ouch."

Morven brushed a strand of hair away from my face. "You're one brave girl, you know that? Not anyone would have the guts to jump out of a flying transport."

"I didn't jump," I said drily. "A body was thrown at me and I flew out." I took a deep breath, glancing at him in my peripheral vision. He was smiling—that silly, teasing grin that would've irked me had I not known him better. "How are you still alive?"

"Got lucky and landed in a dune. But I'll have some lovely bruises come tomorrow morning."

Cade stood over us holding his canteen. "Green cerecite?"

"Gross. Sure." The last time I'd drank it, the stuff hadn't tasted much better than grass clippings. But I'd healed from a nasty broken wrist, so I wouldn't pass it up. He handed the container to Morven, who held it to my lips. I took a sip of the warm liquid.

"You good?" Morven asked.

"Wonderful," I grimaced.

Cade knelt over me, the bright sunlight making his hair look white and glowing, reminding me of the time he'd transformed into a brilliant green dragon. "You'll start to feel better in an hour or two. I gave you a large dose. It'll probably knock you out pretty soon, to be honest."

"Getting knocked out doesn't sound too bad. How's Vevina?"

"About the same as you. She'll be good by tonight, I think. We're lucky I keep a supply of green cerecite on hand."

Clouds covered the sun, blocking out the relentless light. I closed my eyes, the effects of the cerecite beginning to numb the throbbing eating away at the base of my skull.

"Rest." I heard Morven's voice as if from far away.

I woke to a dark sky. Stars flecked the firmament, and I wondered which were real, and which were lights on the dome. Morven sat beside me, hands resting on his knees, as he looked up, peering at the sky with an uncanny intelligence, as if he could see into the galaxies beyond.

He'd been the first to discover we weren't on Earth, and I wondered if there were any more secrets left to be uncovered.

"What are you thinking about?" I asked, my throat dry and voice hoarse.

He glanced at me with wide eyes. "You're awake?"

"Yeah." I answered, then dared to sit up. My head didn't scream with pain as it had earlier, and I managed to move next to him. The desert air held a chill, and I hugged my arms around me. We sat on a hill overlooking the rise and fall of the dunes. Cade and Vevina sat nearby, though their forms were only silhouettes in the moonlight. Their whispered voices carried, but not loud enough for me to understand what they said.

"Is Vevina okay?"

"She's fine. Her hands were messed up pretty bad. Whoever that man was, he can fight."

"He was the man who chased me through the mine. He managed to take the camera with the photos and computer, didn't he?"

"Yes."

My stomach sank. "All that work just to lose it all." But he hadn't taken everything. The pyramid pendant stayed hidden under my shirt. I grabbed the leather cord and pulled it out. Spirals of amber light swirled through the glassy black surface. "At least we have this."

His eyes widened as he looked at the pendant. "You kept it?"

"Yes." I tucked it back under my shirt. "If I can find out what it does, it might be worth something. The trouble is, where do we go now?"

"Go back to Earth like you planned."

I eyed him. "Go back? I've got nothing but this." I patted the necklace under the fabric.

"You remember what the swordfighter looks like, don't you? You'll be able to identify him. Plus, we saw the map of the mines they plan to hit next. That's something."

"Then why do I feel like a failure?"

He wrapped his arm around me, his warmth enveloping me like a blanket. "You're too hard on yourself. You're definitely not a failure."

"I don't know if Vortech will see it that way."

He squeezed my shoulder. His hair and clothes held the scent of wild amber, and I took the liberty to breathe deeply, letting his presence calm me.

"Don't worry about Vortech," he said.

I sighed. "I don't know if we'll ever stop illegal mining. Once we opened the wormhole gateway, we let loose a flood gate. Sure, we might stop these miners, but what about the next? Cade may've been right about protecting Ceres."

"But we couldn't stay secluded here forever. Discovering our way back to Earth was inevitable. It had to happen someday. At least this way, we have some control over who comes and goes."

"You're right." I threaded my fingers through his. "Now we just have to figure out where we're at—which could be literally anywhere on the planet—get back to the capital and make it through the gateway back to Earth. That could take a while."

"Hopefully not as long as you might think."

I glanced up at him. "What do you mean?"

"The stars." He looked at the sky. "The location of Cassiopeia is in the north. Mars is in the west, meaning we're somewhere southeast of the capital. I'd guess we were on the ship for about forty-five minutes. Assuming we were traveling at top speed means we would've made it one-hundred-and-fifty kilometers or so."

"So, do you know where we are?"

"Somewhere south," he answered. "That's about as much as I've got."

I sighed, tucking my knees to my chest. "We could die out here, you know. Dehydration will get to us pretty quickly."

"We won't die."

"How do you know?" I asked.

He smiled slyly. "I'm too smart, for one thing."

I couldn't help but laugh. "Got it. You're taking this whole dying-in-the-desert thing pretty well."

"Maybe for now. Ask me again tomorrow after we've been wandering for fourteen hours, and I won't sound nearly so confident."

A knot of fear twisted in the pit of my stomach. The

expanse seemed to go on forever. If we were lost, then what? A brief vision flitted across my eyes: our dry corpses in the desert, slowly buried by sand.

No.

I couldn't think that way. We'd find our way home. Somehow.

Footsteps shifted over sand as Cade and Vevina strode toward us. The girl hugged her arms around her chest, her eyes darting around. Her tall, thin frame seemed unusually frail in the pale moonlight.

"Hey." Cade sat on the sand beside us. Vevina remained standing, her face drawn, as she stared out toward the horizon. Her body visibly shook, although it couldn't have been colder than sixty degrees out here. Was she in shock?

"Any ideas where to go?" Cade asked.

"North," Morven answered.

Cade nodded. "Unfortunately, we're in one of the most remote parts of Ithical. There may not be a village or settlement anywhere near. Could be more than two days' walk, to be honest. And without water. Well… we'll die."

"Except for you," I said.

"True. But I'll still feel the effects. I could pass out and stay that way until I'm rehydrated."

"So, what do we do?" I asked.

"Start walking," Morven answered. "Straight north. Go as far as we can."

The desert stretched before us like a yawning maw that threatened to devour us.

"How much water do we have?" I asked.

"Only this." Cade pulled his canteen from his jacket pocket and shook it. "Half full and laced with green cerecite. We'll have to drink it in small doses if we don't want to fall asleep."

"Then we'll start tomorrow morning," I said. "With any

luck, we'll find a settlement. Hopefully find the rails and make it back to the capital."

"Not to be a downer," Morven said, "but Ithical isn't a small place. It could be a week or more before we find anything."

A week? We'd be dead by then.

I rested my chin on my knees. A dry breeze stirred, creating swirling patterns over the sand turned silver in the moonlight. Its beauty hid what could become our graves.

6

The dry air sapped the moisture from my skin, leaving my lips cracked. My eyes burned from staring too long into the desert expanse, the sunlight reflecting on the white sand. Sphere-shaped boulders pocked the landscape, glowing in shades of turquoise. Most were small pebbles, but others loomed as large as cars.

I trailed behind Morven and Cade with Vevina beside me. She'd said nothing but monosyllables since we'd crashed, and she walked with her arms crossed over her chest. Her eyes stayed on the horizon.

The two walking in front of us spoke quietly. With nothing better to do than follow behind them, I listened in on their conversation.

"…remember when it was all a wasteland?" Cade asked.

"Some of it. My memories—*Isaac's* memories—are fragmented. There are a lot of blank spaces. Wish I could remember more."

"Nah. It's good you forgot how bad it was. Our living conditions."

"Yeah, I don't remember a lot of that. A couple hundred years tends to do that."

They laughed. It was so odd to hear Morven and Cade getting along. Just a few months ago, Morven would've done nothing but insult anyone who dared start a conversation with him. But so much had changed since then.

We crested a hill and stopped when a gust of wind whipped a cloud of sand in front of our eyes, gauzing everything in shades of tan. When it died down, the jagged peaks of a mountain range came into focus, cutting through the sky on the horizon.

Vevina pointed. "The Spire Ridge Mountains." Blinking, she seemed to come out of a trance. She rounded on us, her eyes bright. "My home is on the other side."

"Are you sure?" I asked.

"Yes. MacKinnon Keep. I'm certain. I would know that mountain range anywhere."

"Then we're in luck," Morven said.

"Perhaps." Vevina's shoulders fell. "But the Mystik creatures infest the mountains now. Some Mystik wolves have attacked our people."

"Strange." Cade rubbed his chin. "Mystik creatures aren't usually dangerous."

Morven shielded his eyes from the sun as he gazed out toward the mountains. "We'll have to be careful."

Cade unhooked his canteen and passed it to us. I took a small sip, doing my best to ignore the bitterness, and passed it to Vevina.

"If the desert doesn't kill us, the wolves will. Is that what you're saying?" I asked.

Morven smiled. "Beats being stuck in a chair. Trust me."

"You might think differently once the wolves attack." Vevina passed the canteen back to Cade. "The only advantage we'll have is that I know the best trails. If we keep to them, we'll have a better chance at evading the creatures. Still, several of our people have been killed recently. This won't be an easy journey."

"We have no other choice." Morven dusted the sand from his leather vest. He started down the hill and we followed, feet shifting over the desert ground. Whirlwinds spiraled lazily around us, appearing and disappearing like ghosts.

I wiped beads of sweat from my forehead, only to feel grit sticking to my skin. Heat radiated from the sand. I focused on details to distract me from the temperature.

A boulder, twenty feet away, half buried in the sand. The sunlight was so bright, it overpowered the stone's glow. If it weren't for the aqua color, it would've looked like any stone on earth.

The call of a bird high in the sky. As I shielded my eyes and glanced up, I caught a glint of turquoise feathers. A Mystik falcon, perhaps?

It still took some adjustment to get accustomed to the creatures of Ithical. Cerecite preserved the DNA of living things, transforming, and recycling the living essence of a person after death. Some of the DNA stayed around to become the building blocks of new creatures—mice and wolves, to name a few, although Cade had managed to be transformed in a powerful explosion, making him capable of changing his form to that of a green dragon.

I grasped the pyramid pendant hanging around my neck. The smooth edges of the stone pressed into my palm. If something was truly special about the pendant, I doubted Cade would tell me. Maybe there was nothing unusual about it, but if that were true, why would the swordfighter have owned it?

A few crystal pillars of salt appeared along our path, white and statuesque as plants.

Evening approached, and the sun dipped low on the horizon, becoming a large, hazy orb. The sky, already tinted purple, became a deeper, unnatural color, one that appeared pixelated in places, completely alien from an Earth sunset.

The others looked at the sky without blinking. To them, it

was what a sky was supposed to look like—what it always looked like.

When we reached the foothills, shadows enveloped us. The air cooled, and sticky sweat dried to my skin. My parched mouth begged for water, but we only had a little left in Cade's canteen, and I wouldn't be the one to drink it. Rocks crunched under our boots as the path slanted upward. Plants began to dot the surface. Leafless trees grew with patches of sickly, yellow bark peeling from the branches.

"What kind of plants are these?" I asked Cade.

"Lokus trees," he answered. "They're the first plants to start growing naturally after we built the shield. They're an offshoot of a plant we engineered using green cerecite. They're not good for much." He plucked a branch from one of the trees that snapped in half with a dry crack. "Firewood, maybe, but that's about it."

As we climbed, the path grew steeper. I slipped on loose rocks, but I managed to keep my footing as we trailed up the switchbacks. The lokus trees grew in thick patches that covered the ground in a network of twisted limbs, hiding the sand, as if we walked through a sea of dead plants. A few other plants managed to grow alongside the trees, grasses and bushes with purple berries.

A rodent-like creature scurried across our path. Its body glowed turquoise green in the dark of night, lighting up the branches beneath the gnarled trees. We reached a plateau overshadowed by steep, craggy hills.

"There might be some caves there." Vevina scanned the shadowed ridges. "We could take shelter for the night, supposing we don't run into any Mystik creatures in the process."

Cade unsheathed his knife. "Stay alert."

The towering cliffs created an amphitheater, magnifying the sounds of our footfalls. Sticks and brambles littered the ground. A few boulders lay along our path, glowing with a fiery aquamarine blue that illuminated the pocked cliffs.

"What about that?" Morven pointed to a cave tunneling into the mountain. "Should we check it out?"

"Fine," Vevina said. "But be careful."

Dry twigs snapped underfoot as we crossed to the cave. Morven grabbed a glowing stone that fit in the palm of his hand, and I did the same. As we approached the entrance, the lights didn't do much to illuminate the area in front of us. When we entered, darkness stretched. The air warmed. Sounds of dripping water echoed far in the distance.

"I don't see any monsters," I said.

"That doesn't mean they aren't here," Vevina replied. "But…" Her gaze trailed to the darkness stretching beyond. "I think we'll be safe enough. We should build a fire to keep away anything that would attack us."

Cade stepped behind us, his boots snapping twigs. He cleared a space on the stony ground. "We can make a fire here. Not sure what we'll do for food."

At the mention of food, my empty stomach growled. After walking the entire day with nothing but a few sips of watery cerecite, hunger gnawed at my insides.

"Hunt?" I suggested.

Cade shook his head. "Mystik creatures aren't edible. We may be able to find some wild rabbits or something, but I doubt much live out here."

"Look for berries, then?" I asked.

"Good idea," Vevina answered. "I saw some wild tayberry bushes along the cliffs."

"I can go look for them," I said.

"And I'll go with you." Vevina walked to stand beside me, her frame willowy and tall, eyes piercing the darkness. Earlier, she'd seemed too shaken to do anything but walk and stare blankly. I wasn't sure how well she'd do in the mountains at night.

"You're sure?" I asked her.

"Yes. This is my home. Or close enough to it." She took a deep breath. "I'll be fine."

"Would you like me to come with you?" Morven asked.

"No," Vevina answered quickly. "That won't be necessary."

I cast her a sidelong glance. Her response confused me. Why had she so quickly dismissed his offer of help?

"Okay." Morven cocked his head. "I'll help Cade gather firewood for the fire."

"We'll do the same as we're gathering berries." Vevina grasped my arm, steering me away from the two men.

I walked with her out of the shelter of the cavern and into the night. The wind picked up, howling through the crags and cliffs. Stars punctuated the sky in bursts of red and blue.

A cluster of pebbles glowed over the ground, lighting our way. On Earth, we would've relied on flashlights, but here, the world provided light when it was needed most.

"These rocks are so amazing," I said. "You don't even have to take a light with you."

She cocked her head. "Cade mentioned you're not from our island."

"I'm from very far away, to be honest."

"He said you came through a gateway to get here."

"Also true," I answered. "And where I come from, it's pretty different. We don't have glowing rocks everywhere, for one thing."

Bushes grew scraggly and sparse along our trail, though some held bunches of orange berries. Vevina gathered her skirt to form a makeshift basket, and we collected what we could.

"Sabine, may I ask you something?" she said hesitantly.

"Of course."

She twisted her finger around her skirt. "What do you think of Cade?"

"Cade?" I asked.

"Yes. Do you find him attractive?"

I grabbed a handful of berries, warm juice running down my fingers, and placed them in her gathered skirt. "He's certainly attractive."

"But… do you think he'd ever… well…"

"Ever what?"

She blew out a frustrated sigh. "Never mind."

"You want to know if he would be interested in someone like you?"

She twisted her skirt until it knotted. "Aye."

"I don't know." I bit my lip, tugging on another berry. Cade had been around for a while—as in hundreds of years. I knew nothing of his past relationships, or if he had any. Did Vevina realize how messed up his past was? Did she realize how messed up *he* was?

But how could I tell her that Cade had gone psycho on me and tried to kill me not that long ago? Maybe that was a conversation for another time.

"Just don't get too attached to him," I said. "Cade's an interesting person."

"What do you mean?"

"I mean you need to be careful around him. Just be sure you know him before you decide he's the one for you."

She attempted to laugh, but it sounded forced. "I only asked if you think he might like me. I haven't thought that far ahead, Miss Sabine. Not that I could care for a person like him in the first place." After cinching up her skirt, she stood, and I followed her back to the cave.

I trailed after her. What did she mean she couldn't care for a person like him? Was something wrong with her? Was she sick with a terminal illness or something? But Vevina didn't seem like the sort of person to open up to me unless she was ready. I would wait her out, then.

The glow of the fire radiated around the cavern, casting mellow light over the previously shadowed spaces. Morven sat on a rock ledge near the flames. When he looked up, his eyes met mine. Dark irises sparkled as he took me in. What was it about Morven Tremayne that completely made me lose my head?

"Hey," he said, his voice deep and sultry.

My heart pattered. "Hey."

I sat beside him as Vevina passed the berries to Cade. Morven gripped my fingers, the heat of his skin spreading to mine.

He leaned over and kissed my forehead. "I missed you."

I shot him a bemused smile. "Missed me?"

"It's been a whole twenty minutes. I get lonely without you."

If that were true, then why had he spent so much time away from me? Was he really so wrapped up in his studies that he couldn't make time for me? Or was there something else going on?

He draped his arm around me, and I rested my head on his shoulder. With his scent, like earthen cedar spice enveloping me, my worries evaporated. Mesmerized by the crackling fire, I sat without worrying—even though I knew there were a million things I should be concerned about, I simply enjoyed the moment.

Cade and Vevina sat across from us, talking quietly as they passed around a few berries. I ate a handful, the sour flavor bursting in my mouth, but my gnawing hunger kept me swallowing eagerly. Our meal disappeared quickly, and we were left to stare at a dying fire. Coals smoldered, and the scent of woodsmoke filled the quiet, damp cave air.

The absence of crickets chirping unnerved me a little. We cleared away the rocks and made pallets on the cavern's sandy ground. Morven wrapped his arms around me, his fingers threaded through mine. Although I was certain I had never slept anywhere so uncomfortable, I closed my eyes and drifted off, the hint of cedar spice lingering in the air.

7

G rowling woke me. I opened my eyes to a cavern lit only by a few glowing coals and cerecite stones. A huge, lurking shadow moved past the mouth of the cavern and disappeared.

Across from me, Cade sat up, the gun we'd taken from the miner clutched in his hands. His blue eyes pierced the darkness as he looked out of the cavern and into the night.

Beside me, Morven stirred.

"What is it?" he whispered.

"There's something out there."

Clothing rustled as Cade gently shook Vevina's shoulder. She woke with a start, her red hair flying around her face.

Another growl echoed outside.

"*Weapons*," Cade mouthed to us.

Weapon?

Sleep fogged my mind. Hadn't I given my gun to Cade? Morven pressed a knife into my hand.

I eyed the weapon sitting in the palm of my hand. "What'll you use?"

Metal glinted as he held up a blade. "I got this off one of the miners while we were on their ship."

I glanced at the knife he'd given me, the wood warm in my hands, the blade straight and tapering at the tip. My heart gave a painful thump as I was reminded of the knife I'd lost, the one Mima had given me. I'd lost it somewhere near the gateway cave, and I still held out hope that someday I would find it again.

Morven's blade felt unfamiliar, the wooden handle unyielding, missing the imprint of my mima's hands.

A massive form—as large as an elephant—lumbered outside, its footsteps slow and deliberate. Sticks snapped. The growling turned to a mangled, animalistic scream.

"That can't be a wolf," I said.

"It's nothing I recognize," Vevina added.

"It's not a Mystik creature." Morven's narrowed-eyed gaze stayed locked on the cave's open entrance. "It would glow."

"Cade," Morven hissed. "Shoot it."

He held the gun we'd taken from the miners. Sand shifted as he stood and crept toward the outside. Morven, Vevina, and I also got to our feet and snuck behind him, weapons held at the ready.

When Cade reached the mouth of the cavern, he stood behind the outcropping of rocks creating the opening. A stiff breeze blew outside, sweeping the sand into clouds.

"I can't see anything," Vevina whispered.

A massive paw with sickle-sharp claws appeared out of the sandstorm and swiped at Cade. A scream ripped from his throat. He fell, dropping the gun. Three gashes bled bright red across his chest.

"Cade!" Vevina knelt by him.

"I'm okay," he gasped, clutching his hands to his chest. "Where's the gun?"

I scanned the ground, my knife held at the ready, and a blood-curdling shriek howled, overpowering the wind.

My mind went into overdrive as I calculated our odds. The cave ended at a dead end. If we retreated inside, we'd be trapped. Outside, the sand made it impossible to see, but we'd have a fighting chance—we might even distract it.

Morven and Vevina both held glowing stones.

"Throw those outside," I told them.

"But we'll be blind," Vevina argued.

"Just do it."

Morven nodded, as if he understood my plan, then threw the rock out into the howling windstorm. Vevina did the same. Only the coals and a few stones on the ground gave us any light.

The sandstorm died down. Quiet descended.

Cade limped to his feet. "Where'd it go?"

"Gather more stones," I said. "Throw them all outside."

Only Vevina gave me a shrewd look as we gathered the stones and started tossing them outside. Snarling echoed as the looming form pounced at the stones. As we threw the rest of the stones, they glowed on the ground, illuminating the beast.

Bingo.

The body of a giant hairless wolf lumbered over the glowing rocks, crunching them under massive paws. Horns rimmed its head—ones that resembled a rhino. Mangled gray flesh hung in chunks from its exposed ribcage. Gray, veiny skin stretched over its skull. Crimson eyes glowed inside its sunken sockets. Revulsion welled inside me.

I'd never seen such an abomination. Its *wrongness* hit me like a tsunami, as if the thing weren't supposed to exist. Madness glinted as it swiveled its massive head toward us.

Cade pointed his gun. He pulled the trigger, but the creature dodged, then charged him. Cade hit the ground and rolled away before wolf's paws trampled him. Vevina grasped her single blade. Shouting, she flung her weapon at the creature.

The knife landed with a sickening thump, impaling the creature's hide. The beast remained immobile, unmoving, as if it hadn't felt the blade's impact.

"*What?*" Vevina backed away.

"How do we kill it?" Morven yelped.

Another blast pulsed. This time, the electric burst struck the creature's head, but it shook off the crackling energy as if buzzing flies. The beast roared so loud my eardrums rang. I gripped the flimsy hilt of my knife. It already seemed inefficient; now it was useless.

"I think we should run," Cade called to us.

"Where?" I yelled back.

"Anywhere!"

The monster dipped its head and charged us. We scrambled out of its path, but its horn impaled my arm, ripping flesh from my bicep. Agony tore through me. The iron scent of blood pervaded the air. Warm liquid trailed down my arm and fingers.

I dropped my weapon and grabbed my arm.

Morven sprinted to me, but then the beast charged, bashing its head into him with a solid thud, throwing him to the ground.

Vevina dashed out of the way as it barreled to her, but it caught her leg with its curving horn. She fell with a strangled scream. Cade blasted another shot, pulling the beast's attention away from Vevina.

"Come get me!" He shot again. Electric waves rippled over its thick frame. It shook its head as if stunned.

"What do we do?" I asked Morven, grimacing through the pain as I clamped my hand to my injured arm.

He shook his head, his eyes wide with fear. "I don't know. Our weapons are useless against it."

"Come to me," Cade shouted, shooting it repeatedly, drawing it away from us.

Vevina crawled to us, a stream of blood trailing behind her. The windstorm picked up. By the time she made it to us, sand blasted our skin. I coughed as it entered my nose and lungs and scoured my open wound. I tasted its grittiness on my tongue.

We'll die here! I gasped for air, trying to think past the pain, the hunger and the thirst, the overwhelming exhaustion. What could we do to stop an invincible beast?

A burst of light sailed over my head.

Fire burned from the tip of an arrow that impaled the creature's hide. The leathery skin burst into flames. The creature raged. Its pain-filled roar rushed in the wind. Another arrow followed the first, sputtering and crackling, as I gagged on the scent of burning flesh engulfing the air in noxious clouds from the beast's body.

Spinning around, I searched for the source of the arrows. The sand still swirled around us, but I focused past it, scanning details, taking in every aspect of the rise and fall of the stones around us, the glow of the stones, the shapes of the rocky desert creations like soldiers at attention.

The silhouette of a man stood on the rocky outcropping. The burst of firelight of another arrow glowed, illuminating a tall, bulky frame and graying beard.

"There." I pointed to the man.

"Who is that?" Morven asked.

"*Grandenpar*," Vevina answered. "My grandfather."

The beast gave one final bellow before collapsing into a charred heap on the ground. We stared past it to the man who had saved us.

"Vevina, you wee lass," he called. "Why ever are you making me save your hide?"

"Grand," she called, waving her arms. "You old fool. Didn't Grandemair tell you not to leave the castle?"

"Aren't you glad I didn't listen to her?"

He marched down the hill toward us, dragging one foot, which gave him an unsteady gait. Still, he walked with confidence, his bow slung over his shoulder, a pride-filled smile stretching his weathered face.

The sky had begun to lighten. Pink tinged the darker gray as the sun rose—at least, what *appeared* to be the sun. I could only imagine the real sun must've appeared much dimmer on a world like this.

The old man nudged the creature with his boot. "Never seen one this large."

"You've seen beasts like this before?" I asked, cradling my injured arm to my chest.

"Aye." The wind stirred the wiry strands of his beard and gray hair. "Nasty creatures, these."

"What are they?" Cade asked.

"Mutated wolves, as far as I can tell."

Morven knelt by the corpse. "This hardly resembles a wolf."

Its smoldering remains put off a repugnant scent that made me hold my breath. Thick bones comprised its charred skull. Horns curved from its nose and head, looking nothing like a canine.

Vevina crossed her arms. "Grand, how did your arrows kill it? We tried with every weapon we had, and they didn't have any effect."

"Aye." He bobbed his head, then touched his bow, his gnarled fingers running over smooth wood. "We had the problem the first time one of these beasts went after our sheep, 'twas nigh six months past. Our arrows wouldn't pierce its hide. Knives and swords, useless. Then I says to meself, Duncan, these beasts come from the north woods. There's got to be something in that forest making them this way. So, I go out there. Do you know what I find?"

He stood as tall as he could with his stooped shoulders.

"What did you find?" Vevina asked.

"A stream full of steaming orange water. Smelled awful. But those beasts had been drinking from it for quite some time. It was doing this to them." He nudged the skull with his toe. "I know that for sure."

"What made the water turn orange?" I asked.

He shrugged. "I can't say. I've never seen anything like it. But I says to meself, if that water is what's making the creatures turn sour, then maybe it will work to kill them the same way. So, I took some of the water, boiled it down until I get this orange substance, and tipped my arrows in it. Didn't work at first, not until I decided to light them on fire." He raised a finger. "That's what finally did it. Killed a beast last week. Now I've killed this one. Orange fire—far as I can tell, only thing that does the trick."

"Well." Vevina placed her hands on her hips. "That's well and fine, Grand, but I'll have you know we've been wandering this waste going on two days now with nothing but a bit of berries to eat. Now, we're half dead from that creature's attack."

"Two days? Why've you been out in this dreadful place for so long?"

"That's a long tale. For now, we'd like to get back to the castle and bandage our wounds."

"Very well." His grizzled hair flounced as he bobbed his head. "Why didn't you say so in the first place?" He pulled out a canteen of green cerecite and passed it around. When it came my turn to drink, I gulped a few mouthfuls of the bitter liquid. Although it burned as I swallowed, the pain in my arm soon subsided.

"Come along," Vevina's grandfather said. "Your grandemair will be happy to see you."

He turned and headed toward the hills. I gave one last look at the creature before following. What did the stream with the orange water have to do with its mutation? The situation didn't sit well with me. On Earth, mutations were usually a result of radiation. The same scientific principles should've applied to Ceres.

Morven grabbed my hand, his warmth coming as a pleasant shock. His crooked smile made my insides flutter.

"What are you thinking?" he asked.

I glanced back at the body. Only a few trails of smoke rose from the behemoth's body. Blackened ribs fanned toward the sky.

"Radiation," I said. "The stream Duncan found must've been the run-off from some sort of radioactive material."

"Cerecite," Morven suggested.

"I don't know. Cerecite has never created radioactive run-off."

"Then it's a mystery," Morven said.

"Yes. We need to find out how the run-off got into the stream. I don't think it's a coincidence that the mutations started appearing around the same time the miners began illegally mining cerecite."

Morven knit his brows, and his dark eyes narrowed, as if he were deep in thought. "If they weren't careful about mining—which they most likely weren't—they could've created an environmental crisis."

"I agree. Maybe we need to check out this stream."

"Yes," he said. "But first, I plan to eat something. I'll start with a loaf of sourdough with generous amounts of butter."

"Mmm…" My mouth salivated at the thought of actual food.

The sun crested the horizon as we reached the hillock's summit. A scene from a fairy tale spread before us. A lake of deep sapphire water reflected the towers of a keep rising above it.

"Welcome to MacKinnon Keep,"

Vevina breathed deeply. Her shoulders relaxed. The breeze stirred, gently lifting the long strands of her hair. She stood as if the weight of the world had lifted from her shoulders. "Home," she said quietly, her voice carried by the wind.

A pang of jealousy pinched me. I had grown so distant from my life in Kansas that Ithical felt more like home. The last time I'd visited with my father, I'd slept on the couch. He'd gotten so accustomed to me being gone that he used my old room for storage, and he treated me like a visitor. And I had to admit, that's what I'd become. A visitor to my home, a place so impermanent, I couldn't imagine living there after spending time on Ceres.

Yet I couldn't forget the memories of home. The scents of fresh baked bread and warm apple pies. Of running barefoot through the fields. Listening to the sound of rain on the tin roof. Sitting in the barn's loft and watching the stars twinkle overhead, never realizing my importance in their place.

Soon, after I'd completed my mission, I would make Kansas my home again. It was the only permanent place I'd known—a home where Mom and Mima were buried, the place where I truly belonged.

8

My arm throbbed a little beneath a clean linen wrap as we made our way through MacKinnon Keep. I counted my blessings for the green cerecite. Otherwise, not only would an infection have been setting in, but the pain would have been excruciating.

Ornate sconces filled with orbs of blue cerecite radiated light through the hallways. Our footsteps echoed in the stone passages with ceilings that rose twenty feet above us. Awe filled me. I felt like I'd stepped back in time to the realm of Scottish kings and castles. Ceres never ceased to surprise me.

I followed the others into an expansive room. A massive hearth took up half the back wall. Sea dragons and crashing waves carved from turquoise cerecite formed the trim and mantlepiece that rose all the way to the ceiling. Flames crackled from the firebox, and wool rugs softened the wood floors. Overstuffed chairs, couches, and roughly hewn coffee tables were arranged near the fire.

"You can sit there." Duncan pointed to the chairs. "I'll have the servants bring in a pint o' ale for you, and some breakfast, I think. Haggis and eggs should do the trick." He chuckled as he patted his granddaughter's shoulder. "Take a rest here, will you? No need for the dining hall this early. 'Tis more comfortable here in the parlor anyway. I'll return in a moment."

"Thank you, Grand," Vevina said.

"Aye. 'Tis nothing."

He ambled out, and we crossed toward the seating area. As I walked, I catalogued the minute details: a chandelier made of antlers. Twelve stones of blue cerecite inside each candle holder, one slightly dimmer than the others. I breathed the musty smell coming from the leather upholstery, the threading bare in places. Seven off-color stones near a bookshelf, lighter gray than the others, square-shaped as opposed to rectangular. Books lined in neat rows on the shelves, ordered by color: burgundy, green, blue…

"Sabine." Morven's light touch on my hand brought me back.

I glanced up, taking in a deep breath as I tried realigning my reality.

"Sorry."

"It's okay." He smiled, warmth exuding from the expression, and that knot forming in my stomach disappeared.

He gave me a questioning glance. "Your ability?"

I nodded. *Ability. Right.* Since I'd used my obsessiveness in finding the lost stones of white cerecite, I'd tried convincing myself it wasn't a curse. But sometimes such an ability got me into more trouble than it was worth.

"You okay?" he asked.

"Yes, I'm fine." I rubbed my eyes. A night of sleeping on the ground had left my muscles stiff and protesting, and my stomach had been grumbling incessantly at the lack of food. "Sorry." I sighed. "Sometimes I'm lousy at controlling it."

Morven took my hand in his and gently kissed my forehead. "You don't need to apologize for being yourself."

At his calming words, warmth seeped through my chest. He gave me strength I didn't know I had. "Thank you," I said sincerely. I reached up and brushed a lock of dark hair from his forehead, my stomach aflutter at the intensity I found in his mesmerizing, intelligent eyes.

It struck me how Morven accepted me wholly—flaws and all—but perhaps that was because I'd given him the same courtesy. I'd treated him as a person while he'd been in his wheelchair, while everyone else had ignored him.

Cade and Vevina's voices drifted as they sat around the fire, and Morven and I joined them. I sank into the couch's soft cushion, the scent of well-oiled leather surrounding me, conjuring memories of the saddles in the barn back home, of horses and fresh hay, and dew-soaked grass slipping under my feet as I carried a bucket of oats with the sun tinting the sky. Of fresh air. What I wouldn't give to smell that again.

Cade and Vevina's conversation broke through my thoughts.

"…near the stream," Vevina finished.

"Can we get inside?"

"It's difficult, but yes."

Cade worked his jaw from side to side. "I'm beginning to hate caves."

I sat up as their conversation caught my attention. "What's this about?"

Vevina explained. "It's the source of the stream my grand was telling us about."

"We need to check it out," Morven said, sitting with his elbows resting on his knees. Tendons flexed in his hands, which had been strengthened by wheeling his chair for so many years.

"We'll have to gather provisions first," Cade said. "Leave at first light."

"Great," I added. "Vortech will be expecting me soon. If the miners are responsible for tainting the water, that could be something they're concerned about." My gaze went to the flames crackling in the fireplace. I prayed Vortech cared enough to do something about it, but my gut told me the company only had interest in protecting itself.

Regardless, I needed to find the source of the tainted water. If Vortech had any concern about protecting this world, at least they'd want to know the truth. They had sent me here to find those responsible behind the illegal mining, and I fully intended to accomplish that mission.

Especially since I'd lost all the evidence.

My heart gave an anxious flutter, and I reminded myself I probably should be careful about mentioning that bit of information. Maybe if I could find more evidence, all would be forgiven.

Who was I kidding? Vortech had never been a lenient employer. If I failed, I'd most likely be out of a job. If it weren't for my familiarity with this world, I had no doubt I would've been sent packing a long time ago.

The thought of leaving Ithical Island and never returning was a frightening prospect. I'd come to think of it as my home. If I left, a piece of me would go with it. Not to mention, I'd fallen for the prince of the island, and being parted from him was torturous.

The doors swung open, and servers entered carrying platters piled with steaming food that smelled of savory cooked meat. My mouth watered, and my empty stomach growled so loudly, I was thankful the others were talking and didn't notice.

They placed several platters on the low tables. I picked up a loaf of round, crusty bread and a portion of thinly sliced meat. The saltiness of the meat burst with flavor, and the buttery bread melted in my mouth. I wasn't sure I'd ever tasted anything so heavenly. Then again, starvation made food taste incredible.

I had the thought that I'd never truly tasted real food until this moment. Canned ravioli and Top Ramen had nothing on this.

Bootsteps echoed as Vevina's grandfather entered the room. A clean linen shirt and leather slippers replaced his animal skin cloak and muddy boots, and a golden brooch glinted from a plaid tartan arranged on his shoulder. He'd gone from a wild man to a refined lord. A rosy-faced woman bustled behind him, her white hair curled around her wrinkled face. Her warm eyes and friendly smile reminded me of Mima, and a pang of sorrow gripped me, causing a lump to form in my throat.

"Vee, you wee girl, come here." The woman shuffled to her granddaughter. Vevina stood, and the two embraced, the top of her grandmother's head barely reaching Vevina's chin. Hands bent with age patted the girl's back. "My, you're not a wee thing anymore, are you?" She pulled away and gently cupped her granddaughter's face. "And what a pretty thing, too."

When the elderly woman pulled away from her granddaughter, she glanced at our group. Her gaze landed on Morven, and she gasped, then gave a bow.

"Duncan," she chided her husband, pinning him with a severe glare. "Whyever didn't you tell me the prince was here?"

"Didn't think it too important, what since he's nearly family," the older man answered, twiddling his mustache.

"*Nearly* family, but not family yet," the woman replied. "Vevina and Morven are only betrothed, and who knows when the wedding will happen? I've been waiting nigh seventeen years come this August."

An awkward silence fell over our group, and I had to do my best to breathe. *Betrothed?* Surely, I'd heard wrong. But Morven's manner toward Vevina made me suspect something had happened between them. Now it all made sense. A wave of cold dread washed over me.

I chanced a glance at Morven. He stood with his jaw locked, the usual defensiveness in his eyes, looking how he did six months ago when he'd been forced to sit in his wheelchair all day. Well, at least he didn't seem happy about it. But why hadn't he ever told me?

"Grandem," Vevina huffed, her freckled face going red. "What a thing to bring up at a time like this!"

"Well." The older woman crossed her arms. "Whyever can't I bring it up? You and the prince never act as if it will happen, but we all know—sure as rain—that wedding is bound to happen sooner rather than later. Being betrothed as children doesn't make it a null ceremony, now do it?" She patted Vevina's cheeks. "Now, enough of this. Why don't you introduce me to the rest of the group?"

Vevina took a deep breath, as if she wanted to say something else, then turned to us and plastered a polite smile on her face. "Everyone, please meet my grandem. Grandem," she pointed to each of us in turn, "this is Cade MacDougall and Sabine Harper."

We nodded in acknowledgment.

"Well." Grandem clasped her hands. "I daresay we weren't expecting visitors, but you're welcome to our home all the same. I pray we'll be able to find changes of clothes for you somewhere in this old place. It's seen six generations, after all. And we're nay keen on throwing anything out." She chuckled quietly. "You may wander the keep and its grounds, but we need you indoors once night falls. As you well know, there's trouble with the wolves."

"We were hoping to travel to the stream in the north forest," Vevina said.

Her eyes widened. "Whyever would you go there?"

Vevina's grandfather cleared his throat. "They're curious about the tainted water."

"Aye, I gathered that. But 'tis a dangerous place."

He waved his hand. "I've been out there and survived. They'll be fine, Lyall."

She gave him a stern glare, then placed her hands on her

full hips. "And what of the caves? They'll not be going there, will they?" She shook her finger in his face. "You know the tales as well as I. 'Tis haunted by the bodach, it is."

"Aye." Duncan's forehead wrinkled as he stroked his beard. "I suppose it is."

A *bodach*? It wasn't a word I'd ever heard before. I guess it must've been a superstition carried over from their ancestors.

"Grandem, you know those are myth," Vevina said. "There's nay such thing as a bodach."

"What say you?" Her stopped shoulders stiffened. "There is such thing. I've been around long enough to know that. Me own grand saw one, sure as day."

Vevina threw up her hands. "That was a hundred years ago!"

"Nay. No less than seventy years."

Vevina sighed, casting a withering glance to our group, still seated on the couch and eating contentedly. "But you'll not stop us. We've got to find the source of that taint, or those wolves will keep attacking us. I fear beasts of bone and blood more than myths."

Grandem chuckled, her voice softening. "You're more like me than you think, Vee. Very well. Travel to the caves if you must but take a bit o' braw with you." Her gaze went to Cade and Morven. "These two will do nicely. Healthy fellas, aye? Braw indeed."

"Grandem…" Vevina groaned.

The old woman's eyes sparkled with mischief. "Aye, I remember being young. Believe it or not, Duncan was once a braw thing, too. Still is, if you ask me."

The aging man's plaid tartan rustled as he gave a deep belly chuckle.

Vevina rolled her eyes. "Don't mind them. Still lovebirds after fifty years of marriage. Never cease to embarrass me, they do."

The elderly couple clasped hands. Adoration shone in

their glances at one another, and my heart gave a painful squeeze. Why had I been so naïve to think I could have a prince like Morven? He'd mentioned his peoples' adherence to the old ways—including betrothals. I should have seen this coming.

I couldn't help but wish that someday I'd be able to have a life like Vevina's grandparents, to spend it with someone who loved me the same way they cared for each other.

I glanced at Morven, at the firm resolve in his eyes, the straight line of his profile, the strong chin and jawline that spoke of masculinity and strength—but not merely physical. Morven was the most honest, intelligent person I knew. And while those traits got him into trouble at times, it allowed me to trust him. Yet right now he didn't dare meet my gaze.

Picturing the rest of my life spent with him came too easily, a picture that seemed so surreal, I knew it could never be reality.

Even if he cared for me the way I hoped, what kind of future did we have? We were from two different worlds. He was destined to be a king. I was tied to a corporation who owned me, and without them, I had nothing. Betrothal or not, we'd never been a good fit. I had plans to return to my home —and he to his.

I took a deep breath to chase away that familiar pang of loneliness. No need to let the betrothal situation distract me. For now, I had a mission to accomplish, and it was best if I stayed focused on it.

For the time being, Morven wasn't married, and I would cherish whatever time I managed to spend with him.

"…we'll have plenty of time to rest up for a few hours…" Cade was saying. "Then go to the caves and be back before dark."

"Take Brutus with you," Grandem said. "He's the most obedient sheep dog we've got, and he'll chase a wolf away sure as day. Mind you, not a giant one the likes we've been seeing, but he'll give fair warning if one of those beasts sneak up on you."

"Very well," Grand said. "Now let them get their rest, Lyall. They've been out in those wastes nigh two days."

"True, But I've got to prepare the bed linens, haven't I? Musty covers haven't been used in years. They'll have to be changed afore anyone can sleep on them."

"Don't worry about the linens, Grandem," Vevina said. "If it's all the same to you, we'll take our rest here."

"What?" Her eyes widened. "On the rugs and couches?"

"'Tis better than the rocks we slept on last night, trust me," Vevina said.

Grandem pressed her lips into a severe straight line. "Ah, very well. Take yer rest here, but I'll at least bring in a woolen plaid or two."

"I'll help you," Vevina said, hurriedly standing, as if she needed a reason to leave the room.

"Very well. Come along then." Grandem bustled to the door, and Vevina followed.

"They'll be but a moment, then," Duncan said. "If it's all the same to you, I'll leave you be. You'll need the rest before heading to the stream."

"Thank you," we answered, then he too left the room, along with the servants who exited with the empty trays behind him.

Morven gripped my fingers and gave me a smile that didn't touch his eyes. "So, you heard."

"Yes," I answered. "I heard."

A twinge of nausea made me wish again for the fresh air of the forests surrounding my Kansas home. "Why didn't you tell me?"

"To be honest, the betrothal was never real to me. I was a kid when it happened. I didn't understand what it meant. After my parents died and my aunt took control, no one talked about it. She'd offended the MacKinnons, as you know. I assumed the betrothal was off. But now, since things with the miners are being smoothed out, and the relationship with the nobles are better, I guess those stupid traditions have managed to survive." He shook his head. "This is a great example of the problem with our system. It's completely arcane."

"But what can you do about it?"

He shrugged. "Nothing for now. Our top priority is to keep Ithical safe from illegal mining. I refuse to consider anything else beyond that." He squeezed my hand. "This changes nothing between us."

I only nodded, unsure what to say. A torrent of bleak emotions warred within me, hollowing me until I felt like a shell without a soul. He hugged me, and I rested my head on his shoulder. A lump formed in my throat as I stared blankly at the fire, my hand in his, the scent of wild forests surrounding me, filling those empty spaces inside me until it didn't seem I was too far from home after all.

9

Tree branches rustled as we walked through the north woods. Although Morven kept shooting sympathetic glances and reaching for my hand, after the revelation of his betrothal, I had turned numb inside. I was doing my best to ignore the prospect of the looming wedding, but my heart had retreated from him.

A playful bark broke me from my thoughts. Brutus, the shaggy-coated, black-and-white sheep dog, followed us. His tongue lolled as he trotted alongside us, smiling happily as we navigated the narrow trail, as if he were born for this.

I patted his head, his fur curly and soft, and he gave me a polite lick. "You're a good dog, aren't you?"

"Don't get too friendly," Vevina called over her shoulder. "He'll follow you around and beg for every scrap of food you've got."

"He's also a fearsome wolf killer," Morven added. "Don't forget."

"Fearsome." I gave him a scratch behind his ears. His fur grew so thick, I could barely make out his eyes under the mass of white fur. "He looks like a big teddy bear to me."

"Are you kidding?" Morven asked. "Look at those massive paws. That'll strike fear into any beast for sure."

I laughed. "Paws? All I see is fur."

Brutus gave a playful woof that carried through the trees. Out here, in nature and away from the castle, it was easy to pretend that Morven's marriage would never happen. I ran my fingers over the green leaves, each one uniform, without a spot of rot. I'd never get used to seeing such perfection. It nagged at me in a way I couldn't describe, although at least now I knew why the plants looked so unusual. They were engineered from green cerecite. This world's natural beauty its seeds and flowers, fruits and vegetables—were nothing more than a man-made product of science.

The trail sloped downward. Moss grew on stones of turquoise cerecite, dimming their glow. Ahead, running water cut through the chatter of birds. We entered a clearing where sunlight bathed the grass and bushes. Steam rose from the stream as it cut through the brambles. When we approached, I inhaled a sharp, chemical odor mingled with the unsavory scent of rotting fish. Brown grass edged either side of the stream, and dead carp and trout bobbed on the surface. The orange-tinted liquid bubbled lazily, as if boiling, giving the appearance of lava.

"Looks like we've found it," Morven said, wrinkling his nose.

"Now we follow it to the caves." Vevina turned on her heel and walked along the stream's edge. "Come," she called over her shoulder.

Twigs snapped under my boots as I followed the others. I did my best to breathe through my mouth, though the chemical odor still managed to burn my lungs. Brutus whined as he sniffed the air, and I patted his head.

"Awful smell. I know," I said.

He only whined once more, though he stayed at our side. Uniform blades of grass carpeted the forest floor. Cade and

Vevina spoke quietly ahead of me and Morven. Vevina talked of her life at the keep, and how she hadn't been back in six months since the miner's revolt. She spoke of her father, and the adoration in her voice was apparent.

Her lashes fluttered, and her cheeks grew rosy as she cast a guarded smile at Cade. I wondered at her feelings for the former miner.

Morven's hand brushed mine. When I turned to him, his bright smile caught me off guard. Sometimes I had to remind myself that this was Morven now—someone who smiled and made jokes, and not the somber prince I'd first met. Still, that spark of intelligence remained in his eyes, and it was that feature that drew me to him most.

"What are you thinking about?" he asked.

I glanced in the direction of the couple walking several paces ahead of us. "Vevina," I said softly, the noise of running water helping to keep them from overhearing me. "I think she's attracted to Cade."

His forehead creased. "Cade?"

"Yes. She mentioned she had feelings for him."

"Feelings for him, huh?" he questioned quietly. "It seems she's taking this betrothal about as seriously as I am." His eyes darkened. "But doesn't she realize Cade can't be trusted?"

"I doubt it. And it's only an infatuation, after all. She doesn't know him well enough to make any sort of judgment on his character."

Morven's jaw ticked. "I still don't understand why we're trusting him. He nearly killed you." He cocked his head, studying me. "She doesn't know that bit of information, does she?"

I hesitated before answering. "No. And I'm not sure I should be the one to tell her."

"If you don't, then I will."

Something inside me rebelled at the notion of telling Vevina of Cade's past. How many times had Cade sincerely asked for forgiveness? How many times had he helped us since then?

"Just wait to tell her," I told Morven.

"Wait?" he questioned. "Why?"

"Because Cade has changed. He's not the same person he was during the miner's revolt. I think we ought to at least give him a chance."

Morven stiffened. "I don't like that idea. What if he hurts Vevina?"

"I don't know if you realize it, but Vevina is pretty good at taking care of herself."

"Maybe." His skeptical tone told me he wasn't fond of my idea—and I had to admit, I could've been completely wrong about Cade. What if he was only pretending to be sorry to gain our trust?

I rubbed my throbbing temples where a headache pounded. Why were some choices so difficult to make? "I'd feel more comfortable if we waited to tell her. At least until we get back to the capital."

"Fine." Morven sighed, looking past me to the dark shapes of trees. "But she needs to know."

"I understand. And I completely agree. But Cade needs a chance at forgiveness, even if it's just a small one." I grasped the pendant around my neck, the pyramid's corners pressing into my palm, a match to the one Cade wore—an object he apparently knew nothing about.

But could that be another lie?

Confusion weighed on me. Maybe it would've been better for Vevina to distance herself from him, but I had to admit that Cade could be charming—and he wasn't bad to look at. Still, I wasn't sure I needed to worry. Chances were Cade had no interest in the girl in the first place.

The path grew rocky. Pebbles replaced grass as we trod up a sloping hill. When we reached the top, an open expanse greeted us. The landscape changed dramatically from verdant forest to rocky wasteland—though that seemed typical for Ceres, especially in places that hadn't been terraformed yet.

The mouth of a cave stood out as a black maw against the backdrop of a cloudless, purple-tinged sky. Orange water streamed from the opening, softly gurgling as it wound its way down the hill and into the forest.

"We'll have to enter quietly." Vevina stood with a straight back as she faced the cavern's entrance, the wind tugging at the long strands of her deep auburn hair. Her willow-thin frame belied her strength. She was the vision of an ancient Scottish princess—one I would be hesitant to cross.

"Wouldn't want to wake the boggart," Cade teased.

"The *bodach*," Vevina corrected. "'Tis nothing to take lightly."

"Do you really believe the legend?" Cade asked.

She shrugged. "They say my great-grand saw one."

I took a step forward, broken shale crunching under my boots as I approached the cavern. Even from this distance, cool air wafted from the open chamber. "The story of the bodach reminds me of the superstitions surrounding the wormhole cave." I glanced at Morven. "Didn't you say those caves were thought to be haunted?"

"Yes." Morven stood next to me. "Odd that both caves are surrounded in superstition."

"It's not a coincidence," Cade spoke up, his piercing blue eyes locked on the tunnel's entrance. "There's usually advanced tech associated with places like this. My guess is there's some sort of spacecraft inside—or at least something associated with Project Ceres."

"You think the miners from Project Ceres came here?"

Cade knit his brows in concentration. "We mined in more than one location. If so, it means this mine would be rich in cerecite ore."

"So… no bodach?" I asked.

"No, though there may be some terrifying rusted miner's equipment from the future."

"Which may explain how the bodach legend got started," I said.

"Possibly," Cade said. "But then again, we're going into this blind. Who knows what's lurking inside?"

"None of my people have ever gone in there," Vevina said.

"Then we'll be the first to find out," Morven added.

We started toward the entrance, though Vevina stayed a few paces behind us. When we entered, her wide eyes darted to the walls of slate, the crumbling stones littering the ground, and the glowing spheres like mushroom tops, as tall as dinner tables, lighting our way.

We followed the path of the trickling stream through a narrow passage. The scent of chemicals made tears spring to my eyes, and I held my arm over my nose, praying the fumes didn't kill us. When the path widened, the odor lessened. The floor sloped dramatically downward, and in some places, we were forced to climb on hands and knees.

The thunder of a waterfall boomed from the passageway ahead. Misty spray dampened the air. After following the stream until it turned to a flowing river, we stopped at the base of an underground waterfall that fell from a hundred feet above.

I took in the sounds of the water, the droplets of mist dancing, and the glow of the stones spiraling upward, situated in the cavernous dome above.

"A dead end?" Cade called.

Around us, the room seemed to box us in, but the waterfall had to come from somewhere. "I don't think so." I gazed to the top of the waterfall. Slick rocks comprised the wall. "Climbing to the top would be suicide. One missed step and we'd fall to our death."

I allowed my ability to surface, and it came in bright

contrast, like a light switch when turned on to reveal the smallest of details.

A glint of turquoise caught my eye. A dark spot in the wall juxtaposed the lighter stones around it. An opening?

"Through there." I pointed past the waterfall to the darker area. "It might be a passageway."

The others followed as I picked my way over uneven stones. I slipped but managed to keep my balance. By the time I made it up the slope, my lungs burned from inhaling the chemical mist.

"I don't know how safe this air is," I shouted over the waterfall's roar.

"I agree," Morven said as he climbed behind me. "If we don't find something soon, we'll have to go back the way we came."

I glanced toward the passageway leading behind the waterfall. Beyond it spanned blackness, and I couldn't be sure what lay inside.

"We'll need to be quick about it," Vevina shouted.

I led the way. None of the glowing stones appeared here, so I was forced to press my hands to either side of the slippery walls to keep my balance. Panic unsettled me as I pondered what we might discover, or if the floor opened to a giant pit, or if we happened to encounter another wolf.

The footsteps of the others echoed behind me, and Brutus' panting filled the air. His padded paws shifted over the loose shale.

Fresh air rushed past, replacing the stifling odor of fumes. I breathed it in. Though a mechanical undertone still carried on the chilly draft, I preferred it to the alternative. Light came from ahead, illuminating the hard lines of the walls and floor.

A frigid breeze bit at my skin, and when we neared the exit, I was shocked to see snow. A white blanket covered the landscape of gently sloping hills, punctuated by turquoise stones.

"Snow?" I questioned, bending down and touching the white powder. Its iciness chilled my fingertips.

"We should've worn our coats," Morven suggested.

"Where'd it come from?" I asked.

Brutus sniffed it, then trotted toward a drift, his muzzle damp, his nose topped with a snow puff.

This planet had the weirdest weather patterns.

Cade nudged the snow with his toe. "We must've hit the outer rim."

Outer rim? Memories flooded back. When I'd first come to Ceres, my guide Ivan had taken me through the snowy tundra before arriving on the inner continent. An image of a map of Ceres also flashed in my mind's eye. The island was surrounded in a barrier of snow—but since we were on a planet, and not an island, how did that translate? Were there perhaps north and south poles? That was a question I couldn't answer, but perhaps Vortech could.

"Up there." Cade pointed to a hilltop.

I followed his line of sight to a narrow spindle rising into the sky. "An antenna of some sort?"

"Looks like something Project Ceres would've built. We should check it out."

We trudged up the hill. Snow cushioned our footfalls. Brutus gave a playful *whoof*, his giant tail wagging his entire shaggy body. Chills bristled my skin, and I rubbed my arms for warmth.

The structure came into view: a squat black building that stood out against the backdrop of a white void. The snow grew deeper as we hiked. Its wetness soaked through my pants and shoes, freezing my calves and shins.

When we stopped at the top of the hill, my breath came out in puffs of frozen air. Shivers racked my body, and my teeth chattered. I focused on the building to distract me from the cold.

One door. Metal. Rust around the frame. No knob. A control pad with buttons covered in a layer of ice. No other entrances, at least from this vantagepoint.

I crossed my arms, breathing shallowly in the thin air, as we approached the door.

"No knob," I said through chattering teeth. "No windows either."

Morven stepped to the control panel. He used his elbow to knock the ice away, and it fell to the ground with the clatter that sounded of broken glass. I stepped closer to inspect the rusted buttons.

An open gap remained where one of the switches had once been. The letters above it had faded so badly, they were unreadable.

"I don't know if we'll get in through here," Morven said.

Cade stepped toward it. "I remember control panels like these. But that was a long time ago…" His voice drifted as if he were caught up in a memory. He ran his fingers over the open slot. "We need a key."

"What kind of key?" Morven asked.

He shook his head, allowing his fingers to trail over the empty niche the size of a half-dollar. "Something about this size." He sighed in frustration. "I remember coming out to a place like this once. There was trouble with a generator, and they wanted my team to repair it. Our supervisor opened the door…" He tapped his chin, then shook his head, his shoulders slumped. "Something was weird about this place."

"Look over here." Vevina's voice carried from the far side of the structure. Cade, Morven and I followed the source of the sound until we reached her. She stood looking over a stream of orange sludge cutting a path through the snowdrift. It trickled from a hole in the building's outer wall, then continued down the hill and to the cavern we'd come through.

"At least now we know where the chemicals are coming from," Morven said.

"Yeah, which means it's even more important that we get inside," I added.

Vevina glanced toward the building's entrance. "We could try breaking down the door."

"Maybe," Cade said. "But those doors are three feet of solid titanium reinforced with yellow cerecite. I don't think we'll be getting it open. But… if that's our only choice, I guess we should try."

The others wandered back to the door while I stayed behind.

The black metal building loomed, taunting me, the antenna protruding from the top like an alien structure. A faint buzzing came from it. Something inside must've been functioning.

An idea niggled at the back of my mind. Something bugged me about the control panel—something that seemed familiar. I wandered back to the door as the others stood by it. Cade grunted as he rammed his shoulder into the metal.

Facing the control panel, I studied every aspect. *Flecks of rust around the edges. Faded words. The top of a T, an A, and L.* Other than that, nothing was discernible.

I ran my fingers over the panel. Divots pocked the surface. Preserved by the cold, the metal could've been three-hundred years old. Cold steel chilled my fingertips. I inspected the opening where the buttons were missing, but as I studied it, realized perhaps nothing was missing. Perhaps it was built purposely this way.

A square-shaped opening, tapering to a point inside the metal.

I grasped the pendant around my neck. Was it possible?

Without overthinking it, I cradled the pyramid that had been warmed by my skin, then I inserted it into the opening.

The screech of grating metal echoed. The others jumped away from the door as it began to slowly slide open.

"What did you do?" Cade asked.

I held up the pendant. "I found the key."

10

S tale air wafted from the opening doorway. The grating of metal set my teeth on edge. Bits of rust fell from the frame and rained onto the floor beneath. A blue glow shone faintly from inside, illuminating the dark shapes of machinery and control panels.

"Is it safe?" Vevina asked, her eyes wide.

"I don't know," Morven answered. "But there's only one way to find out." He stepped into the room, and we followed. Beeping came from a screen to the left, and a gray glow came from around us in every direction. The circular space disoriented me, and I had to face the open doorway, allowing the snow-covered landscape to keep me grounded.

"Is this a screen?" Morven asked. He walked to a gray wall and touched one. Light blossomed from the walls, displaying a view of the surrounding landscape, as if he'd opened windows rimming the room to reveal the outside scenery. Lines and dots appeared, outlining the hills. I turned a complete circle, staring in awe. The glow of sunlight bathed my face.

"I thought this building didn't have any windows," I said.

"It doesn't." Morven knocked on the wall, and a metallic clanging echoed.

Fluorescent lights buzzed to life from the machines beneath the window screens.

"I remember this," Cade whispered to himself, the glow surrounding him, giving his eyes an eerie blue hue. He walked to a control panel and pressed his hand to a flat disc. "This is the east generator. It's one of four located in the north, south, east and west. They power the shield covering the planet." He went to a panel and pressed a button. The scene switched from a view of the surrounding hills to a telescopic view of the planet from space. A shell of purple light, resembling Earth's atmosphere, encased Ceres.

Vevina jumped back. "What happened?"

"I switched the view," Cade said. He pushed another button and four dots appeared around the perimeter of the planet. Cade pointed. "Those are the locations of the shield generators."

He flipped a switch that echoed with a hollow click. Three of the dots turned green, and one changed to yellow.

The dots flickered faintly under a layer of dust clinging to the screens.

"Is that where we're at?" I asked, pointing to the yellow light.

"Most likely," Cade answered.

"It's yellow," Morven said. "Is that because this generator is damaged?"

"I think so," Cade answered.

"That's our world?" Vevina asked hesitantly.

"Yes," Cade answered matter-of-factly.

"But…" She stepped closer to the screen, staring at the glowing purple orb.

Questions swam through my head while we gave her a moment to absorb what she was seeing. I knew we were on Ceres; knew we were under a dome. But so much of this was foreign. An image of standing in the field near my home flashed in my mind's eye. The fresh scent of wheat. Puffy clouds in the sky. Sunshine on my skin. A place that was normal. A place where I didn't have to question the realities of the universe. Now, everything felt so strange, I had trouble accepting what I saw as truth.

Cade was standing near Vevina. The woman's face had gone white, and she could do nothing but stare at the screen with a slacked jaw and wide eyes. Cade was speaking softly to her. "…been misled our whole lives. When our ancestors came to this island, they crossed through a portal that took them here. Ceres. Another world, millions of miles from Earth."

Vevina reached out and touched the screen. Her fingers smeared the dust and created a rippling wake that made the planet's image seem to waver.

"How is this possible?" she asked.

"It's a long story," Morven said. "But if I ever get my way, and we introduce a university to our world, I hope we'll be able to educate our people about the truth."

Vevina didn't make a reply. She only stood staring at the screen, her mouth gaping, as if she couldn't believe what was right in front of her eyes.

"What now?" I asked after giving Vevina a moment to process. I imagined her shock must have been overwhelming. Even so, we had more important matters to handle. "How do we repair this place?"

Morven spun around, inspecting the walls and floor. "There's got to a be a leak in here."

We searched the room with him. I allowed my ability to surface as I scrutinized every nook and cranny.

"How would this place last so long?" I ran my fingers over the flat plane of metal panels. "It had to have been here hundreds of years sitting abandoned. Wouldn't it have stopped functioning a long time ago?"

"It's powered by a specially engineered type of yellow

cerecite called pharocite," Cade answered. "It'll power the generators another five-hundred years, give or take, as long as nothing disrupts the pharocite—but I suspect this one has been disrupted."

"Which begs the question—how did it get disrupted?" I asked.

"No idea," Cade answered.

"We need to find out where the pharocite was stored," Morven said, addressing Cade. "Any ideas where to look?"

Cade shook his head. "Only the engineers would have known the location of the power chamber. Search the room."

Empty footsteps echoed as we combed through the open chamber. As I paced, the chemical odor grew stronger. I followed the source of the scent until I reached a blank wall panel. Orange ooze crusted the base of the metal paneling.

I knelt to inspect it more closely. A tiny fissure cracked the base of the wall where the substance leaked. "Over here," I called over my shoulder.

The others gathered around me. Morven knelt by me, then removed his knife from the sheath on his boot. He stuck the blade into the crack. Bits of rust flaked off until he created a hole.

Wires of red and blue peeked from the opening.

"I'll bet the pharocite was kept behind this wall," Morven said.

"Agreed," I said. "Will we have to break it down?"

Cade inspected the wall. "Not necessarily. Look for a control panel or a latch. We may be able to release it and open the door."

I searched with the others around the room. Running my hands over the cold metal, I scrutinized every detail, allowing my ability to work without hindrance. My fingers brushed over a bump in the wall. Vibrations pulsed under my fingertips as I moved my palm from one side to the other. I focused on the areas where the pulses were the strongest, stopping in the middle of the blank metal wall.

I knocked on the panel. Clanging metal echoed. Cade stood behind me.

"What are you doing?" he asked.

"There's something behind here. It's vibrating. It could be the control panel, but I wouldn't know how to access it without breaking down the wall."

He worked his jaw back and forth as if in concentration. "Press your hand to the wall. Hold it flat with all five fingers extended."

I gave him a questioning glance, but I did as he said. With my hand against the metal, I held my palm and fingers flat.

A click echoed. Blue light shone from under my hand.

"I think that did the trick," he said. "It's a handprint lock. Good work finding it."

"But how did it recognize my fingerprints?"

He pointed to the pendant around my neck. "I suspect it scanned that and allowed you access."

The metal moved inward, then lifted with a mechanical hiss. A pressurized burst of air issued from the opening doorway to reveal a closet-sized room.

Wires and cords comprised the chamber surrounding a glass box, though the top was busted open, and shards littered the floor.

An orange ooze leaked from several of the hoses, and I held my nose against the scouring scent of chemical acid.

I took a step inside. "Looks like we found where the pharocite was kept."

"Yeah," Morven answered. "How is this place even functioning without it?"

"There's a few shards left." Cade pointed to a group of orange crystals crusting the inside of the glass. "But it won't last long."

Vevina, who'd managed to pull herself away from the

image of the planet on the screen, shot him a questioning glance. "Meaning what?"

"Meaning that once these crystals' energy is drained, the shield generator fails. It'll open a hole in the atmosphere. This area of the planet will be left unprotected."

A prickle of fear shot down my spine. "But if that happens…" I trailed off, my mind whirling with the implications of the shield failing.

"If that happens…" Morven continued. "A fourth of our world dies."

"How do we find the missing pharocite?" I asked.

Cade narrowed his eyes. "We find the miners who stole it. And soon."

"How do we know it was the miners and not someone else?" I asked.

He pointed to the pendant I wore. "Because that's the only way to get inside, and the swordfighter was the last person in possession of it."

I clutched the pendant, its sharp angles pressing into my fingers. "How did he get this pendant to begin with? Where did it come from?"

Cade shook his head. "I've told you everything I know."

"But you have one just like it?" Morven questioned.

Cade's eyes darkened. "Yes, but I've had it for a very long time. Since I first came to Ceres."

"Which begs the question," I said, "how did the swordfighter get his?"

"I don't know," Cade said. "I don't have any answers. Not yet. But I can tell you how we'll find out. We need to find where the miners are located."

"On Earth," I answered. "The miners I saw in the cave spoke with Arabic accents, meaning they can't be from Ceres. The have to be from Earth. I was hired by a woman named Anna Johnson who wanted me to research the three founders of Vortech. She suspected one of them may've been funding the illegal mining." I sighed, looking at the broken case that once held the pharocite. "I'll have to go back to Earth to do more research. And I need to report back on everything I learned. The swordfighter was hired by someone. We need to find out who."

Vevina pursed her lips, knitting her brows as she inspected the ooze leaking from the cables. "What do we do about this?"

"I can repair it temporarily," Cade answered. "We can at least stop the leak from polluting the stream. Hopefully stop the mutations. But if we want a lasting fix, we'll have to replace the pharocite."

"I'll help you," Vevina said. "That is—if you could use my help."

"Eventually yes," he answered, kneeling by the busted hose. "But we'll have to go back and gather tools and something to replace this with." He nudged the busted hose.

"And I need to get to the rails," I said.

"I agree." Morven glanced at the doorway behind us. "I don't like what's happening. We've got to stop whoever's doing this. They obviously have no respect for our world, and they'll do whatever it takes to achieve what they want, even if it means destroying us."

"But what would they want with the pharocite?" Vevina asked.

"Same thing they wanted with the yellow cerecite they've been stealing from the caves," Cade answered. "Using it to power something."

"Power what?" I asked. "Another gateway?"

"No. Only white cerecite is powerful enough for that. They're using this for something else."

I stood straight. "Then we can't waste time. I've got to get back to Earth. Cade, Vevina, we'll go with you back to the keep, but after that, we'll need to part ways. I intend to find out who's behind this."

"Agreed," Cade said solemnly. "And do it before they

destroy our entire planet. This—" he pointed to the eroded tubes, the foul-smelling pollution, the wires severed in half and leaking as if broken arteries, as if the life blood of Ceres were spilling onto the cold cement— "is only a sample of what's to come."

11

The long hike back to the keep went by in a blur. My thoughts grew dark at the implications of the stolen pharocite. What was really going on? The miners were not only stripping the planet of its resources but taking the source of its protection? Without the shield, Ceres became a desolate rock. Was that their intention? It made no sense.

Guilt weighed on me, causing a sour taste in my mouth that I couldn't swallow. Maybe I should've never opened the wormhole portal between our two worlds. If I'd kept it closed, this wouldn't have been happening. Maybe Cade was right to have tried to kill me. Sure, I would be dead, but he would've protected his world, and none of this would've been happening. And Vevina walked in a daze, making me feel even worse.

The air warmed as we made it back to the forest surrounding MacKinnon Keep. Morven grabbed my hand, and I peered up at him in confusion.

He squeezed my fingers. "You looked worried."

"I am." I sighed, the tree branches towering over us, the leaves turned bright emerald in the evening sunlight. "If they destroy the shield, there's nothing to protect us anymore.

Everyone dies. A whole civilization is wiped out, and Earth would've never even known it existed."

"Have you thought perhaps that's their purpose?"

I gave him a shrewd glance. "What do you mean?"

He pursed his lips and shook his head. "I'm not sure," he muttered, almost to himself. His eyes stared straight ahead, and the dark depths of his irises got a faraway look, as if he were staring into some unknown plane. He got that look sometimes—as if he could see things others didn't.

"Morven," I said. "Do you think someone wants to destroy Ceres?"

"Not destroy it," he answered. "Erase it. As if it never existed."

This had gone way beyond stealing cerecite for bombs or trading it for money. "Why do you say that?"

"I don't know yet. But we need to find out. I'm going with you to Earth."

I shot him a questioning glance. "Can you do that? Don't you have things here that need your attention? You're the king now, aren't you?" I conveniently left out mentioning anything about planning a wedding.

"My official title is king elect until my aunt decides to relinquish all powers of the throne. And to be honest, I'd like to avoid the palace right now. Since Aunt Tremayne is getting along with the other nobles—including Vevina's family—she's been hinting at planning the wedding. I'm hoping that if I avoid the court, she'll forget about it. At least for now."

"I doubt she'll forget about it entirely," I said, unable to keep the bitterness out of my voice.

"True, but I'd like to avoid the palace all the same. That way, I'll be able to help you try to find out who's plotting to destroy our world." He shrugged. "I've got nothing better to do."

"Nothing better to do, huh?"

"Well, and I'd like to spend time with you." His dazzling

grin caught me off guard and stole my breath. He kissed my forehead. "Maybe steal one of those, a few times."

I playfully jabbed his shoulder. "Stop it. You're supposed to be getting married to Vevina. And we're supposed to be catching dangerous criminals."

"Then that's all the more reason to have fun while we still can." He brushed a kiss over my lips. Tingles spread like wildfire through me. His warmth and the scent of amber and spruce enveloped me. With his hand in mine, with him by my side, how could I ever want for anything more? He was like air, like life. I felt more at peace with him around than I did on anyplace in either world. But … "while we still can?" The thought made a jolt of unexpected reality race through my heart. My palms grew sweaty, and I unthreaded my fingers from his. He knitted his brows in confusion as I pulled away.

"Something wrong?"

I didn't know how to answer. Through the gaps in the trees, the keep appeared. Cade and Vevina were nearly at the doors. My pounding heart was proof that I was getting too close to him. How could I do that at a time like this? Maybe Morven saw our relationship as something casual, something he could easily discard when it was time for him to marry someone else. But if I let him get too close to me, I would never be able to let him go. My feelings for him were too powerful.

I sighed, hoping I could be honest with him without hurting his feelings. "I think I'm falling for you, and it kills me to say this, but I think we should be friends. Nothing more."

He didn't answer. His eyes remained locked on the keep, and the wind stirred strands of his dark hair across his forehead. "You really feel that way?"

"Yes." The words were almost too painful to speak. "I think it's best to keep our distance."

"No." He shook his head. "You're only saying that

because of the stupid betrothal, but what if I could stop it from happening?"

"If you stopped it, then what? You'd make your aunt angry; you'd upset the noble families all over again. Sometimes you have to put your country before yourself."

He clenched his jaw and didn't speak, as if he knew I was right, but didn't want to admit it.

"I understand," he finally said, then turned away from me and walked ahead, tears pricking at my eyes, though I did my best to push them down, to suppress those old, all-too familiar feelings of loneliness.

Vevina's grandmother greeted us at the door, and I spent the rest of the day feeling numb as it went by in a flurry of activity. I didn't speak to Morven much, and when I went to sleep that night, in the quiet comfort of the castle, I thought of nothing but him, and the image of the hurt in his eyes stayed with me, lingering like a waking dream.

When morning arrived, we said our goodbyes to Cade and Vevina, then took the train that ran on rails of yellow cerecite to the capital. The sun shone over the uniformity of the green trees and perfect grass, and I couldn't help but feel that this place was a utopia built to hide the truth—a place so perfect, no one bothered to dig deeper and uncover their reality hidden beneath a seemingly perfect facade.

"There's a storm coming," Morven said as we approached the palace, a towering structure of three tiers decorated by rooftop gardens and trickling waterfalls. Dark clouds blocked out the sun, and the air held the scent of rain.

When we made it inside, Morven gathered his things, and I collected what little I'd brought with me. He wished his aunt goodbye. Since he'd been traveling so much, she didn't question his choice to leave for a few days. Her once stone-cold eyes now warmed with compassion, and she gave him a hug before he left.

"Come back safely," she said. And that was it.

We made it to the rails leading to Edenbrooke as midday approached. Bodies crowded the rail coach, and Morven and I had to stand in a passageway, pressed into a corner. My body was pressed up helplessly against his.

When evening arrived, still dark with the threat of rain, we made it to the gateway cave. Cool air replaced the heat of the desert. Lights glinted from newly installed walkways, handrails, and a metal staircase leading down into the heart of the cavern.

"It's changed so much since we first came here." My voice echoed as we stepped into the main chamber. "It doesn't even look like the place it was."

A cavernous room surrounded us. Vortech had built a shell of reflective metal panels leading to the gateway. In the distance came the sounds of drills and clanging engines. The legal mining took place not far from the gateway cavern, and Vortech kept a minimal profile by staying so remote.

"Yes," Morven answered, his voice distant, his jaw locked. He hadn't uttered more than a few words to me since we'd left the capital.

"I upset you, didn't I?"

He gave me a quick glance. "No."

"No?"

"I've been thinking a lot about what you said. And you were right. Every word." When he looked at me again, a hint of life returned to his eyes. "I have a duty to serve my people, and that includes marrying Vevina. Maybe we're not meant for each other—at least, not right now, not with my life here and yours on another planet. Not with the sort of problems we're trying to sort through. But that doesn't mean we can't work together." His fingers brushed mine. The warmth of his skin melted the cold shell covering my heart, and I wanted him so badly, pain tugged at my heart.

I knew truly keeping my distance from him was impossible, but I couldn't get so involved that I lost track of my mission.

We walked up the metal platform leading to the renovated wormhole portal. Blinking lights surrounded the outer edge of the rectangular gateway. I'd taken this path more times than I could count, but even now, the view never ceased to amaze me.

How far I'd come since the beginning.

Morven took my hand and kissed my fingers, his lips feather-soft on my skin, and I had to remind myself to breathe.

"See you on the other side."

I took a deep breath to calm my fluttering heart.

Without another word, we stepped through the portal.

12

Cold wind slapped my cheeks as I stepped through, fast as a blink, onto the platform to Champ Island. The hum of bustling machinery filled the air. Dump trucks loaded with cerecite ore moved on track wheels over the snowy landscape. They drove out of a row of portals just like the one we'd stepped through. Vortech was nothing if not efficient. Why build one portal when you could have twenty?

Morven and I stood on an open platform overlooking Champ Island. Round boulders pocked the snow drifts, dark lumps of stone dotted with yellow and black lichen. Unlike those on Ithical, the cerecite in these formations, being away from Ceres for so long, had burned out and no longer glowed.

I rubbed my hands together for warmth. Morven stayed at my side as we headed for the tents and buildings looming ahead. The island looked nothing like the sparsely populated place I'd come to six months earlier. Instead of a single struc- ture built on a blank canvas of snow and ice, tents and portable buildings dotted the landscape. The *V* Vortech logo was printed in bold black on the canvas and aluminum comprising the structures.

A man wearing a bulky fur-lined coat stepped out of a building and waved us toward him.

"Sabine Harper," he called, muffled by the scarf over his face. Dark goggles covered his eyes.

"Yes," I answered through chattering teeth.

"This way please. You, too." He motioned to Morven.

We followed him into the warmth of a tent where a spiral staircase led down a metal-lined hole in the ground.

"Down here," he said.

"Where are you taking us?" I asked.

"We've relocated the base of operations belowground," he yelled over the noise of machinery coming from outside.

The air warmed as we made our way down. I held to the handrail as we descended into the bowels of the island. When we stepped to the floor, fluorescent lights and tarps dotted the walls. Desks and computers were placed in rows, and we dodged them to make it to the back of the room.

The man removed his hood and goggles, and I couldn't mistake his scruffy face, leathery skin, and fatherly expression for anyone else than Logan.

"Agent Logan! Why didn't you say it was you?"

A grin stretched across his weathered face, and he spread his hands. "I assumed you'd recognize me."

"Under all that?" I motioned to his hood and glasses.

"Well," he sniffed. "Come on and give me a hug."

I leaned in and he hugged me, reminding me of my dad, all stiffness with a soft edge. He smelled of the outdoors, and his friendly smile put me at ease.

"What are you doing here?" I asked.

"Still working for Vortech, of course. Can't seem to find anything better. That vacation in Hawaii? Yeah, never happened. Too much work to do." He motioned to Morven. "Welcome back to Earth, Your Highness."

"Thank you, but there's no need to call me that, especially here."

"True. I heard things are smoothing out with the miners."

"Yes. Let's hope they stay that way," Morven answered.

"Well." Logan stood tall. "Ms. Johnson has been waiting for you. She's just through this room and down the hallway." He motioned to a door behind him. "I'll take you to her."

He turned and walked us to the door. After opening it, he led us into a room where a few people wearing Vortech lab coats milled about, arranging objects on shelves. I recognized some of the gears and broken machines as artifacts from the gateway cave. One of the devices had even played a hologram meant for recruiting miners to work on Ceres.

"What's happening in here?" I asked Logan.

"We decided to catalog the artifacts we've been unearthing in the gateway cave. We've found so many unusual items, it didn't seem right to toss them aside. You could think of this as a makeshift museum." He smiled. "It's not every day you find ancient materials from four-hundred years in the future."

I gave him a sidelong glance. "That would have sounded really strange if I didn't know the truth."

"Aren't you worried about the consequences?" Morven asked.

Logan scrunched his forehead. "What do you mean?"

"These items come from the future," Morven explained. "If you learn how they work, and introduce the tech into your society, you could irrevocably alter that future."

"Ah," Logan said. "But who's to say this didn't already happen? Perhaps in the future, these items were already discovered, which is how they were invented in the first place. You never know. Now." He waved us forward. "Follow me. We've got more pressing matters to discuss."

He led us toward a door. I lingered a moment, marveling at the technology we only barely understood. Had Vortech discovered any of these technological secrets? If so, that was a lot of power in Vortech's hands—which was a thought that terrified me if I pondered it too long. They already controlled the cerecite.

I turned away from the stacks of gears and broken screens to follow Morven and Logan into a small room. A tarp hung on one wall, and utility lights hung from tripods. The air held the scent of metal shavings and grease. A single folding table had been situated at the room's center, and several folding chairs surrounded it.

Anna Johnson paced, her high heels clicking on the stone floor, her red lips drawn into a line. She wore her auburn hair in a bobbed haircut. Gray strands streaked along her temples. Her eyes widened, wrinkles scrunching on her forehead as she watched us enter the room.

"Harper, thank goodness. We just about thought we'd lost you." Though her words hinted at concern, her exasperated sigh revealed frustration. "Logan, leave us."

"Of course." He turned and left the room. The heavy door thudded as it shut with a click behind him.

"Well." She motioned to two folding chairs across the table from her. "Have a seat. I've been waiting a long time for you to return. What happened?"

I shot a quick glance at Morven. He nodded as if to encourage me, and I started at the beginning, briefing her on every detail, including how the palace had been attacked, how the photos and computer had been stolen, and how we'd found the source of the polluted stream.

She pinched her lips at the mention of the swordfighter.

"You believe it was him who stole the yellow cerecite from the shield generator?"

"We're almost certain," Morven answered.

She fisted her hands as she continued pacing. "Zentoku Uzamaki," she said with venom in her voice. "We call him Zen."

I sat up straight. "You know him?"

"Yes. He's been on our radar for many years because he's

stolen secrets from Vortech in the past. He's impossible to catch. And we don't know much about him except he comes from Tokyo and he's a talented martial artist."

"That's it?" I asked.

"I'll give you the files on him. You may be able to glean more than what I've told you. But I'll warn you, Zen is a ghost. He's impossible to track down."

"Great," I muttered.

"It gets worse." She shot me a somber glance, brows drawn together. "I'm convinced he's been hired by someone in our organization. I'm giving you access to all Vortech's files on this matter. I can't do any of the research myself, not if someone on the inside is watching. I'm personally funding you using a secret account, so nothing is tied to Vortech's purse strings. You're working on my dime, and I expect you to keep this investigation quiet." She stopped pacing and pressed her knuckles to the tabletop. "Find out who Zen is working for. Start by researching Vortech's two other lead founders— Vincent Fernoulli and Yusuf Barnak."

"What can you tell me about them?" I asked.

Her eyes darkened. "They've both got dirt on their hands. Fernoulli inherited his wealth from his father in the automotive industry before he became a partner in Vortech. He would've had an easy time funding any sort of business dealings on Ceres. He was convicted of fraud once in the eighties, but never served time. Of course, affording the best lawyers may've had something to do with that.

"Barnak gained his money in the Saudi Arabian oil industry. Like Fernoulli, he has the means necessary of funding illegal mining operations on Ceres. He's also been tried for a host of crimes, including embezzlement and money laundering, but he was never convicted.

"I need to know which of them hired Zen."

I sighed, staring at the wall behind her. The ticking of a clock came from somewhere in the room, although I couldn't see its source. Pressure weighed me down, and I had the feeling I was drowning. Vortech was an industry I didn't want to be involved with any longer than necessary.

"What happens if I say no?"

"Then you'll lose your job. Your contract will be voided, and it will be as if we never met. This is your decision, Harper. But let me assure you that we need you. I need you. You have a gift for seeing things others overlook. Barnak and Fernoulli are hiding something. I need you to find what it is."

I felt as though I stood at a crossroads. If I accepted, I would have guaranteed income. I could pay for Dad's cancer treatment if he ever needed it again. Saying no meant I would be free from Vortech, but was I willing to give up so soon? There was more at stake now—the entire life of a planet and the tens of thousands of people living there.

"Fine," I answered. "I'll find out who hired Zen, but I'll need more than just the information on Fernoulli and Barnak. I'll also need access to your records as well."

Pencil-thin eyebrows rose. "Mine?" she huffed.

"You hired me to investigate the three founders of Vortech. That includes you."

Wrinkles deepened as her brow creased. "Fine," she spat. "But you'll find nothing on me."

"We'll see."

She crossed her arms. "And this conversation is to remain strictly confidential. Both of you. Revealing any information will land you in a dangerous predicament. I hope you understand the consequences. Whoever hired Zen is a dangerous person. They won't blink twice to make sure you're dead if they find out I've hired you. Is that understood?"

I stiffened at the word *dead*. Fear made my skin grow clammy. I'd gotten in over my head. "Perfectly."

"Good. I'll have a chopper fly you to the mainland. From there, you're free to visit your home should you choose, as I realize you've had no downtime for a while."

I eyed her. Something didn't add up. "You're letting me go home?"

"Yes."

"Why?" I demanded. "What's the real reason?"

She pursed her lips before answering. "I need you off the grid and away from prying eyes. Your remoteness in Kansas is the perfect location."

Right. I knew there had to be some reason other than Anna Johnson's benevolence. "Not LA?"

"No. Fernoulli and Barnak will know to look for you there, assuming they've realized I've hired you, which they won't as long as you stay invisible." She tapped her fingers on the table in a nervous gesture. "Oh—and one more thing." She reached into her pocket and pulled out a thin white flash drive. "You'll need this. There's a program on here that will keep you incognito. Use it before starting any research you plan to do online. I don't want anyone finding out where you are or what you're doing."

"Got it." I took the device and put it in my pocket.

"You need to know that Vortech's founders are subject to certain policies," Anna continued. "As such, we have very little freedom. We're required to relinquish all our financial information to be available in the Vortech database. You'll be given high level access to it. Find out who hired Zen. That's all I'm asking."

Almost too easy. "After I do this, will I still have job?" I almost didn't ask the question, but I knew better than to burn my bridges with Vortech.

"Yes, if you complete this mission, you'll be given the opportunity for another."

Did I really want it? Weren't there any other options left for me? If I were being honest, my one wish was to cut my ties with Vortech and settle down somewhere far away. Truth be told—somewhere with Morven. But of course, future was a fairy tale.

"When does the chopper leave?" I asked.

"Whenever you're ready." She leaned forward, pressing her knuckles to the table. "Contact me as soon as you have any pertinent information. I intend to capture Zen as soon as possible."

"I will."

She waved her hand. "Good luck, Harper. I'm personally counting on you too see this through."

Morven and I stood, then left the room and made our way to ground level. The rest of the day went by in a blur. We ate and changed into warmer clothes. When we finally got settled on the chopper, Morven sat beside me and looked out the window. Snow spiraled around the chopper, and ice crystals danced on the wind as we took off from the helipad.

A ray of sunlight broke through the clouds, making the ice sparkle around us in a kaleidoscope of colors.

"Beautiful," he sighed.

I almost agreed, only to notice his gaze wasn't on the view, but on me. My cheeks heated. Our gazes locked, and my heart sped. Denying my feelings for him had become impossible, so I tentatively reached out for his fingers. It seemed the only thing I could do in such a situation.

Morven didn't say anything as I held his hand. He gave a slight smile—a gentle curving of his perfect lips.

"I knew you couldn't resist me for long," he whispered with a sly grin.

I gave him my shrewdest glance, although kept my hand in his. "Didn't I ask you to keep your distance?"

His smile held a hint of mischief. "I'm choosing to ignore your request."

I couldn't answer, and I didn't want to pull my fingers from his. Truthfully, I wanted him close to me forever.

"Just for today, Sabine," he said, his smile fading, though I noticed the intensity—and an edge of worry—clouding his eyes. "We can be together for today."

Outside the window, the snowbanks appeared far below the chopper. Morven's words stuck with me. If we were together just for today, shouldn't that be enough?

As we climbed to higher altitudes, clouds surrounded us, erasing Champ Island, as if it had never existed. An unexpected shiver ran down my spine. If I failed at this mission, if whoever had hired Zen found me, what happened then? Anna Johnson was using me because I was unknown, because if I happened to mess up, erasing me wouldn't be difficult. I was expendable, and maybe that was the exact reason Anna Johnson had hired me. I wasn't a diplomat or a sought-after assassin or informant. I was a nobody from Kansas.

The chopper rose above the clouds, but we'd flown too far away to see the island. An ocean of dark, churning water spanned so far, it seemed as if nothing else existed.

13

My backpack's straps dug into my shoulders as I walked the gravel drive to the porch. Why did my bag seem so much heavier now? I felt as though I carried more weight on my shoulders now that I'd become Vortech's pawn, and the problem was, I didn't know how to untangle from their web.

Faded yellow leaves fluttered from the wispy branches of the willow trees leading to the farmhouse. The air held the scent of autumn. Morven walked beside me, his fascinated gaze going from the sky to the trees to the grass. Yellow spots blighted the blades, and weeds grew in patches along our path. A dead branch hung from a tree, and he brushed his fingers over the withered leaves, his face brightened with wonder. The stem snapped as he plucked a brown leaf from a branch.

"So strange." He ran his fingers over the brittle plant.

"It's funny." I smiled.

"Funny?"

"Most people on Earth view dead things as unwanted. You look at it like it's gold."

"Well, it's not what I'm used to. It's different." He gently grasped the stem and placed the leaf behind my ear, his warm fingers brushing my skin, sending butterflies dancing through me. "Lovely." He smiled.

I gave him a confused glare. "It's dead."

"It's the color of your eyes."

"Wow. Thanks." I hoped he heard my sarcasm.

He grabbed my fingers and we laughed, and my worry about finding Zen's boss and saving Ceres faded. Here, under the shade of trees, with the birds chirping and a gentle October breeze cooling my face, peace replaced the fear gnawing at the pit of my stomach.

We made it to the porch and climbed the steps. I knocked twice, the rusted screen rattling in the door frame before it was thrown open.

Dad stood inside, a dark silhouette barely illuminated by the light through the doorway. He wore his standard overalls and stark white shirt that smelled of bleach, but a twinkle lit his eyes that I'd never noticed before.

I straightened my backpack straps. "Hi, Dad."

He stepped out and hugged me, catching me by surprise. So much had changed since I'd first told him I'd passed Vortech trials. Stopping a second solar flare had allowed my worry for him to fade. When he stepped away, he focused on Morven.

"You've come back, huh?" Dad asked.

Morven stood tall. "Yes, sir. I couldn't stay away. You've got a nice place here."

I bit my lip to hide my smile. Morven could be a gentleman when he was motivated.

Dad plucked the leaf from behind my ear. "What's this?"

"Oh." My cheeks heated. "Nothing."

He raised an eyebrow, then shrugged and dropped the leaf on the porch. "Well, come inside. I've got a lot to tell you."

A lot to tell me? Curious, I stepped inside. I supposed six months was too long to be gone without something of consequence happening.

When I entered the front room, nostalgia overwhelmed me. Even so, being gone for so long had changed me, and I wondered if this place would ever feel like home again.

Morven looked around the room with guarded fascination. His dark clothes blended in with the shadows, as if he weren't here, as if he really did belong in a different world.

"Come in the kitchen," Dad said. "I've got something for you."

"For me?" I laughed. "It's not Christmas."

"Doesn't have to be."

We wandered into the kitchen where a narrow box sat wrapped in shiny reindeer paper. "I guess it is Christmas."

The paper crinkled as I picked up the rectangular gift. It weighed heavy in my hands. I shook the box, and something rattled inside.

"What is it?"

Dad motioned to the package. "Open it."

Ripping the paper, I revealed a white cardboard box. As I opened the lid, the gleam of a blade shone from the velvet-lined bottom. I ran my fingers over the silver dagger. "A new knife?"

"Yes," Dad said. "Since you lost the first one."

Emotions warred in me as I held the box, not yet daring to remove the blade. "Are you sure about this? You realize I lost Mima's knife—and that was an heirloom."

Dad waved his hand. "Mima would have wanted you to have a replacement."

The silver inlay of a wolf decorated the hilt, and a ruby sat in the place of the eye. "It's beautiful. This must have cost a fortune."

Dad chuckled. "Then it's a good thing my farming is picking up."

I eyed him, then glanced back at Morven, who stood silently in the corner, watching our conversation with guarded fascination. I turned back to my dad. "You're being honest?"

A smile I hadn't seen in ages tugged at the corners of his mouth. "It's true. Thanks to you, I was able to afford the new combine. Pulled in more corn and wheat than I have in the past five years. Soybeans aren't far behind."

"Dad, that's great." Pride swelled in my chest. I hadn't realized how much it would mean to experience Dad's success. He'd been struggling with the farm for so long. For him to be successful now seemed almost unbelievable.

"I've got better news."

"What is it?" I asked.

He cleared his throat, as if trying to decide to tell me. "Well…"

"Go on," I nudged.

"I'm not sure if you'll like it."

"Dad, I think I can handle it." I finally dared to pick up the knife. The handle wasn't worn like my old one, which had been held by Mima so many long years ago. Would this new knife really be a replacement for my old one?

"I'm getting married," he blurted.

"Married?" I nearly dropped the knife. "Are you joking?"

"Her name's Helen. Met her online."

"Online?" I laughed. "Dad, you don't even know how to open your email."

"I do, too," he argued. "Had to learn to do it myself when you left. She's from Denver," He spoke with pride, smiling as if this was all normal.

I dropped the box on the table, and the knife fell out and hit the linoleum with a loud clatter. "Dad, why?"

"Why do you think?" he asked.

"I don't know."

"You've been gone so much… and I can't do this anymore." His voice cracked. "It's hard to admit it, but I've been lonely."

"Lonely?" I questioned.

He nodded. "There's more."

He can't be serious. "More?"

"I'm selling the farm. It's time. I've finally gotten ahead, and I can't live this way anymore, wondering when the next flare will hit. Wondering if we'll have enough to get us through. Wondering if the cancer is coming back." He absent-mindedly rubbed his chest, as if the cancer were lurking just beneath his skin. "I'm moving to Denver with Helen soon as the harvest is over, then I'll put it up for sell soon as winter hits."

"Dad…" Gently, carefully, I stretched my hand out to his to soften my words. "Your home was here—our family home for the last four generations. If you sell the farm and moved away, are you ready for that? I thought you loved the farm."

"I did. But now… it's just become a burden, and without you here to help, it's too much."

Unable to speak, I only sank into the kitchen chair—the old one with the missing spindle. The wood creaked as I sat awkwardly on the edge.

Morven rested his hand on my shoulder. I grasped his fingers. He was the last thing in my life I wanted not to change.

Denver?

Out the window over the sink, the tree branches stirred in a gentle breeze. A few leaves got tugged away. Little by little, the branches would soon become bare until the leaves made piles covering the ground, only to rot away and become part of the soil.

"I need to take a walk." I stood. "Give me some time to process this."

"You want me to come along?" Dad asked.

"No. That's all right." I shot one last glance to Morven, unsure what to say to him. Not wanting him to see my raw emotions, I brushed past him and headed out the door. Metal springs squeaked as the screen slammed behind me. I marched outside, down the porch steps and onto the drive.

Rain scented the air, and a line of dark thunderheads approached on the horizon.

The barn loomed ahead, and I followed the path toward it, my shoes shifting over the loose gravel. Footsteps echoed, and I turned to find Morven jogging toward me.

"You don't need to follow me," I called over my shoulder.

He caught up to me. "No, but I want to."

Charging ahead to the barn, I ignored his question.

"Sabine," he persisted.

I shook my head. When we entered the barn, the sweet scent of hay brought back an onslaught of memories. Jumping from one bale to the next. Helping Dad fix the tractor. Being too distracted by all the details in the wood beams and engine parts to be any help.

My eyes misting, I blinked past my tears to focus on the ladder leading to the loft. Hay cushioned my footfalls. The gusting wind outside created a shrill wail. When I reached the ladder, I grabbed a rung and climbed until I made it to the shelter of the loft.

Neat stacks of square bales surrounded me, and I sat on one that faced the open window. Morven climbed up and sat beside me. He didn't talk. Didn't ask any questions. And I felt grateful for that.

A light rain pelted the tin roof. The scent of ozone wafted from the open window, and a damp breeze helped cool my overheated skin. I threaded my fingers together, clenching them until they throbbed.

"You have a home here, don't you?" Morven asked.

That stupid lump in my throat made it hard to speak, so I managed a nod. I'd been away from this place for so long, I'd forgotten to call it home. But sitting here, surrounded by the scent of hay, with the patter of raindrops and the gray clouds blocking the sky, reminded me of all the things I would miss.

Selling the farm. He's selling the farm.

"I don't understand," I finally managed, picking at the

loose stalks, counting them. *One, two, three…* until I finally managed to swallow back my tears and make my brain think logically. "Why now? He bought the new combine. Things were finally starting to work out. I don't think he understands how much this place is a part of him. It's the lousiest timing ever."

"Maybe it's the best timing," Morven suggested, his gaze fixed on the window—on the storm clouds flashing with an occasional burst of lightning, though we were too far away to hear the thunder. The wind ruffled his dark hair framing his angular face. Despite my heartache at Dad's confession, my stomach still gave that inexplicable flutter whenever I was near Morven.

"What do you mean?"

"Well, I'm not an expert on how your economy systems work here, although I have to admit, I *have* been doing a great deal of research. Won't he make a profit now that it's mostly paid off?"

I picked at the hay. "I guess so."

"And he's getting married."

"To someone I don't even know, and moving to Denver." I sighed. "This is my fault. If I hadn't gotten the job with Vortech, he wouldn't have been able to pay off the farm. And he wouldn't have been able to…" I waved my hand, unable to speak that stupid *M* word.

"Isn't that a good thing?"

"No. Our home is here. He'll hate living in a city. He needs open spaces and room to breathe."

"He needs that? Or do you?"

I shot him a dark look, but my anger lasted half a second before his words sank in. "Maybe we both do," I admitted. "I've got to convince Dad not to sell the farm. He doesn't understand what he's losing by doing this. He'll never be happy in a city. The only times I've heard him curse were when we were driving through traffic on a busy highway. He hates cities more than Mom did, and that's saying a lot. His home is here. *Our* home is here."

"Yeah, but you have to admit, you haven't been spending that much time here lately."

I placed my fists under my chin. "Maybe I should. I'll tell Vortech I can't work for them anymore. I'll start helping Dad with the harvest. I'm pretty good at…" I breathed an exasperated sigh. "At something."

Morven reached for my hands. His warm fingers rested on my cold ones, and my cramped joints relaxed at his touch. He took my hand in his, and with that one gesture, my pent-up anxiety melted away.

"Maybe you should give him a chance to live his life, Sabine."

"But his life is here."

"Is it? What's that saying I've seen on that plaque hanging in your kitchen? Home is where your heart is? You never know. You might love wherever you're going next. Denver, is it? Where is that? Far from here?"

"Might as well be on Ceres." Except Ceres felt more like home than even here, and that wasn't something easy to admit. "My dad belongs here, Morven. If he's gone, where does that leave my family? Mom and Mima are buried there." I pointed to the road leading to the cemetery hidden by the willows and cottonwoods. Their marbled gray headstones must've darkened in the drenching rain.

"You think you'd be letting go of their memory if your father moves away?" Morven asked.

"I don't know." I shifted as the hay poked uncomfortably at my legs. "Maybe." But wouldn't Mom have wanted him to be happy? I shook my head at such a thought, though it needled at me until I had to admit that maybe Dad getting remarried was the best thing that had happened to him in a very long time.

Morven squeezed my fingers. "I know this is upsetting to

you. I don't like seeing you this way." He tucked a strand of hair behind my ear. "What can I do to make you smile again?"

I couldn't answer as Morven pulled me to him. He placed his hand behind my head and gently rested my cheek on his shoulder. The familiar scent of evergreen forests calmed me. My stomach danced with the pattering of butterfly wings as he held me to him. Biceps hardened by his time spent in the wheelchair cushioned my neck and shoulders. He leaned in and brushed a kiss over my forehead, his lips feathery soft on my skin.

I sucked in a stuttered breath at his touch.

With my senses heightened, my anger slipped away. His eyes locked on mine. His dark pupils reflected the storm clouds. His gaze drank me in until I felt we were the only two people in the world.

He leaned closer until he brushed his lips over mine. Pressing a kiss to my lips, he tasted of peppermint. My heart pattered so furiously I was surprised it didn't break out of my chest.

He cupped my cheeks, his hands warm, his fingers slightly callused as I pulled away from him.

His fingertips trailed my cheek, wiping at the dampness left from shed tears. I couldn't admit it to him—and perhaps I never would—but if home was where the heart was, then I'd found it with him.

14

I'd returned to the house only to grab some food and my laptop, then I'd escaped back to the safety of the barn with only a quick "hello" to Dad. My emotions were too hard to sort out for me to have a conversation with him.

Morven rested by me as I sat in the loft, a bale of hay supporting me as I leaned against it. My laptop propped on my knees, I inserted the flash drive, then clicked Vortech's website. After entering my credentials, a message waited from Anna Johnson.

CONFIDENTIAL INFORMATION-DO NOT SHARE
VINCENT FERNOULLI
YUSUF BARNAK
ANNA JOHNSON

Links underlined each name. I clicked Vincent Fernoulli first. A picture appeared on the screen. A distinguished-looking man wearing a tux smiled with too-white teeth. White strands grew along his temples, contrasting his thick black hair perfectly sculpted with gel. Wrinkles creased the skin around his deep-set eyes.

Scanning the information came easily, and I sped through birth certificates, financial documents, and business mergers until a picture of the man's life came into vivid detail. Born in Northern Italy. Graduated from Oxford with an undergrad degree in computer science and a master's degree in business. Obtained a doctorate in computer engineering. Began his career as a computer technician, later hired by Vortech where he quickly rose in the ranks and became the lead developer of Vortech's *Agent Fifteen* program. Married and divorced five times. Currently remarried to a wealthy heiress of a well-known fashion company.

"Interesting." Morven's voice pulled me from my thoughts.

"What is?" I asked.

He pointed to the screen. "He owns a collection of more than fifty Ferraris. Those are cars, right?"

"Yes. Expensive ones, too. I guess having a career like his will get you places." I rested my chin in my hands, my eyes going bleary as I stared at the screen. "There's nothing linking him to Zen. Nothing I can tell so far, anyway."

"Money?" Morven suggested. "He obviously has a lot of it. People like that tend to never have enough and want more. Maybe he's greedy and wanted more wealth from mining Ceres?"

"Maybe." I tapped my fingers on the keyboard, staring at the man's picture—his perfect white teeth, and not a single hair out of place. I wasn't convinced I'd found the right person, though at this point, I wouldn't discount anyone.

"Who's next?" Morven asked.

"Yusuf Barnak." I clicked the link. A picture of a heavyset man with a goatee displayed on the screen. Like Fernoulli, graying hair and wrinkles placed him in his late fifties. Unlike Fernoulli, he didn't smile. His thin lips pressed to form a severe line. Thick eyebrows framed deep-set eyes.

I scanned his bio, which listed him as a lead member of the Vortech corporation. He came from a rich Saudi Arabian oil family. He had three wives and fourteen children, and there were rumors he had ties to several terrorist organizations, though the sources for that didn't appear in the research Anna had sent me. He was also a philanthropist and had donated millions to numerous charitable organizations. I narrowed my eyes and studied the list of organizations. *Cancer Care for Kids*, *El Salvador Helping Hands*, *Volunteers Building Homes*, *Stamp Out Hunger*… Twenty-three charities in total. Seemed like a long list. Could his donations be a front?

"Saudi Arabian." I mulled over the information. "The miners in the cave spoke with Arabian accents. Coincidence?"

Morven's brows lowered. "Possibly, but not likely."

I pointed to the screen. "It says he may have ties to terrorist organizations. If so, mining cerecite on another planet would be a good way to fund it. But…" I scrolled down the page, looking for any other keywords about terrorism, but found nothing. "There's nothing concrete here. If he does have shady connections, there's no proof. We'll have to dig into this. There may be something here. In the meantime, we need to switch gears and look into Anna Johnson."

"She wouldn't have hired you if she were up to anything."

"Doesn't mean she's innocent." I clicked the link leading to her info. My shoulder muscles cramped as I sat hunched over my computer, and the screen's light burned my tired eyes.

Yawning, I scanned over Anna's information. Born in San Diego, graduated top of her class, had a degree in microbiology, became an intern for a lead research firm, worked in the science field until she moved to intern for Vortech. Rose to the top of the ranks. Never married. No children. Dedicated to her career. It all sounded a little too neat, like it was sugarcoated.

"She's left out the good stuff." Morven sat back and crossed his arms. "Where's the dirt?"

"Not surprising." I exited the screen and shut my computer with a click. "I doubt she'd send me anything incriminating. She may not be responsible for illegal mining, but she may have more to do with it than she's telling us."

When I closed my eyes, black-and-white words swam in my vision. "We'll have to dig up more information on her. That'll take time." I rubbed at a knot in my neck, then exhaled a long breath and turned my attention to the open window. The rain had stopped, replaced by a chill breeze carrying the scent of moist autumn air.

Crickets chirped a staccato cadence, and far in the distance came the hooting of an owl. Stars twinkled in the satin blackness of the universe. Morven's gaze went to the sky, where he looked with fascination at the pinpoints of light burning millions of miles away.

"You're lucky your world isn't built with a shield. You can see the stars the way they're meant to be." He pointed to a bright star on the western horizon. "Venus," he said. "The Mayans thought of it as the morning star, the sky god and the most powerful deity, as powerful as the moon or sun."

I eyed him. "Where do you get this stuff?"

"What do you mean?"

"You're like an encyclopedia."

"You forget I was stuck in a wheelchair for half my life. What else did I have to do but read every book available? Plus, I like astronomy." He pointed to another group of stars. "You see the Big Dipper?"

"Yes."

"It comprises Ursa Major. The story goes that Zeus was smitten by a nymph named Callisto. Zeus's wife Hera got jealous, as she usually did, and she turned Callisto from a beautiful nymph into a bear. Later, Callisto birthed a son, the baby bear, or Ursa Minor." I followed his finger to a smaller grouping of stars. "Hera was furious. She tried to kill Callisto and her son. Zeus found out what Hera was up to. To protect them, he placed them in the night sky to live eternally."

His gaze softened, and his voice struck a chord deep inside me.

"Interestingly enough, Jupiter's fourth moon is named

after Callisto. You can see it there." He pointed to a star on the western horizon. "Just there, see? It's a planet, so it doesn't twinkle the way stars do."

"I see it." A chilly breeze gusted inside, and strands of loose hair tickled my nose. Morven drew his fingers along my cheek until he tucked the strands behind my ear. I rubbed my hands over my bare arms for warmth. He pulled me to him. His warmth surrounded me, and I breathed a contented sigh.

My tense shoulders relaxed as I stared out at the stars, at the Big Dipper forming the bear, the little dipper comprising the baby bear. I closed my eyes, and Morven's story echoed in my head. The mother and son sent to live eternally in the sky —a place Zeus thought they would be safe.

Zeus did it to protect them. But what if that was a life they never wanted?

15

I woke in my childhood bedroom, and for half a second, I could almost imagine I was young again. My sleep-fogged brain begged me to stay under the covers where it was warm and comfortable, where a gentle rain sang a familiar lullaby as it pattered on the tin roof, where the scent of lavender dryer sheets brought memories of Mom tucking me in.

With my eyes closed, I imagined her sitting on the edge of the mattress, reading from my favorite book of fairy tales. Maybe that's all I had left of her. A fairy tale. That wasn't my life anymore. It never would be.

From the kitchen, Morven's laughter mingled with Dad's monotone voice. I rubbed my eyes and stared around my room filled with shelves and labeled boxes. It looked nothing like the place where I'd grown up. I'd been lucky Dad had fit my old bed back in the space. Otherwise, I'd have been back on the couch.

Dad's unexpected news had derailed me from the reason I'd come home. I was here to research the Vortech founders. Nothing else. And while my heart wanted to be part of a whole and complete family, to spend time with Dad the way things were when Mom and Mima were around, that would never happen.

Plus, Morven was here.

My insides tied into a knot at the thought of him chitchatting with my father. Was I ready for Morven to become familiar with this side of my life? I'd only told Dad a little about what had happened on Ceres between me and the Ithical prince. Talking freely about my feelings for Morven didn't come easily. And now, with Dad getting remarried, it was only more complicated. Worse, the memory of Mom was left to turn to dust in her grave.

The knot lodged in my throat was proof I wasn't ready for Dad to remarry. Too much was happening all at once, and I didn't even know where my home was anymore.

My feelings kept tugging me back to Morven. Spending time with him in the barn gazing at the stars was an experience that had imprinted on my soul, one I knew I would never forget. When I had to let him go, how would I do it?

After showering, pulling on a sweatshirt and a pair of jeans, and grabbing my laptop, I made my way to the front room. I'd pulled my hair into a damp knot at the nape of my neck, and hadn't bothered with makeup. Worrying over my appearance seemed laughable after everything Morven and I had been through. He'd seen me covered in dirt and gore. Still, a hint of anxiety pulled at me, reminding me he wasn't truly mine. With his elevated status—prince of an entire planet—I would possibly be never worthy of him, and maybe I should've been more concerned about how I looked.

Breathing a lengthy sigh, I pushed away the negativity looming like a stalking shadow. *None of that really matters. Morven likes me for who I am. Focus on Vortech. Find out who hired Zen. Worry about everything else later.*

Dad and Morven sat at the kitchen table eating bowls of steaming oatmeal while the sun streamed in through the fluttery yellow gingham curtains Mom had put there. Memories punched me at the sight of the windowsill—the place where Mom had put her apple pies or freshly baked bread. I could almost smell the warm apples and cinnamon, and nearly taste the soft bread in my mouth.

"Back to the barn?" Dad asked, breaking me from my thoughts.

I held up my laptop. "I've got more work to do."

"Don't you want breakfast?" Morven asked.

I grabbed an apple from the fruit bowl. "I've got it."

"Busy day, is it?" Dad asked.

"Yeah." I held up my laptop, its weight seeming heavier, as if it were a wedge between us.

Morven stood, thanked Dad for the breakfast, and we walked out the door. The sunrise painted streaks of gray and pink across the sky. It had stopped raining, but hazy clouds hid the horizon, and a humid fog lingered. My feet slipped over damp leaves and twigs littering the ground.

When we reached the shelter of the barn, the air warmed, and we made our way up the ladder and to the loft. It didn't matter how many times I came here, the scent of fresh hay mingled with morning dew would always remind me of home.

After getting situated on a haybale, with Morven beside me, I opened my computer and logged onto Vortech's website.

"What am I doing?" I mumbled.

Morven clasped his hands on his knees. "What do you mean?"

I didn't want to get into my real problems, so I settled for something less personal. "I don't understand why Vortech put me on this case. I'm not qualified. What if I screw up? What if whoever hired Zen finds out what we're up to and comes after us?"

"Sabine." He rested his hand on my shoulder. "I know how you feel. I'm the king elect of an entire nation, remember? If anyone feels unqualified, it's me."

I looked into his eyes—dark and full of intelligence.

"That's not true. You've been preparing your whole life to rule."

He shook his head. "That doesn't matter. Vortech trusts you. They know you're capable. Plus, you know how to keep things quiet, which is precisely what they need in the current climate. And you've got your gift to help you. I think you're more capable than you realize."

"My gift." I sighed. "Right." Shaking my head, I focused on the computer's screen. I was overthinking things as usual. Without Morven here, I would've been a total mess. I rested my fingers on his.

"Thank you." I gently squeezed his hand. "I hope you realize you help me keep it together. When you're around, I'm not a total basket case."

A smile tugged at the corners of his mouth, showing his dimples. "A basket case?"

"Yes, my gift isn't overwhelming with you near. I think you're good at keeping me sane."

He kissed my forehead, his lips soft and warm on my skin, sending a trill of anticipation pulsing through me. "I don't know how I managed it, but you're welcome." He nodded at the screen. "Where are we starting?"

Reluctantly, I pulled my attention back to my task. "Vincent Fernoulli." I clicked his name. "We didn't find anything linking him to Zen, which may mean he's good at covering his tracks. Plus, I want to know where he got all his wealth. Some of this doesn't add up."

Anna's information linked to a classified document titled FERNOULLI, V. WEALTH MANAGEMENT. The screen filled with documents after I clicked the button.

"Wow," I breathed, scrolling through pages of files.

Morven leaned forward.

"Fernoulli's a busy man. He's got financial investments all over the world." I allowed my photographic memory to process the list, recording to memory the research firms, tech endeavors, and multi-million-dollar corporations. The bottom of the screen showed links to his banking accounts. Thirty-seven of them. "We'll have to comb through this. If he hired Zen, he'll pay out of one of these accounts."

"Let the computer do that," Morven said. "Set it up to search for keywords. Link Zen's name and any of his aliases and see if it finds anything."

"Good idea." After opening the files, I typed in the keywords. The search came up with zero results. "Nothing. If he's paying Zen, it's either under another name, or it's not from one of these accounts."

Morven tapped his fingers on his knee as he sat deep in thought. "Zen," he drew the name out. "He's our key. If one of Vortech's founders hired him, they would've met him at some point. What else do we know about him?"

I rubbed my forehead, the image of Zen flashing in my memory. The intensity in his eyes. The promise of violence should I cross his path. "He's a skilled fighter. Martial arts of some type. Anna said he's from Tokyo. What else do we know?"

Morven knit his brows, a clump of dark hair falling over his forehead. "He knows how to fly a transport. That's a difficult skill to learn. Aircraft on Ithical are more complicated than on Earth, so he would've trained on Ithical. There's no way he could've learned it on Earth. It takes most Ithicans years to learn the techniques of flying a transport."

"But the gateway has only been opened a few months."

"Yeah." Morven clenched his jaw. "Something doesn't add up."

I stared out the window. The fog thickened, leaving the sky hidden in a damp mist. Its chill seeped through my clothes and burrowed under my skin. A crow flew past, its wings beating the air, a shrill caw echoing in its wake.

"I'll have to email Anna. See if she's got anything else on

Zen. In the meantime, let's take a closer look at the second founder, Yusuf Barnak."

Clicking his name, I searched through the files. A headache pounded behind my eyes. "I feel like I'm going in circles. There's nothing concrete on anyone. It's like they've all got their secrets and they're efficient at keeping the dirt out of sight."

"Then we've gotta dig up the dirt."

"How?"

He pointed to the screen. "Start there. Saudi Arabia. You said the miners were speaking with Arabic accents, right?"

"Yeah."

"Then that's our link. Yusuf Barnak and the miners on Ithical must be connected."

"Maybe. But if that's true, we'll have to prove it."

"Where do we start?" Morven asked.

"Money," I answered, my fingers flying over the keyboard. I clicked on YUSUF BARNAK-FINANCES. "If he's funding terrorists, his money has to come from somewhere. We'll follow the dollar trail."

The page loaded. Only fifteen financial institutes were listed, as opposed to Fernoulli's pages of finances. "Should be less complicated," I said, then clicked on the first link.

Scanning over the information, I searched for anything out of the ordinary. Lists of credit card transactions, investments, and bank statements scrolled past until my eyes blurred.

"See anything?" Morven asked.

"Nothing yet."

"Well." He crossed his arms. "I'm not much help. Your monetary system is completely foreign to me. Everything on Ithical is based on a system of cerecite credits."

Breathing a frustrated sigh, I scanned the list for a second time, but nothing stood out.

"Nothing?" he questioned.

"Nothing."

"Then we're looking in the wrong place."

"What do you mean?"

He motioned to the screen. "Start from the beginning. Anna Johnson feels certain someone from Vortech is funding the illegal mining on Ceres. Whoever that person is will be doing it for a reason. They'll be benefitting from it."

I tapped my fingers on my lips as I mulled over his words. "I'm looking in the wrong place. I'm looking for funds being withdrawn when I should be looking for unusual deposits." Glaring at my computer screen, I was starting to hate those lists of files. "Guess I'll have to go over this again."

Morven squeezed my hand. "You've got this."

"Yeah, I guess." Muscles knotting in my neck, my eyes blurry, I launched Fernoulli's links first, focusing only on the money coming in. My hyper-focus allowed me to scan every detail and inconsistency, mentally tallying each transaction and deposit. By the time I reached the end, the sun had crested, and the fog had burned away, leaving the sky clear and blue. The apple I'd eaten was long gone, my stomach empty.

At some point, Morven had left. I couldn't blame him. Funny I couldn't remember him leaving, but that was the problem with having a super-focused crazy brain like mine.

Placing my computer aside, I stood and stretched my sore muscles. In the barn below, footsteps crunched over straw. I looked down from the loft to find Morven heading toward me, a plate balanced in one hand and a thermos in the other.

"Lunch?" he called up to me. "Your da made it for us."

Da? Right. Sometimes I forgot he came from a different world and used uncommon words.

He smiled up at me as he climbed the bottom rung, then passed up the plate of food and canteen. Reaching down, I grabbed them from him.

Scents of spiced meat and grilled onions filled the loft.

When Morven reached the top, he perched on the edge of the hay bale beside me.

"You must've read my mind," I said. "How did you know I was starving?" I took a bite of the fajita, tender meat and grilled onions falling apart in my mouth. I savored the spicy tang of jalapeño sauce before washing it down with a sip of lemonade from the canteen.

"You were so engrossed in your research, I supposed you wouldn't mind if I went for food. Your da is an amazing cook, by the way."

I couldn't hide my smile. "*Dad*," I corrected.

"Oops." He laughed. "Dad. Right. Forgot which words you use here."

"It's okay."

He nodded as he chewed, then his eyes widened, his cheeks reddened, and he grabbed for the canteen.

"Hot," he breathed before grabbing the drink and guzzling it.

I took another bite to hide my smile.

"Wow," he said after wiping his mouth. "That's incredible."

I gave him a puzzled glance. "You like it?"

"Sure. After I get past the part where my taste buds are burned off, it's great." He cleared his throat. "Tell me about your dad." He waved his hand, hiding his cough as he attempted to nibble another bite.

"What do you want to know?"

"I don't know. It seems like you care a lot for him." He frowned. "Different than my relationship with my aunt."

"Yeah." I took a bite, pondering how much I wanted to open up to him. "Dad was there for me after Mom passed, but..." I took a deep breath, that well of emptiness opening when I thought of the dark time after Mom's death. "After some time, he got distant. Retreated into his work. I didn't see him much. We lost touch. I admit I wasn't useful helping him on the farm." I shrugged. "When I got back from Ceres last time, I felt like we reconnected, like for the first time in my life, he got me. But now… he sort of blindsided me with this whole getting married thing."

"You're angry at him for it?"

I paused before answering. "Not exactly." My stomach suddenly sour, I placed my half-eaten food on the plate. "I worked so hard to keep our family together. Risked my life, saved our world from a solar flare, and barely made it home in one piece. I did it for him. Now he's leaving it all behind." I picked at the long blades of hay, dry and stiff under my fingers.

Morven leaned forward and placed his chin in his hands. "But he's not leaving you behind."

I shrugged. Morven was hitting on a topic too raw for me to process. Maybe it was time to change the subject. Focusing on the computer, I turned away from him. "I should get back to this."

"You're sure you don't want to talk about it?"

"Positive." I kept my eyes on the computer and didn't meet his gaze. *Focus. Yusuf Barnak.* I scanned over the bank deposits, searching only the ones from the past six months since the gateway had been opened. Lists of names and businesses blurred past.

Scanning it twice helped me memorize each word until I built a mental picture of Yusuf's earnings. When I went over it a third time, the name *FINANCIAL ENERGY INSTITUTE* stood out. There were three deposits, starting six months ago.

"How many mines have been raided since the portal opened?" I asked Morven.

"Three, I think. If you count the one you recently discovered. Why?"

I pointed to the institute. "He's gotten three payments from this place in the last six months. There aren't any other payments from them before that date." Clicking on the link, I inhaled sharply as I looked at the sum he'd gotten from the three transactions. "This would pay college tuition to an ivy league school. Twice."

Not that I'd thought of college since I'd started working for Vortech. Getting an English degree was nothing but a distant dream.

"That's interesting," Morven said. "What do you know about Financial Energy Institute?"

"Nothing. Never heard of them."

I opened my web browser and typed in the name. Only a few sites popped up. One caught my attention. *Financial Energy Institute embroiled in legal battle.*

After clicking the link, I scanned the article. Alarm bells rang in my head as keywords popped out. *Links to terrorist organizations. Funded for chemical weapons experiments. Tied to Tokyo Tech.*

"This might be it," I said. "This might be our proof."

"You're sure?"

"I think so. Look at this. Yusuf Barnak received three payments from Financial Energy Institute, who are associated with terrorist organizations and chemical weapons firms. He must've mined the cerecite, then sold it to them. They're also tied to a company called Tokyo Tech. Zen is from Tokyo. That must've been how the two met. That's the connection we've been looking for."

Morven's dark eyes narrowed in contemplation. "You might be right," he admitted. "But there're still some things that don't add up. How did he pay for the mining project to begin with? Those kinds of things take money, and a lot of it. The drills and machinery cost millions of cerecite credits. Where did he get the funds for it?"

"I don't know. There's no record of it. But there's always a chance he's got accounts in remote locations unknown to Vortech. It's not likely, but it's possible."

I stretched, my muscles stiff and protesting. I'd been stuck in this barn so long I'd lost track of time.

"Should we contact Anna and let her know what we found?" Morven asked.

"I don't know yet. I'm not sure we have enough."

"She didn't want irrevocable proof. She wanted to know who Zen is working for. We found it."

Wind rushed through the window, carrying a Sycamore leaf to the hay-strewn floor. I picked it up and rolled the stem between my fingers. On one side, the leaf appeared robust and green. On the other, its veins and edges had turned brown. Something about this situation was sitting well with me, like there was a piece of information we were overlooking.

With a sigh, I tossed the leaf to the ground. Rubbing my eyes, I stared at my computer's screen one final time. "You're right," I said. "I'll contact her. She needs to know what we found."

I launched my email server when a message pinged. Anna Johnson's name popped on the screen, followed by an urgent message.

Before I could click on it, my video phone opened, and Anna Johnson's name appeared in bold.

When I clicked to answer the call, Anna's face appeared in my video window. Dark circles ringed her wide eyes, and her usually neat hair was disheveled.

"Harper," she breathed, her voice edged with panic. "Did you get my message?"

"I saw it just now, but I didn't get a chance to read it. What's going on?"

"They found me. They know what I did."

I shot a confused glance at Morven. "Who found you?"

"Zen's people," she seethed. "I shouldn't have trusted anyone. I should've known."

"Anna, slow down. What's happening?"

"The shield! They destroyed a shield generator. Ceres is under attack!"

Morven stiffened. "What?" he demanded.

"It's Zen. We weren't fast enough. We should've expected this. They destroyed the shield in the northern hemisphere. It's a remote location. Still, at least a dozen were killed. Our team is working now to repair the atmosphere, but it's still too toxic for human survival in that area for a mile radius. The technology is completely foreign. Even working with local engineers, repairing it is nearly impossible."

Morven fisted his hands. His jaw clenched as anger burned in his eyes. "I've got to get back. I have to help repair the shield."

"You?" Anna questioned.

"None of your people have studied the shield biometrics. They'll kill themselves if they don't calibrate it correctly. The shields were built with tech from four-hundred years in the future. Contact Cade McDougall. He can help. We're the only two who understand the technology."

"Our people are qualified—"

"No," Morven interrupted. "There's no way they understand this level of tech. Get me back there. I can help."

"Fine," she relented. "I'd better not have to warn you about how dangerous this is. I can't be held responsible for your safety. The atmosphere is toxic. There's radioactive fallout. I refuse to be blamed for your death."

"Trust me. You won't be."

I sat up straight. "I'm going, too."

"You, Harper?" Her eyes narrowed. "Why?"

"Because this is my fault. I should've been researching who was mining on Ceres sooner."

She raised a pencil thin eyebrow. "Did you find out?"

"Yes. I'm almost certain it was Yusuf Barnak. He's the only one with ties connecting him to Zentoku."

Anna's shoulders relaxed, and her eyes softened. "Good. That's more help than you realize. With that information, we can stop another attack before it happens. In the meantime, we have to repair the shield."

"Agreed," Morven said with steel in his voice. He clenched his jaw, and anger radiated from his dark, livid eyes. "How quickly can you get us back to Ceres?"

"I'll send a chopper immediately. It should arrive this evening and take you straight to this outpost. I'll be waiting for you." Anna ended the call, and we stared at a blank screen.

My mind reeled. Was Anna safe? I hadn't even had a chance to ask her.

I imagined the hole in the shield, the atmosphere leaking into space, replaced with a void of radiation. Outside, the cornfield spanned to a perfect blue sky. Shaking my head, I tried to breathe through the panic coiling around my heart, constricting with each breath I took.

"Why?" Morven rubbed his forehead. "Why would anyone do this?"

"It doesn't make sense. If Barnak was financially gaining from illegally mining cerecite, why damage the planet? What reason would he have?"

Morven's knuckles turned white as he clenched his fists. "I don't know. But we'll find them. I swear to you we'll stop them. Whoever it is, they'll pay."

His deep tenor resonated with power. Fear tingled down my spine.

"We've got to get back," I said. "We've got to make this right."

Morven's eyes darkened with an intensity I'd never seen before. "We will. I promise. We will make this right."

16

Wind whipped the chopper as a snowstorm spiraled around us. I tightened my grip on the armrests. My insides lurched as we hit another air pocket.

"I'll never get used to this," I said through clenched teeth.

Morven gave a half smile, though worry clouded his eyes. "Champ Island is an awful spot for a gateway."

"Agreed."

I ground my teeth as the chopper dropped. Outside my window, a red light blinked from the top of an antennae—the only beacon against the backdrop of white. Whirring blades came as a muffled roar through my headphones. The pilot's voice cut through the noise.

"Almost there," she said.

Wind gusted around us, although we managed to maneuver toward a helipad. The faint letter "H" appeared hundreds of feet below us. After a few tense seconds of descending, with my stomach jumping to my throat, the chopper landed with a thud on the ground.

With shaking fingers, I unlocked my seatbelt and glanced at Morven. "We made it," I said.

"Yeah, and most importantly, we're alive," he added.

After climbing out of the chopper, we made our way down the path leading to a bunker. Buildings made of corrugated metal blended into the landscape of Champ Island. Blue tarps covered some of the structures. They gave the only color against the white void, and they flapped in the wind as we made it to the entrance.

I opened the door and walked inside the building with Morven following.

"No one here to greet us?" he asked as we stared around the empty room.

"I guess not."

We made our way through the room, down the hallway, and into the area housing the artifacts from the gateway cave. I briefly glanced at the objects before entering the next room.

Shouts echoed from down the hallway. Morven and I ran down the corridor to a doorway at the end. After hefting open the partition, we stepped into an enormous room filled with people who scrambled past us. The room's back wall glowed blue, indicating the portal. Ceres was just on the other side.

We brushed past the Vortech employees and stepped toward the portal. Anna Johnson waited nearby, her high heels clicking as she paced over the cement floor. As we walked closer, the portal wavered with a strange warbling sound, like hearing vibrations underwater.

"What's happening?" I asked. "Is something wrong with the gateway?"

"I don't know," Morven answered.

It wavered again, this time louder. Several people emerged from the gateway. Blood streamed from a man's nose and mouth. He gasped and fell to the ground. A woman and another man followed behind him. Their clothes were blackened, and ash covered their faces. Blood poured from wounds in their chests and necks, as if they'd been caught in an explosion.

Anna yelled for the medics. Several people wearing white

jumpsuits rushed forward. Morven and I stepped aside to let them through, and Anna spotted us, her eyes widening, as we crossed the distance to her.

"Harper, I'm so glad you've come." She glanced at Morven. "You, too."

"What's going on?" Morven asked.

"We've sent in twelve people to assess the shield generator." She nodded to the people who had just stepped through the portal. "These three are the last to make it back. It's unstable and too dangerous for us to send anyone else through. I'm afraid we've lost. We'll have to secure the area, make sure the contamination doesn't leak, then work on making sure this doesn't happen anywhere else. At this point, I don't see how we'll ever repair the shield—not with how dangerous it's become."

Morven cursed under his breath. "That generator is close to several villages, including the settlements of most of our miners. If we don't repair it, without the shield protecting them, they and their families will die."

"I understand," Anna said. "But it's too risky to send anyone else through." She pointed to the three people lying on the ground, blood saturating the bandages being applied by the medics. "You can see for yourself how dangerous it is."

"I understand, which is why we'll need protective gear to get through, including oxygen breathing suits."

I eyed him. "Spacesuits?"

He shrugged. "More or less. With that generator out, we've basically reverted the northern portion of Ceres to a desolate, oxygen-starved rock. There won't be much atmosphere." He turned to Anna. "Do you keep any suits like that on hand?"

"The closest thing we have are the survival suits. They're equipped with oxygen masks. I'll have them brought to you."

"Good." Morven spoke with an authoritative tone, speaking with the training of a king of Ithical. "In the meantime, we need to contact Cade MacDougall. He remembers more about the construction of the generators than me. He'll know how to fix them, and we'll need an extra suit for him."

"We've already contacted him," Anna said. "He should be arriving at the generator site soon."

Morven nodded, then Anna motioned to several of her people who rushed forward. She gave them hasty directions, and a few minutes later, they returned with the survival suits. The next few minutes went by in a whirlwind of activity, and before I felt ready, I stood in my suit beside Morven as we faced the gateway a wall of blue that made our reflections waver.

"Start the countdown," one of the men yelled by the control panel. Another man pushed a button, and lights glowed around the outer shell of the gateway.

Anna paced nearby. "Are you sure you want to do this?"

"Yes," I answered. The bulky survival suit weighed me down, and the oxygen mask and goggles made me feel as if I were about to step into the place Ceres had been before the settlers arrived—an alien world devoid of life, a place hostile to humans.

Morven took my hand, his gloved fingers grasping mine. "We're ready," he said.

"Fine, but don't forget I warned you. If anything goes south—I mean *anything*—you're to return here as soon as possible. Don't do anything risky."

I traded a glance with Morven. If Anna knew anything about either of us, she'd know she was asking a ridiculous question. We'd nearly died once in the gateway cave, been attacked by miners, and almost lost our lives.

"We'll do our best," I answered, and we stepped through the portal.

17

Pressure squeezed my lungs as I passed through the portal. When Morven and I stepped out from the confines of the blue void, we entered a room like the east station generator where we'd first found the tainted liquid leaking into the water. Unlike the first station, the smoking remains of this shield generator sat in a smashed heap around us. Noxious smoke rose from the pile of twisted wires and busted metal. Crackling flames engulfed most of the electronics. The air smelled of fumes, making my eyes water. Orange liquid oozed from the busted shield generator.

As I breathed through my oxygen mask, my goggles fogged. When we took another step, I floated an inch off the ground as gravity failed. Morven took my hand and guided me away from the portal.

"Over here," someone called.

We rounded to find Cade standing on the threshold of an open doorway leading outside. A snowy landscape spanned behind him, and a dark sky filled with stars stretched to the horizon. Morven tossed the survival suit to Cade. It glided through the air until Cade caught it. He hastily pulled on the oxygen mask before putting on the coveralls and goggles, and then he stepped into the room.

"How did this happen?" Morven asked Cade as we approached him, his voice muffled by the mask.

Cade pointed to the ceiling. A star-filled sky appeared through several blasted-open holes. "They must have shot it from the air. My best guess is they used the cerecite transport, flew overhead, and targeted it from there. But I can't understand what sort of weapon they used." He knocked on a wall partially standing beside us. "These walls are reinforced with a mixture of yellow cerecite and titanium. A bomb made of yellow cerecite wouldn't have any effect, and a nuclear bomb would have laid waste to the place."

"What about the pharocite they stole from the first generator?" I suggested. "Could it be made into an explosive?"

Cade tilted his head. "I suppose it's possible. To my knowledge, it's never been done before." He unzipped his jumpsuit and reached into his shirt pocket, then pulled out a small glass vial filled with a few orange crystals. "I harvested these from the east generator. If we repair this generator—which is a big *if*—then we can use these for its fuel. Theoretically, we'll be able to repair the atmosphere." He pointed to the holes leading up to the star-filled sky. "You'll be interested to know it's actually noon right now."

"So, we're seeing the actual sky not hidden by the dome," Morven said.

"Yes," Cade agreed.

I wiped my goggles and looked with wonder through the blasted holes to the sky above. Stars twinkled so brightly they could have been jewels. My breathing sounded too loud with the mask covering my face, and my breath fogged the lenses, so I turned my attention to the broken generator. Glass shards and metal pieces lay scattered over the ground. Given how much I knew about tech from the future, I wouldn't be much help in this situation. "Morven, how much do you remember about this machinery?"

He shook his head. "My memories—*Isaac's* memories— are still fragmented, but some of it has come back to me."

"Good," Cade said. "Because you and I are the only people on the planet capable of fixing something like this."

A rumble shook the room as a metal panel crashed to the ground from overhead, and we jumped away from it just in time. Flames licked at the air, but soon died out.

"At least the lack of oxygen is good for something." I pointed to the dying flames. "Although there's still just enough oxygen to keep the fires burning a little."

"Yes, but if we get the atmospheric pressure fully functioning, we won't have that advantage," Cade said. "This place could blow up, and all our work repairing the generator would be for nothing."

"Then I'll work on putting out anything flammable," I said.

Morven glanced at the broken machine behind him. "And we'll work on repairing the generator."

As I took a step toward the pile of smoking metal, my stride made me float. "I've got to get used to that," I mumbled to myself, then grabbed a low-hanging beam. I pushed on it until my momentum shifted downward and I landed on the ground, then I scattered ash over the small flames until they died out.

Morven's and Cade's voices came as muffled sounds from behind me. I worked on making my way from one pile of debris to the next, smothering flames here and there. In a few places, the flames sparked, but I managed to put them out before they could burn brighter.

As I worked, I glanced at Morven and Cade hunched over the generator, speaking quietly to one another. It hadn't been long ago that Cade had been responsible for poisoning Morven's food to keep the prince from remembering his past as Isaac the miner—and consequently forgetting about the gateway cave.

Not only that, but Morven had never been cordial to Cade. In fact, sometimes he'd been downright rude. Six months ago, I would have never believed they could get along. Seeing them now gave me hope for the future—that maybe people and situations could change, that perhaps somehow, by some great miracle, Morven and I could be together.

I wasn't sure how much time had passed when Cade moved toward me, walking with long strides that made him rise off the ground before landing again.

"Morven's going to ignite the generator," he said. "We'll need to stand outside while he does it."

I glanced to the room's center where Morven stood. The glass cylinder had been repaired, as had the surrounding metal instruments holding it in place. Three small crystals gleamed from inside the transparent tube.

"Will you be okay?" I called to Morven.

"I'll be fine." He cast a sidelong glance at the crystals. "I'll move away from it as soon as I can."

I wasn't appeased by his answer, but I'd learned that arguing with Prince Morven Tremayne was a waste of my time, so I followed Cade outside the open doorway. We stepped onto the snowy terrain, our boots crunching the ice-crusted ground. Despite my survival suit, the cold air seeped through the layers of fabric and around the edges of my oxygen mask, making a chill burrow under my skin.

"Start the countdown," Cade yelled.

"Okay," Morven yelled back. With a click of a button, lights ignited around the cylinder's casing. Morven backed away until he stood beside us. We waited in silence, the lights slowly blinking on and off.

"Is it working?" I asked.

"I don't know," Cade said, his voice tense. "It should have ignited by now."

"Unless it's misaligned," Morven said. "Which is entirely possible."

Wind blustered with an eerie shrieking.

"Should we check it again?" Morven asked.

"No," Cade answered. "Give it more time."

The seconds stretched, and I hugged my arms around me for warmth. The flashing lights grew brighter, and a mechanical roaring came from the generator.

"Get back," Cade yelled.

We jumped away just as the lights grew blindingly bright, and the roar turned to a deafening clatter. I clamped my hands over my ears. Above us, a blanket of purple stretched, covering the stars. The roar decreased to a low hum, and I moved my hands from my ears.

Overhead, the sky turned brighter, and the intense purple color faded until it resembled the real sky—mostly blue, with only the smallest tint of lavender.

"Looks like it worked," I said.

"For now, at least," Cade said. "This is a temporary solution. Those crystals won't last long. A few weeks, maybe. A month at most."

"Then what do we do?" I asked.

Cade bit his lip, as if deep in thought. "We'll have to go back to the palace. I've been working with cerecite a long time. I know how it functions. It shouldn't be too hard to create pharocite."

"But you've been creating plants," I said. "Do you really think you can engineer pharocite?"

"It's made from yellow cerecite," Morven said. "I think I remember a little about the engineering process. Maybe I can help."

"Good," I said. "Now let's get back to the palace. It's freezing out here."

"The quickest way is back through the portal," Cade said,

waving us forward. "We can go back to Champ Island then find a closer portal from there."

We followed him just as the sky darkened. Was the generator failing already? But as I looked up, the dark, blocky shape of a cerecite transport flew into view. Its engines roared with a low rumble as it descended.

I clenched my fists, and my heart rate quickened. "Zen."

"Zen?" Cade raised an eyebrow.

"That's the name of the man who's been attacking the generators," I said. "Looks like he couldn't stay away for long."

"He must have been nearby," Morven said. "He probably saw when the shield got repaired and came back to finish the job."

Cade cursed and pulled a gun from his belt. "What weapons do you have?"

"None. Even so, nothing will be of much use against that." I pointed to the transport, which was slowly descending. Wind blustered from the transport's turbines until the sound became deafening and the transport loomed above us.

"We should run," Morven said.

Morven and I turned to go, but Cade stopped us with a wave of his hand. "Wait," he said.

"What?" I asked. "Why? Cade, we've got to get out of here!"

"No." He peered up at the ship, which now hung suspended above us, unmoving. "I'm calling their bluff."

Wind screamed around us, and snow blustered to create a blizzard, but the transport held steady.

"I doubt they have the weaponry to destroy the generator from their ship," Cade yelled over the wind. "Which means they'll have to send someone inside to destroy it." He hefted his gun. "I'll be ready for them. Wait for me."

He held his gun to his chest and dashed back toward the shield generator.

Morven cursed. "We can't let him go in there alone."

A man's silhouette dropped from the overhead transport. He hung suspended from a wire until falling to the ground. I caught a glimpse of the person before he turned and dashed behind Cade into the shield generator. There was no mistaking the braided goatee and hooded eyes that made my blood run cold.

Zen.

18

"We have to go after him," I yelled to Morven over the rumbling engines of the transport hovering above us. Snow blustered as I ran toward the shield generator station. Cade and Zen had already disappeared inside the dark building.

Morven chased after me as I dashed toward the entrance. When I stepped inside the building, my heart pounded, and the roaring engines were muffled by the surrounding room. The darkness blinded me, and I could barely make out the shapes of hulking machines.

Shouts came from the far side of the room, and I followed the sounds until Morven grabbed my hand.

"What?"

He put a finger over his lips. "We've got the element of surprise going for us. Let's not ruin it."

I nodded. We moved quietly, although with the whirring of the air transport coupled with the hum of the generator, I doubted either Zen or Cade could hear our footfalls.

We hid behind a massive machine that hummed with a deep base sound. As I peeked around it, I found Cade facing Zen, who held twin swords. A wave of dread flooded through my blood at the sight of the weapons. They glittered with a thin line of yellow along the sharpened blades. Swords made with yellow cerecite? With those, he could poison his opponent with only a scratch from his blade. Yellow cerecite was the only substance capable of killing Cade.

The glow of the orange crystals illuminated Cade as he stood pointing the gun at Zen's chest.

"Not another step," Cade said. "I've killed to protect this world, and I'll do it again if you force me."

"But we want the same goal," Zen said, his voice deep and edged with warning.

"The same goal?" Cade spat. "You're lying. How could you possibly be protecting Ithical? You've destroyed two shield generators."

"For good reasons," Zen said.

Morven and I inched our way toward the two, although we kept our distance and approached quietly, stopping behind the larger machines.

"What reasons?" Cade demanded.

"Not *my* reasons..." Zen held perfectly still as he spoke, his swords held protectively crossed in front of him. "I obey Aeon Orion. Only he knows the truth."

"Who is he?"

"My master."

Cade narrowed his eyes. "He told you to destroy the shield generators?"

"Yes." Zen shifted his weight, his stance that of a practiced fighter. "His goal is to erase this world, make it so Ithical never happened. This is *Finem Nunquam*, the *End of Never*, and it starts with me. Stand aside." He waved his swords at Cade. "Allow me to destroy the power source, and I will let you live."

Cade flexed his jaw. Anger simmered in his eyes. "Good luck with that. I've got a gun. You've got knives. Take a wild guess as to who wins this fight."

"Very well." Zen gave a polite bow of his head. "If that is the way, then I wish you peace in the afterlife."

Zen rushed at Cade in a flurry of spinning swords. Cade fired off a shot. A silver ball of light hurtled from Cade's weapon, straight for Zen's chest, but Zen moved so lightning-fast, the shot bounced off his swords and ricocheted to the ceiling. Chunks of metal rained down, as did a volley of sparks.

Cade fired again, and Zen narrowly avoided the shot. Zen maneuvered toward Cade, his swords waving in a practiced dance. With each step, he gained an inch toward the power source.

"We have to stop Zen," I whispered to Morven.

"How? We have no weapons."

"Then we'll have to distract him long enough for Cade to get a clean shot," I explained.

"All right," Morven agreed. "What do you have in mind?"

"I'm not sure." I searched for anything that could cause a distraction. Sparks still fell from the ceiling, and below them were piles of twisted metal. "What if we disable the power source, just for a minute?"

"Risky," Morven answered. "But not a bad idea."

"We have survival suits and Zen doesn't. He wouldn't be able to breathe. At least, not very well," I added. "If you disable the generator, how hard would it be to bring it back online?"

"Not hard," he answered. "All I would have to do is misalign the crystals, then realign them once we want to start up the generator again."

Another shot fired from Cade's gun, but Zen spun out of its path with amazing speed—so fast I wondered if he were human.

I tiptoed behind the hulking machines until we reached a pathway leading to the power source. Morven led the way, and thankfully, while Zen and Cade fought, they didn't notice as we slipped to the generator.

With the press of a button, the lights surrounding the generator dimmed, and Morven reached inside and moved the crystals slightly aside.

The constant droning of machinery ceased. The lights went out, plunging us into darkness. I hastily pulled on my mask and goggles just as the oxygen slipped from the room. Sounds of struggling ensued, and Cade cried out with a shriek that raised the hairs on the back of my neck, as if he'd been mortally wounded.

I did my best to peer into the darkness, but without the lights of machinery, and the glow of the atmosphere gone, all I could make out were the silhouettes of the two men still fighting.

Someone choked and backed out of the room. Zen, hopefully.

"Help…" a weak voice called, and I recognized it as Cade's. I rushed forward, pressing my hands to the sides of the machines as I lifted off the ground. When I came closer to the room's center, an ice pick seemed to puncture my heart me at the scene I found.

Cade was lying in a pool of his own blood. His left arm was mangled and severed at the elbow. His oxygen mask was thrown to the side.

With stiff fingers, I managed to grab the mask and pull it over Cade's face. Morven hovered behind me. In the blink of an eye, he pulled the belt off his jumpsuit and wrapped it around Cade's bicep to stop the flow of blood.

"He took it…" Cade whispered, and even in the darkness I could see his face was so pale I feared he would pass out at any moment.

"Took what?" I asked.

Cade shook his head, mumbling incoherently.

"We've got to get him back to the palace," Morven said. "He needs green cerecite or else he'll die."

"I'll take him," I said. "Follow behind as soon as you can after you realign the generator."

"No," Morven said. "If I realign it, Zen will only return to finish the job."

"Then what are we supposed to do?"

"I don't know," he answered. I'd never seen such panic in his eyes. His world was being destroyed and he knew it. Worse, there was nothing he could do to stop it. "All I know is we need Cade if we want to stop Zen. Help me get him back to the palace."

We lifted Cade to his feet. With the loss of gravity, we floated up with only a little effort, and made our way to the gateway portal. The mangled stump of Cade's arm hung limply at his side.

19

<hr>

Morven and I sat at Cade's bedside. Sunlight streamed inside through the many windows ringing the tower room. The scents of greenery and earth filled the airy space. Everything about the room spoke of order—the flagstone floor without a speck of dirt, the solid oak dresser and heavy desk devoid of a spot of dust, ink bottles arranged in a neat row, and flowerpots filled with plants arranged neatly on the windowsills.

I'd always known he loved gardening, but the care he put into every plant was obvious. He'd created frilly blooms of pink and yellow, and exotic-looking fruit with purple, spongy rinds. By the way Cade cared for the plants, it was easy to see his love for this world. All he'd ever wanted to do was protect it and keep it filled with beauty.

But had he ever accomplished his goals? Yes, Ceres was lovely in places, but it was obvious it could be so much more. The fruits and flowers he'd cultivated could transform the world into a garden utopia. And if Zen and his master got their way, Ceres would cease to exist. The implications of Zen's words still sent a shiver down my spine.

A breeze wafted through the room, tugging at the loose

strands of blond hair on Cade's forehead, a blue checkered blanket covering his prone form. He lay with a bandage around the stump of his arm. Beside me, Morven stood and paced the room. After the encounter with Zen, we'd reentered the portal and made our way back to the palace, where Cade had been treated with green cerecite. He'd been sleeping ever since.

A knock came at the door, and Morven opened it to reveal Vevina holding a tray of food.

"Mind if I come in?" she asked.

"Not at all," he answered, then led her inside. Worry creased her brow as she took in the gardener sleeping on the bed. She placed the tray on his bedside table, then smoothed a hand over the blanket covering his chest.

"I thought he would've woken by now," she said softly.

"We thought the same," I answered.

"What if he doesn't make it?" she questioned, her eyes lit with anxiousness.

"He'll make it," Morven stated matter-of-factly. "He's been through worse."

"Worse than this?" Vevina reached out and tentatively touched the bandage wrapping the stump of his arm. "How will he ever do his gardening now?"

"I don't know," Morven answered. "But we need him for more than gardening. He was supposed to help us create pharocite. Now, I'm not sure."

I rubbed the sore muscles in my neck. "Give it time."

Morven shook his head. "The one thing we don't have."

I tapped my fingers on my knee. Ever since Cade's fight with Zen, something had been bugging me. Cade had mentioned Zen taking something, but what? His arm? No. That didn't make sense. Cade meant something else—something Zen had taken with him.

Out of a nervous gesture, I clutched the pyramid pendant around my neck when it hit me. His pendant. Standing, I reached forward and felt for the leather cord around Cade's neck.

"What are you doing?" Vevina asked.

"Looking for his pendant," I answered.

"Is it gone?" Morven asked.

"Yes," I answered with a sigh of disappointment. "Zen must have taken it."

"Meaning what?" Vevina asked.

"Meaning he has the ability to open another shield generator and remove the pharocite," Morven answered, scrubbing his knuckles down his face.

My heart sank as I fit the pieces together. "He's already taken out two generators." Clutching my pyramid pendant, I paced the room as I mentally retraced Zen's footsteps. "He originally used this pendant to unlock the east generator. He didn't have the key to the other generators, so he used the stolen pharocite to create a bomb."

"Then he used the pharocite bomb to destroy the north generator," Morven chimed in.

"Exactly," I answered. "But that means he needs the key to either the south or west generators. He'll repeat the process of stealing the pharocite from one, and then create a bomb to destroy the other."

"And he stole Cade's key," Vevina said. Wind gusted through the open windows, tugging strands of red hair across her face, highlighting the concern in her eyes. "But which generator does it open—the west or the south?"

"South," I answered after pondering for a moment, stopping to stare out the window. Beyond the city lay miles of greenery stretching to the purple-tinged horizon.

"How do you know that?" Morven asked.

"Because I remember when I first went through the portal to get here. I came through a shield generator station located in the south. The gateway portal had been busted up, and I later learned that Cade was the one who'd destroyed it. Although I suspect he left the shield generator intact, or else there wouldn't have been any atmosphere out there. Cade must have had the key and used it to get inside, then destroyed the gateway portal."

"Why would he do that?" Vevina asked.

"He was trying to protect our world," I answered. "Every Vortech agent who came before me was trying to find the seven cerecite stones and reopen the gateway leading to Earth."

"But Cade knew a gateway would lead to destruction," Vevina surmised. "And it looks like he was right."

Morven crossed his arms. "It's possible we could try to apprehend Zen at the south station and stop him from taking the pharocite—if we even have the time to do it, which I doubt."

I propped my elbows on the windowsill. "It would be smarter to wait. Once Zen has the pharocite from the south station, it will take time for him to engineer a bomb. We know it took him several months to engineer the first bomb he made from the pharocite stolen from the east station."

Morven paced to the window, sunlight shining over his tall frame. "Since he's done it once before, let's assume it takes him less time to engineer the second one. Even so, we'll still have a few weeks at least to apprehend him. If only we could find him and stop him before he ever tries to destroy anything."

"Do you have any idea of where to look?" Vevina asked.

"No clue." Morven locked his jaw, and he stared out the window. "I wish I knew."

I tapped my fingers on the windowsill, the faint scent of the metallic atmosphere wafting from outside. "He said he served Aeon Orion. Have you ever heard that name?"

"No," Morven answered, and Vevina shook her head.

"Neither have I," I admitted. "But if we want to find Zen,

finding out who he serves is a good place to start. If that's Yusuf Barnak, then we need to know for sure."

"He also mentioned a project," Morven said. "The End of… Never. Was that it?"

"Yeah. End of Never. Odd name. We'll need to look into them both, and hopefully stumble on Zen's hiding place in the process." I turned away from the window to sit by Cade once again. "There's so much I wish you could tell us…" I whispered to him.

"We should get to the library," Morven said, taking my hand.

"I agree," I answered, then turned to Vevina and opened my mouth to question her when she spoke up.

"I know," she said with a wave of her hand. "I'll let you know the minute he wakes."

"Thank you," I answered before I grabbed my backpack sitting by the doorway, then exited the room with Morven.

The hallway felt unusually empty as we walked. I slung my backpack over my shoulder, feeling the weight of the laptop inside. What research could I possibly uncover about Aeon Orion and the End of Never? I couldn't stop replaying what we'd learned about the shield generators, and I still didn't have a clue about how to stop Zen from destroying the last two.

Worse, seeing Vevina had stirred up a host of emotions. Imagining her and Morven together left a bitter taste in my mouth, and I'd rather focus on learning more about Zen and stopping the destruction of Ithical.

"Are you thinking about Zen?" Morven asked.

"Yes," I lied. "Some things just aren't adding up, you know?"

"I'm thinking the same thing," Morven said. "If Yusuf Barnak is Zen's employer, what's his motivation? Why destroy Ithical? It's a rich source of cerecite. We've made it possible for legal mining to take place. If he plays his cards right, and he mines cerecite legally, he's poised to make billions off this place. Why take all that away?" I bit my lip in concentration as we took a set of stairs down to the second tier. The carved wooden doors to the library were just ahead, illuminated by sconces burning blue cerecite. Flickering flames caused shadows to dart over the doors' engravings. "I'm not sure Barnak is Zen's employer. I'm not sure if any of the three founders are."

Morven gave me a puzzled glance. "You think it could be someone else altogether?"

"Maybe." I shrugged. "But if that's the case, we're still not any closer to finding out who it is."

Morven reached the doors first and pulled them open to reveal the library. We wandered through the stacks until we reached the back of the room where Morven's table sat piled with books and scrolls.

He cleared away the clutter, and I opened my backpack, then placed my laptop on the table's center. We situated our chairs in front of the screen, then I launched the program linking me to Vortech's database.

I typed the words END OF NEVER into the search engine.

Zero results.

"I can't say I'm completely surprised," I mumbled, then typed AEON ORION with the same results.

"Nothing on Vortech's database," Morven mused. "But this is a limited search. What happens if we Google it?"

I raised an eyebrow.

"What?" he asked.

"*Google it?*" I couldn't keep a grin from spreading across my face. "Now you really sound like you're from Earth."

"I may have spent some time there." He nudged me.

"You didn't waste any time picking up the lingo, did you?" I teased. "But you're right. I can use the flash drive Anna gave me to connect to the web." I exited the Vortech browser and launched the search engine, then repeated the process of typing the phrase and name.

Three sites popped up. Soundcloud, a Latin translator, the keywords out of order, but then I found one that listed both the phrase *End of Never* and the name *Aeon Orion*.

"Got something." I pointed to the screen.

"Let's see," Morven said, and I clicked the link, pulling up a website from a scientific journal.

"The author's name is Aeon Orion," Morven said. "Weird."

I scrolled down, using my ability to scan the important information. "It's a thesis on how time travel is possible. 'Some state that hypothetical particles and states of matter would violate laws of physics, but this is untrue. The collision of two black holes could create enough energy to break the time barrier. What if this same power were harnessed in a more stable source?'" I quoted. "Interesting. It almost sounds as if he's talking about the seven cerecite stones."

"I don't think that's a coincidence."

"Yeah." I thrummed my fingers on the table. "But how does Aeon Orion know about cerecite?"

"Maybe there's some clue in the article," Morven suggested. "Something that's not straightforward."

"It's possible."

"There's gotta be information we're not seeing. Look for any words that are repeated or out of place. You can scan for it, right?"

I scanned through it twice, then a third time. I almost closed out the page when something hit me. "Look," I said to Morven. "There are only four numbers mentioned in the article. 2, 4, 4, and 7. In that order."

"And?" Morven lifted an eyebrow.

"When was the wormhole first created?" I asked.

"In the twenty-fifth century." Morven frowned. "I don't know the exact date."

"Yes, but Cade told me he was born in the year 2437. Exactly ten years before 2447."

"Meaning what?"

"Meaning the author of this article could have been hinting at the year the wormhole was created. Cade said he was born in 2437. Supposing he was in his twenties when he first came to Ceres, that would put the wormhole's creation around the year 2447, which are the only four numbers in this article—which ironically—happens to be about time travel." I spoke quietly. "What if Aeon Orion is a time-traveler?"

Morven shook his head. "I don't know, Sabine. That seems like a stretch."

I sat back in my chair and rubbed my eyes. "Is it? Maybe. Morven, isn't there anything you remember from the future and your first life when you were Isaac? Do you remember anything about when the wormhole was created?"

"Not really." He shook his head. "I remember emotions mostly. Lots of stress, hard work. Pain. Some happy moments here and there. The bigger details are cloudy at best. Living on Ceres wasn't a great life." He hooked his pinkie through mine. "I hope my life as Morven Tremayne will be better."

Would it be better, though? If he had to marry someone he didn't love, what sort of future could he expect? Assuming he still had a world to live in.

I grabbed my computer and shut the lid with a click.

"Why'd you do that?" he asked.

"Because I'm tired." I rubbed my eyes. "Tired of working. Tired of being afraid. Tired of feeling like we'll never win!" I threw my hands in the air, the burst of emotions—of frustration and stress—came from months of bottling them up. "I feel like since Vortech hired me, I've forgotten how to live and be happy. Let's do something fun."

"Something fun?" he asked. "Like what?"

"I don't know." I waved to the windows. "Go exploring on the velocipedes. Something."

He arched his brows. "Our world is on the brink of destruction, and you want to take a ride?"

I sighed. "I know it sounds ridiculous. It's just sometimes, I feel like I've forgotten how to live." I folded my hands on my lap.

Morven squeezed my shoulder. "I wish I could." He shook his head as a pained expression crossed his face. "But Aunt Tremayne asked me to help her."

"Help her with what?" I asked.

"The word is getting out about Zen and how he's destroying the shield generators, which is why she decided to move forward with the wedding plans." He sank in his chair. "She wants me to marry Vevina in one week."

"What?" My heart sank. "A week?" He couldn't be serious.

"I know." He sighed in defeat. "There's not much I can do about it at this point. Everyone is onboard with this wedding. Well—everyone except me and Vevina. Even her family is putting on the pressure for us to get married. The unity of Ithical is at stake. They want to observe traditions and keep the status quo." He clutched my hand. "Which is why the wedding will never happen."

"Come again?" I asked, surprised.

"I refuse to marry Vevina, and my wedding day is the perfect time to break tradition. Sabine—I've given this a lot of thought."

I didn't like the twinkle in his eyes—mischief laced with a stubborn streak. "Given *what* a lot of thought?"

"I'm going to marry you."

Shock slapped me. I could have fallen out of my chair. I would have questioned him, but words escaped me.

"It's the right thing to do," he continued. "I've got to make everyone understand that we can still keep traditions while starting new ones, too. Arranged marriages are such an outdated notion, they're laughable. And that's just the start of it. We need to abolish the monarchy. We need an academy. Our people need to know our position in the universe—that we're here on Ceres and not on some island on Earth. There's so much more we could learn about cerecite and how it works. If we had a proper place to study it, think of all the advancements we could make."

The passion in his voice told me he must have been pondering this for a long time. And I had to admit—his passion was contagious. My heart leapt to know he'd imagined marrying me. But would he ever convince his aunt, Vevina's family, and the entire population of Ithical that he was right?

"Morven," I said gently. "I agree with every word you've said, but how do you plan to pull this off without starting an all-out war?"

"I don't know," he answered honestly. "I'll find a way." He nudged me with his shoulder. "Maybe I'll skip out on wedding plans and take you up on that ride."

I nudged him back. "Maybe you should." Just as I pulled my computer off the table, my Vortech bracelet buzzed, startling me. Vortech had replaced the tech-jewelry months ago, so they rarely ever used it.

"What's that?" Morven nodded to the bracelet. "A message?"

I nodded as I pressed the disc to answer the call.

"Harper," Anna's voice came through. "We've got him. Yusuf Barnak is here at the Ceres station. Vincent is also here. I need you. Come here as soon as possible."

"Why do you need me?"

"To present the evidence you found. I need all the help I can get."

A lump rose into my throat. I wasn't prepared to go up against the most powerful leaders in Vortech. I could easily lose my job if Yusuf knew I was working for Anna to bring him down. Then again, wouldn't this be a good opportunity to confront him? If he was indeed Zen's leader—if he was Aeon Orion—then I would find out for sure.

"I'll be there soon," I told her.

"Good," she answered, then ended the call.

"Well." Morven folded his arms across his chest. "That was unexpected."

"Not necessarily." I stood and grabbed my backpack, then stuffed my computer inside. Morven also stood.

I cast him a quizzical glance. "Where are you going?"

"I'm coming with you."

I motioned to the hallway leading to the door. "Don't you have a wedding to plan?"

He waved me off. "This is more important. I'm sure Aunt Tremayne will understand."

"Yeah," I said with sarcasm. "Sure. She'll understand completely."

He placed an arm around my shoulders. "I'll tell Vevina before we go, and she can relay the information to my aunt. Aunt Tremayne listens to Vevina better than me anyway. She'll make her understand."

"I guess we'll find out," I said, slinging my backpack over my shoulder.

Snow drifts piled on either side of our path leading to the bunker. It always took me some time to adjust from one world to another. Ceres was a place filled with warmth and near-perfection, yet also filled with air that reminded me we were under a dome. Earth was filled with bitter cold and unpredictability, yet it gave me a sense of freedom—and of home.

The hatch to the metal bunker loomed ahead. Guards waited around the doorway, their bulky, black uniforms contrasting against the snow. One of the men nodded as Morven and I approached. The mechanical door opened with a hiss. We stepped onto a metal grate, and the door sealed shut behind us. The warmth came as a relief, and I dusted the snow off my clothes. As I turned to the walkway ahead, to the guards lining the passageway with rifles held at the ready, anxiety pulsed through my veins. Their gazes lingered on me for too long.

Something about this entire situation was off-putting. Swallowing hard, a cold sweat dampening my palms, I wondered, could Anna be setting me up to take the fall if anything went south? If so, I needed insurance to make sure nothing like that happened. I had no way of getting a lawyer now. If I wanted to be on top of my game, I had to think outside the box.

Morven rested his hand on my shoulder as we crossed through another doorway and entered the makeshift artifact room.

"Are you worried?" he asked.

"Never," I teased, straining to smile, then shook my head. "Terrified. Vortech has so much power over me—too much power, really. What if Anna Johnson is using me as her scapegoat?"

"You think she's setting you up to take the fall?"

"Not necessarily. But if things go badly, I wouldn't be surprised if she tried to place all the blame on me." I bit my lip, pondering my situation. "Anyway, that's why I need to prove who Zen is working for."

"How do you plan on doing that?"

"I'm not certain yet." Wandering through the stacks of artifacts gave me an idea. Something about these items called to me, and I wasn't sure what drew me to them, but I knew my answer to solving the mystery of Aeon Orion's identity lay here. Rust clung to my fingertips as I started rifling through the objects, mentally cataloging each one—the size, shape, and possible function.

"What are you doing?"

"Looking for our answer," I told him. "If Aeon Orion comes from the future, then something here will prove it." I sounded more confident than I felt. There was no guarantee I would find anything of value, but if I didn't find something soon, I had no way of proving Orion's identity. If Yusuf Barnak was indeed the man we thought, we had to know for sure.

Recognizing a familiar object, I paused to stare at it. The sheet of bronze was flat and a little wider than a plate, with hairline circuits on the surface, and the words *PROJECT*

CERES etched into its surface. I picked up the device and turned it over, revealing a blank screen with buttons surrounding it. My heart leapt with excitement. I knew the worth of what I held in my hands, and I wouldn't hesitate to use it.

"I remember this." Morven motioned to the device. "We found it in the gateway cave the first time we went there."

"Yes." I hefted the artifact. "This is it. This is the object that will prove we're right."

"Are you sure?" he asked.

I took a deep breath. "I hope so, but we'll know the truth soon enough." I didn't want to say any more. But if this artifact was the object I remembered, then we were one step closer to finding the true enemy among us.

Morven and I left the room and entered another hallway. A pair of guards led us to Anna's office, blue tarp still hanging on one wall, floodlights still attached to tripods, their harsh brightness glaring over the folding table and metal chairs where two men sat.

Anna stood as we entered, her black pant suit pristine and her bobbed hair styled artfully to frame her face. There was no trace of the frightened, harried woman I'd spoken to last time. The shrewd look in her eyes reminded me of a panther, and I fought my nervousness as she pinned me with her stare. *Don't mess this up*, she seemed to warn me.

The guards spread out, and Anna paced around the folding table where the other two Vortech founders sat.

"Agent Harper, Prince Tremayne," Anna said. "You made it. Thank goodness." She motioned to the two unoccupied chairs, and we sat. I kept the device on my lap, sizing up the people sitting around me. The man across from me was heavyset, with thick eyebrows and a mustache. He smoked a cigar, and its scent perfumed the room. I recognized Yusuf Barnak from his profile picture.

The man beside him wore a fitted suit. He looked like a

sixty-something Hollywood celebrity, with obvious plastic surgery plumping his face, and his hair gelled and styled until it could have withstood any storm Champ Island could throw at him.

"Agent Harper," Anna began. "I'd like you to meet the founders of Vortech. Yusuf Barnak." She gestured to the man with the cigar. "And Vincent Fernoulli." She pointed to the other man.

Vincent threaded his fingers together on the tabletop. "It's a pleasure to finally meet you," he said with a plastered-on smile, his voice holding a slight Italian accent.

"Pleasure?" Barnak snorted. "I disagree. She's the one who started this mess." He took the cigar from his mouth and pointed it at me. "Are you the one accusing me of stealing cerecite?"

"Don't answer that," Anna snapped. "Yusuf, you know better than to challenge her. If you must know, Ms. Harper was hired by me."

"Hmph," he snorted. "Figures." He stuck the cigar between his teeth. "Well, can we get this over with? I've got to be at a meeting in Dubai in twelve hours."

Anna placed both hands on the table, her expression stern. "Yusuf, that's enough. This is a serious matter. When we opened the wormhole portal to Ceres, the most important requirement was keeping the cerecite protected and not over-mining it. Yet here we are, faced with the fact that someone is illegally mining and possibly using it to create bombs which have already been used to destroy two shield generators."

"Where's the proof of this?" Yusuf crossed his arms over his wide chest.

"We've seen it ourselves," Morven spoke up. "And as the prince of Ithical, I hope you'll believe me."

Yusuf's eyes narrowed, but he didn't speak.

"Still," Fernoulli said, frowning. "Yusuf is right. If we're to take this seriously, we need proof that the illegal mining is indeed happening."

"Will these work for proof?" Anna picked up a manila folder sitting on the table. She pulled out a stack of photos and scattered them over the table. The familiar images I'd taken in the cave of the miners came as a shock, and I sucked in a breath of air.

Those pictures had been stolen by Zen. How had she gotten them back?

Yusuf grabbed the photos and flipped through them. "What are these?" he demanded.

"Your proof," Anna answered, "Agent Harper risked her life getting these for us. They were taken in a cave not designated for mining, and no one in these images is a member of the Vortech dig team." She paced behind the table, her high heels clicking over the cement floor.

"Fine," Yusuf barked. "Someone is illegally mining. But I hope you're not implying that I'm somehow behind this."

"I wish it weren't true." Anna crossed her arms. "But unfortunately, I knew that if illegal mining were to take place, you two would be the only ones capable of doing it. You're the only ones who have the knowledge of how the gateway functions, and who have access to it. You also have the funds to command such an operation."

Vincent barked a cheerless laugh. "How did you reach that conclusion?" He leaned forward, pinning Anna with a dark glare. "It seems to me you're levering this situation for your own purposes."

"I would never do such a thing," she seethed, then continued her pacing.

I rubbed my forehead where a headache pounded. I'd never known there was so much bad blood between the founders of Vortech. Morven grabbed my hand and looped his pinkie through mine.

"Reminds me of my aunt," he whispered.

"It's a wonder Vortech functions with so much distrust."

Anna and the two men continued their back-and-forth until Yusuf pounded his fist on the table.

"Enough." His face had gone red. "Why have you brought us here, Anna? Your baseless accusations are getting us nowhere. Either tell us something important or we're leaving."

"Baseless?" she asked. "Hardly. I've had Agent Harper do some research. It seems you bear the brunt of the guilt. Tell me, what is the Financial Energy Institute? And how is it you've been paid by them three times in the last six months? Guess how many mines have been raided in that time?"

Yusuf's face flushed and his gaze slid sidelong to me. "How did you get that information?"

"It doesn't matter." She pursed her lips. "What does matter is the truth. Tell me, Yusuf. Where did these funds come from? Are you profiting from the sale of cerecite?"

He locked his jaw. "You had no business looking into my personal finances."

"We have no personal finances," she said. "You know that. Everything we own belongs to Vortech."

"This is ludicrous." He spoke with livid passion. "How dare you demand I come here so you could berate me? My finances are my business, not yours."

"So, you don't deny the money came from the sale of cerecite? In that case, tell me who you hired to mine it for you? Was it Zentoku Uzumaki?"

"What?" he blanched. "How dare you accuse me of hiring him? Is this because of my nationality? I'm of Middle Eastern descent, so you assume I must be aligned with terrorist cells? You've gone too far, Anna, even for you." His voice held a dangerous edge. "You know me better than that. All my life, all I've ever done is fought the stereotype, and now you accuse me of hiring terrorists as if it's nothing. This is too much." He shook his head. "You'd best tread lightly if you wish for our partnership to continue."

Anna stopped pacing and held perfectly still, her eyes boring into Yusuf's, as if she were shocked by his reaction. Did she expect him to admit his guilt? Maybe with the evidence she was presenting, that was exactly what she'd wanted. But even I had to admit that our case against Yusuf was shaky at best.

Vincent leaned forward in his seat. "I agree with Yusuf," he said. "These accusations have gone too far. His financial dealings were none of your business, and you have no proof connecting him to Uzumaki."

"Anna," I said with an even tone, hoping she'd start to calm down. "I've brought something that might help."

Anna gave me a sharp look.

"Yes, let her speak," Yusuf said. "I myself would like to know what evidence you've concocted. Anything other than proving my innocence will be a waste of time."

"I brought this." I placed the metal device on the tabletop, scanning the faces of the three Vortech founders as I did, looking for any subtle reactions.

Anna placed her hands on her hips, her gaze calculating, as if I weren't abiding by her narrative. Still, I pushed forward.

"Morven and I found this in the gateway cave the first time we went there. It's a recruitment hologram for Project Ceres."

"What does this have to do with illegal mining?" Yusuf demanded.

"That's a great question," I answered calmly. "And it's something that's been bugging me since I discovered Zen in the mine. Why would anyone want to illegally mine Ceres? Vortech has worked hard to keep a minimal profile, to help support the miners living there, and to make sure not to take too many resources. What motivation did anyone have for stealing cerecite? Then I remembered something on my way here." I tapped the device. "Something mentioned on this hologram."

"Well, don't keep us waiting, Harper," Anna said tensely. "What does it say?"

I cast a quick glance at Morven before pressing the button. Faded colors hovered above the screen until they took shape. The gray stone walls of the gateway cave came into focus. Conveyor belts carried loads of oar from dump trucks into pressure washers. On the other side, round spheres rolled down the chutes and into spaceships. One of the ships rose off the ground and blasted through the open gateway.

The image froze. NASA: PROJECT CERES appeared in blocky letters above the hologram screen.

"I don't get it," Yusuf said. "What's so special about this?"

"Keep watching," I told him.

Peppy electronic music played a soft background noise as a woman began speaking. "Welcome to Project Ceres…" She spoke with an Indian inflection. "You are part of an elite group of astronaut pioneers…" She continued explaining the benefits of becoming a miner on the dwarf planet Ceres, how cerecite was first discovered, and listed its benefits. The part I was waiting for came next, and I prayed I'd remembered it correctly.

"…costs of shipping and production almost bankrupted operations, but a solution became available with the invention of Dr. Fernoulli's wormhole gateway portal…"

I pressed a button to stop the recording.

The name *Fernoulli* echoed in my head. Was it a coincidence that the founder of Vortech shared the same name as the wormhole's inventor? If so, I needed to know the truth.

"How long have you been in this timeline, Mr. Fernoulli?" I asked. "Or should I call you Aeon Orion?"

I expected him to argue. Honestly, he could have yelled to high heaven that it was merely coincidental that his last name and the name of the wormhole's inventor were the same. I fully expected him to point that out. And I'd gone even farther by accusing him of being Aeon Orion, the leader of the group bent on destroying Ceres. That had been more than just a leap—it was a suicidal headfirst dive. I had no evidence except for a last name spoken on a hologram from four-hundred years in the future. But he sat in silence, his hands folded on the table, as he stared daggers through me.

"Is it true?" Yusuf finally asked. "Are you the person mentioned on the hologram?"

We waited in silence for his answer, and it was only now I noticed how quiet the room was, without even the ticking of a clock to chase away the absence of sound.

"It's true," he answered after a long pause, his tone perfectly level.

My mind reeled. Yes, I had suspected it, but for him to acknowledge it came as a shock.

"How?" was my only question.

He spread his hands. "I invented the gateway," he stated matter-of-factly. "It's arguably the most powerful creation in the history of humanity. A creation such as this has to be protected, and so, I'm protecting it. I stepped through it, from the twenty-fifth century to now. I've been in this timeline for the last thirty years."

"What are you saying, Fernoulli?" Anna asked, her voice quiet and shaded with disbelief.

"I created Vortech after I arrived, precisely for the reason of not just protecting the gateway, but more importantly, for protecting the timeline."

Dark brows hooded Morven's narrowed eyes. "How exactly are you protecting it? By destroying my world? You're behind all this, aren't you? It was you who hired Zen. You've been mining Ceres to create bombs that will destroy it. Why? What could possibly drive you to do such a thing?"

He leaned back, a resigned look on his face. "Because Agent Harper opened the gateway." He pointed to me. "I knew it was inevitable. When I arrived on Earth thirty years ago, I created Vortech. Not long after, we sent agents through the gateway. No one returned. Still, I knew that one day, we would find an agent who could discover the seven pieces of white cerecite, open the wormhole portal, and bridge the gap back to Earth. That's the reason I bided my time, waiting for the moment when Earth and Ceres became connected."

I rubbed my forehead. Acid burned my throat, and I had trouble wrapping my mind around what he was saying. He was from the future, *and* he created the gateway? Even if it was all true, I still couldn't fathom why he wanted Ceres destroyed.

"When Agent Harper returned through the gateway, I knew my time to act had finally come," he said.

"Act on what?" Morven demanded. "You still haven't given us a single good reason for taking out our shield generators and attempting to destroy our world."

"Not destroy it." He held up a finger. "Erase it. In four hundred years, Earth will know nothing of the Ithican civilization that once existed on Ceres. Your people will leave nothing behind, and it will be as if Ceres was always a desolate rock floating in the asteroid belt, and nothing more."

A cold stone of shock sank to the pit of my stomach. "But why?"

"Because," he answered, his shrewd eyes boring into mine, "if I don't act, the timeline will be irrevocably damaged, and I will never invent the gateway. The explosion sending you and Cade MacDougall back in time will never happen. The immigrant ship will have never landed on Champ Island. The survivors will never make it to the gateway. You will have never existed. Don't you see? I'm not destroying your world." His voice held a sharp edge of warning. "I'm saving it."

21

Sitting around the table with Morven and the founders of Vortech, I rested my forehead in my hands. Fernoulli's revelation was all too much. How could any of this be true? Worse, I blamed myself. If I'd never opened the gateway back to Earth, Fernoulli would have no reason to destroy Ithical. But he'd known the gateway would eventually be opened. If it weren't me who had done it, someone else would have.

No one spoke. I supposed we were all too shocked to make a reply. What could anyone say? Vincent Fernoulli was going to destroy Ithical and everyone on it.

Morven's hands shook as he sat rigidly beside me. "You're killing thousands of people to accomplish this."

"And if I don't…" Fernoulli said, "then your ancestors die out on the ocean, and your people never exist."

"No." Morven slammed his fist on the table. "There's got to be another way. I refuse to sit aside and watch as you destroy every man, woman, and child on my home world."

I took Morven's hand in mine and gently squeezed his fingers. "Morven is right," I said. "There's got to be another solution than killing every person on Ceres."

"Find a solution," Fernoulli said, "and I'll listen. Otherwise, I've hired Zentoku Uzumaki to engineer another bomb formed from a combination of pharocite and yellow cerecite. Once he's created it, he'll take out the remaining shield generators, and Ceres will become the world it's meant to be—devoid of life—the world my people discover four hundred years from now."

My mind raced. This couldn't be happening. All those people! How could he possibly live with himself, knowing he'd killed them? But in his mind, he was saving them.

"What if we create a new timeline?" Morven suggested. "One where we don't destroy Ceres?"

I eyed him, as did the others in the room.

"Is that even possible?" Yusuf asked.

"It's never been done before," Fernoulli said. "But alternate realities have been proven to exist. During my time, NASA conducted a study in Antarctica that used positively charged ions in the atmosphere—ions similar to those used in the creation of pharocite. They detected neutrinos passing through Earth's atmosphere and then back again. After the study, one of the scientists created a device that split the neutrinos and changed the entire nature of their makeup. Granted, this was on a microscopic level."

"Meaning it may be possible?" I asked.

Fernoulli scratched his chin. "If so, it would require an enormous amount of power."

"Like the power harbored in the seven cerecite stones?" I questioned.

"Yes," Morven answered. "The seven stones have enough energy to power the gateway, which means they could also theoretically initiate a new timeline."

"Meaning we both get what we want," I said to Fernoulli. "You destroy Ithical in this timeline…"

"And we save it in the new one we create," Morven finished for me.

For the first time since I'd sat at this table, a spark of hope warmed my chest. Was it possible? Could we use the seven cerecite stones to create an alternate reality? If so, Fernoulli would know. He'd created the gateway. He knew more about the application of theoretical physics than anyone.

"Interesting." He tapped his fingers on the table. "With enough energy, dividing our reality may be possible. But even with the power contained in the seven stones, it's not enough. We would need some sort of device to amplify their inherent energy."

"What if we used the shield generators?" Morven suggested. "They've been amplifying the pharocite for centuries. Could they do the same for the seven stones?"

"That might work. But to initiate a rift in the timelines, we would have to create an unprecedented explosion. Once a white cerecite stone is placed in each threshold, they would have to be set off at precisely the same time." He pursed his lips in concentration. "The ensuing explosion should create enough energy to bisect the timelines."

"What are you suggesting?" Anna's voice took on an accusatory edge. "Setting off a massive explosion on Ceres? Absolutely not!" She thrust her finger at him. "You've already admitted to destroying two shield generators. How do we know you're not using this as an opportunity to finish off the rest of the world?"

"If that were true, I wouldn't be sitting here right now, would I?" He crossed his arms.

"You're discussing setting off a massive explosion based on an untested theory." Anna stood and placed her hands on her hips. "If this goes wrong even in the slightest, you'll not only destroy the Ithical civilization, but you'll also destroy the entire planet of Ceres. It will become nothing more than a collection of rocks floating in the asteroid belt."

"I agree with you," he admitted. "If we fail at this, the consequences would be unfathomable, which is why we must not fail."

Anna clasped her hands so tightly, her red fingernails dug into her flesh. "I forbid you from doing it."

"If you forbid him," Yusuf said, "he'll still destroy the planet."

"Not if he's locked up." Anna's eyes flicked to the guards standing on either side of the door. They'd been silent since they'd entered, rifles at the ready.

"Lock me up?" Fernoulli laughed. "Where? How? The nearest prison is hundreds of miles away, and we're at a Vortech facility where the entirety of the people working here are loyal to me. Even if you did manage to lock me up, it would make no difference. Zentoku will finish my plans for me. In less than a week's time, the shield generators will be destroyed, and all of Ceres will die, preparing the way for the future."

"This is insanity," Anna hissed between clenched teeth. "I've trusted you all these years and you've done nothing but betray me. You deserve a fate worse than imprisonment. If you step out of the doors of this facility, I'll have you shot on the spot."

A bemused smile tugged at the corners of his mouth. "You never were convincing with your threats, Anna."

"That's because I've never had cause to follow through. Until now. You don't want to do this, Vincent. The only choice you have is to call off the attacks on the shield genera- tors and leave Ceres in peace. Otherwise, I'll have no choice but to stop you by any means necessary."

"Any means necessary?" He crossed his arms. "I'd love to see it. I've already admitted I'm a time traveler. Trust me when I say you won't be successful in stopping me. My knowl- edge and expertise go far beyond yours."

"We'll see," Anna spat, her tone laced with venom.

"But what if he helps us divide the timelines?" I asked.

"It's too risky." She shook her head. "The proposal to use

the shield generators and amplify the cerecite is untested. I won't allow it to happen."

"That's a shame," Fernoulli said. "I thought the proposal to divide the timelines was brilliant. Even so, you won't stop us, Anna."

"You're wrong." She stood perfectly still with her hands clenched at her sides. "You'll regret ever coming to our century. I'll make sure Ceres stays safe."

"Then stop me." Fernoulli stood abruptly, his chair falling backwards in the process. The challenge in his voice was unmistakable, and Anna's eyes widened for a fraction of a second, as if she weren't prepared for this show of power.

"Stop me, Anna," Fernoulli challenged. "This is your opportunity." He crossed his arms as the room remained silent. "There, you see?" Fernoulli gave a confident smile. "There's nothing you can do. Have a nice day, Anna. Yusuf." He gestured toward me and Morven. "I'll follow you two back to Ithical. It's imperative we set up the shield generators as soon as possible."

"*Don't* walk out that door," Anna warned. "You'll regret it."

"I regret nothing, Anna, except perhaps hiring you." He crossed the room and passed the guards, but he paused before opening the door. "Are you coming?" he asked us.

Morven shot me a questioning glance. I debated whether to follow Fernoulli or stay with Anna. Either choice carried dire consequences that could go horribly wrong. But in the end, it was only Fernoulli who had the power to stop the destruction of Ceres. For all of Anna's talk, she was powerless to stop someone as intelligent and capable as Fernoulli.

I stood, and Morven stood with me. We exited the room without another word from Anna. Perhaps she was too shocked to speak. Or perhaps she knew our fate was inevitable.

22

"When we get to the gateway, I want you to run," Fernoulli said as soon as he, Morven, and I stepped out of the hatchway of the Vortech facility. "Go straight to the palace. I'll follow shortly."

I gave him a sharp glance. "Why?"

He shook his head. "Just do as I say. We've angered Anna Johnson, which is something I swore I would never do. She carries more loyalty than either me or Barnak. Without her support, Vortech is no longer mine to control. It's hers now."

"But you're Vortech's founder," Morven pointed out. "You were bluffing?"

"Everyone on this island is more devoted to her than to me. It's my own fault. I never interacted with the employees the way she did. She carries a level of respect far above mine."

I didn't admit it out loud, but he was right. I'd never met Fernoulli until today, and I'd only ever worked directly with Anna. If I hadn't known the circumstances, my loyalty would still lie with her.

Even so, I had to admit that I didn't fully trust Fernoulli. I didn't agree with his tactics. Part of me felt as if I were working with the enemy. Someone who considered wiping out an entire population to be a viable solution was a person I would never agree with—no matter his motives. It bugged me that I was working with such a person, even if it were to save Ithical—at least in one timeline.

But what other choice did I have? If I aligned myself with Anna, there was no chance we would be able to stop Fernoulli. He was right. His knowledge and expertise far outweighed ours, which meant I had no choice but to work with him.

Conflict warred within me, but only for a moment. I'd made my decision, and I would stick with working alongside Fernoulli if it meant I saved Ithical.

Gunshots rang out behind us.

Shocked, I glanced over my shoulder. Four armed guards stood aiming their weapons at us. I spun around and focused on the gateway bunker, a stark steel building against a backdrop of white.

"Run," Fernoulli yelled.

Morven and I dashed over the snow-packed ground toward the bunker looming ahead. Icy particles battered my cheeks, and fear rushed through my veins, propelling my movements.

My heart pounded as I grabbed the lever and tugged the metal hatchway open, but not before an explosion of shots rang out. Bullets ricocheted off the building. My feet slipped over the snow-packed ground.

Another shot blasted. Fire radiated through my shoulder. I gasped before falling to the ground. My face hit the ice. Pain spread like poison through my shoulder.

"Sabine." Morven grabbed my uninjured shoulder and hauled me to my feet. He ran with me inside. Fernoulli stayed behind, and he pulled a gun from a holster hidden under his suit jacket. Shots blasted from his weapon.

"Get to the gateway," he yelled over his shoulder. "Now!" He closed the distance between us and slammed the door closed. It echoed with a permanent thud. Buzzing filled my ears at the sudden silence.

"We can't leave without him," I gasped between breaths, my voice echoing through the room. Dizziness clouded my vision, and I found it difficult to draw in a breath. Had the gunshot punctured my lungs?

"But we can't wait for him either," Morven argued. "He knows where to find us."

"But if they kill him…"

"Then there's nothing we can do about it. We've got to get you to the palace, Sabine. You need green cerecite."

Ahead, the blue glow of the gateway radiated. The dizziness worsened. I felt as if I were staring into a narrow tunnel right before the world went black.

23

I woke to a room lit by moonlight. Silver-white beams drifted inside through a single window set in the stone wall, illuminating a chamber filled with rows of crystal bottles that lined the surrounding shelves. Green liquid swirled inside their depths. The calming scents of lavender and healing herbs filled the room, and I breathed deeply, hoping to clear my head and remember how I'd gotten here.

The last thing I remembered, I'd been with Morven racing toward the gateway portal. *I'd been shot*, I reminded myself.

As I moved, my stiff shoulder protested, and I lay back on the bed.

"You've got a nasty wound there," a female voice came from nearby. I focused to find Vevina standing by a washbasin. She smoothed her hands down a white apron that she wore over her plaid dressing gown. "The weapons on your world are vicious things."

"I agree," I managed, my voice hoarse. "How long have I been here?"

"Several hours. Don't you worry, though," she said, her Scottish accent carrying through her words. "You'll be right as rain come morning. Morven managed to get you here to the healer's room in time. The healer was here earlier, Miss Margaret. She said the bullet grazed one of your lungs, but the green cerecite has already begun to heal you. Miss Margaret asked I stay here and keep watch over you." She patted my good shoulder. "You'll still need to rest." She picked up a cup from the bedside table and handed it to me. "And you'll need to drink this."

"Green cerecite?"

She nodded, and I took a sip. The overpowering flavor tasted like bitter grass clippings, and I did my best not to grimace. I counted my blessings Morven had gotten me here in time. If I'd been on Earth, I'd been taken to the Champ Island medical bay and would have most likely bled out.

Attempting to sit up once again, I pushed past the stiffness in my shoulder, and I managed to prop my back against the padded headboard. A warm, balmy breeze blew through the window, ruffling the delicate white drapes. "Where's Morven?" I asked after swallowing a few mouthfuls.

"He's with Cade," she answered, taking the cup from me.

"Cade's awake?"

"Aye. He woke shortly after you and Morven left. He had some interesting things to say." She stood stiffly. Her voice held a tone of caution.

"What do you mean?" I asked.

"He knew the name Aeon Orion," she explained. "He'd heard it in the future. He's not who you think."

A drop of fear trickled down my spine. "Then who is he?"

"He's a powerful time traveler. He engineered the wormhole gateway, and he trained Zentoku Uzamaki to be not only his bodyguard, but his assassin. Zentoku is a weapon—a very powerful one. They'll do whatever it takes to protect their timeline. Sabine, I don't know what you've found out, but I know this—Aeon Orion can't be trusted. He'll stop at nothing to make sure this world no longer exists."

"We know who he is," I said. "Orion's real name is

Vincent Fernoulli. He's the lead founder of Vortech. Morven and I found out the truth already, and we've decided to work with him."

Her forehead creased. "Work with him?"

"I know how it sounds." I held up my hand. "But hear me out." I explained Fernoulli's plan to destroy the shield generators and make Ceres uninhabitable.

"He thinks he's paving the way for the future?" Vevina questioned, her red hair fanning around her face, her eyes shadowed with worry.

"Yes," I answered. "He'll destroy this world no matter what, which is why Morven and I proposed a new plan."

"What plan?" she asked.

Footsteps came from the doorway, and Morven and Cade stepped inside.

"A plan to create a new timeline," Cade said.

Morven crossed the room and sat on the bed, then took my hand, his dark eyes warm and filled with concern. "How are you feeling?" he asked quietly.

"Sore," I answered. "But better."

Cade sat in the chair beside Vevina. His cobalt eyes looked milky blue in the moonlight, and he cast a guarded glance her way. He held his bandaged arm stiffly at his side.

"They already know everything," she said, voice soft as she spoke to him.

Cade nodded. "Morven explained as much, which is why we've been doing some research."

"Researching what?" I asked.

"The four shield generators," Morven answered. "We already know two are barely functional. There's not enough pharocite in either one to create the kind of explosion we'll need."

"I know," I said. "But that's why we'll be using the white cerecite, right?"

"Not exactly," Cade explained. "White cerecite is powerful, yes, but in order to initiate the kind of explosion we'll need to create an alternate timeline, we'll need double the amount of pharocite."

"Didn't you say you might know how to create more?" I asked.

"Yes, it's possible," he said. "But with this?" He held up the stump of his arm. "It will take more time than I anticipated."

Morven squeezed my hand. "With Anna Johnson coming after us, I don't know how long we'll have. She knows we've come here to the palace. I imagine Fernoulli is trying his best to keep her and her Vortech guards from coming through the gateway, but they'll get here eventually."

"Then we find someplace to hide," I suggested. "We'll figure out how to create the pharocite, and we'll set up the bombs to create the new timelines."

"For that to happen, we need Fernoulli," Cade explained. "He's the only one with the knowledge of how to make any of this work."

"But he stayed behind," I said. "Morven and I don't know if he made it through the gateway, and we don't even know if he's alive."

"I doubt he's dead," Cade said. "He's survived for this long. He would never get taken out that easily. He'll know how to find us when the time is right."

"Then what do we do?" I asked. "Where do we go?"

"Back to my grand's keep," Vevina suggested. "There are miles of tunnels beneath the place, some leading near enough to the east shield generator. We'll be able to access the pharocite if we need it. They'll never find us there. It's the perfect place."

"But would you really want to put your family in danger?" I asked.

"Danger?" She brushed her hand through the air.

"Hardly. They're hardened farming folk. They've been through a scrape or two well enough."

Morven crossed his arms. His chest rose and fell as he breathed. "This is all quite convenient, isn't it?" He shot a pointed stare at Vevina, and a look passed between the two.

"What is it?" I asked. "Why is it convenient?"

"The wedding," Vevina explained. "My parents and Queen Tremayne decided it would be best to hold it at the keep. They think it's better to show solidarity for the people rather than relying on the monarchy, so my family's keep is becoming a symbol of the people."

"And it just so happens to be the place where we're planning to escape," Morven finished for her.

"Ah." Any time the mention of the wedding came up, I felt as if I would be sick.

"Then it would be best to find somewhere else to hide," I said. "Once Anna finds out where the wedding has been moved, she'll know to look for us in the keep."

"Not necessarily." Cade held up a finger. "I would argue it to be the last place they would look. It's far too obvious. And even so, Vevina's right, those old keeps are built on miles of tunnels. They would be hard pressed to find us."

I bit my lip in concentration, but focusing at a time like this wasn't easy to do. My head spun with dizziness, and my shoulder ached. How could I know if we were making the right decision?

"The wedding is taking place in three days' time," Vevina said. "And I know as well as Morven that we'd rather see it not happen, but we may not have a choice in the matter."

I rubbed the knot in my neck. "If we divide the timelines, then what will our world be like? Will it be the same?"

"Theoretically, it should be," Morven answered. "If it goes as planned, we won't see any differences. Minute ones at most. The biggest difference is that the Ceres in our timeline won't be destroyed."

"Meaning the wedding still happens," I stated.

"Yes. The wedding still happens," he echoed.

I rubbed my eyes where the headache pounded. We could come up with a plan to prevent the destruction of an entire civilization, yet we couldn't stop a marriage between two people who had no love for each other. Sometimes the universe seemed so unfair.

I tried to swallow that hardened knot that had risen into my throat, but the unjustness of it was too much. I wanted Morven more than air, more than life itself. If I couldn't have a future with him, what was this all for?

He took my hand once again, holding it tenderly as if it were the last time we would be together, knowing as well as I did that soon, we would be apart.

"We should escape when we're ready," Cade said. "We'll have the protection of the cover of night if we leave soon. Sabine, do you feel up to traveling?"

"No," Vevina answered, interrupting my reply. "She's only just woken. She's in no condition to travel."

"Vevina, I'll be all right," I said resolutely. "We're not safe here, and Cade's right. We should go now while it's dark."

She crossed her arms. "Then you'll be bringing ample amounts of green cerecite with you. It's nearly seven hours travel to the keep by rail."

"It'll be quicker if we take the velocipedes," Morven suggested. "Plus, we'll be less conspicuous that way."

"All right," I said. "Let's do this."

Morven helped me stand, and my shoulder throbbed whenever I shifted, but I managed to pull on my boots and leather jacket and make it into the hallway. Shouts came from somewhere below. I glanced at Morven. "What's that about?"

He shook his head. We continued down the hallway until we reached the open staircase looking over the second tier.

My breath caught in my throat. Several guards lay dead

on the marble floor. Blood seeped from wounds in their necks and backs.

Vevina unsheathed her knife. "We're too late," she hissed. "They've already found us."

"This way," Morven murmured hastily, spinning around, and guiding us back the way we'd come, past the healer's room I had been in, and to another doorway at the back.

Gunshots rang out behind us.

"It's Anna Johnson's people," I whispered. "She must have killed Fernoulli."

24

My heart pounded with a staccato tempo as we raced through the palace. I ran with only the thought of escaping. Nothing else mattered. Gunshots rang out, and I worried at who else was being murdered in cold blood because the situation with Anna Johnson had gotten out of control. One thing I knew—I would never trust Vortech again. They had used me for far too long, and I refused to be their pawn a moment more.

Morven dashed down the stairs, and Cade, Vevina, and I followed. Adrenaline masked the pain of the gunshot and fueled my movements. We rounded a corner, and I recognized the stark stone hallway leading beneath the castle to the garage housing the velocipedes.

Only a few sconces lit our path, leaving most of the passage in shadows. The blue glow of cerecite looked eerie in the deserted hallway. Hollow footsteps rang out through the domed corridor. The doorway loomed ahead, and we ran for it just as shouts echoed behind us.

Red laser lights from the guards' guns cut like needles through the dark corridor, sweeping the air, aiming for us.

"Stop," a man's voice called. "Agent Sabine Harper, stop now or I'll shoot."

Fear punched me at the sound of the man's words. I halted and spun around to face three men wearing tactical gear. The white *V* Vortech logo stood out on their vests.

"You're wanted by Anna Johnson," one of the men bellowed.

"I know," I said calmly, although inside, terror filled me, turning my skin clammy.

"Then you'll come with us back to the Vortech Facility on Champ Island."

I took a step backward to the door. Morven, Cade, and Vevina stood beside me. How fast could we make it through to the velocipedes before the guards caught up?

"You'll come peaceably," he barked. "Don't move!"

I fisted my hands. "If you wanted me to come peaceably, then you wouldn't have come with guns and killed every person in the palace you encountered."

"Stop talking," the man snapped.

Locking my jaw with determination, I spun around and barreled through the door. Shouting came from behind as my friends dashed through the doorway with me. After we were inside, Morven slammed the door closed and pulled down a metal bar to lock it.

A row of velocipedes sat behind us, and we ran to them. I hardly had time to remember how to ride one as bullets ricocheted outside the door, but with my injured shoulder, I worried pushing the handles forward would be a problem.

"Over here," Morven called as he sat on one of the vehicles, one looking like a motorcycle with a row of caterpillar-like wheels beneath. He patted the seat behind him, and I sprang onto it, grasping him around the middle.

He kicked open the gateway leading outside the palace, and the doors sprang apart to reveal an empty road leading outside the palace. A half-moon hung above the outline of buildings.

Cade and Vevina also shared a velocipede, with Vevina in front, and Cade behind her, grasping her slim waist with his good arm.

We took off without a word. A chill wind stole my breath as Morven pushed the handles forward. I darted a glance over my shoulder, just as two soldiers managed to break through the door. We sped around the building and out of sight, and I focused on holding on to Morven.

We rode through the city and past tall homes until we crossed a bridge, and the structures became more spread out and stood only one story tall. When we passed under the city gates, the world stretched out before us in a black void, high-lighted only by our headlamps cutting through the darkness.

As my pounding heart slowed, I finally managed to let go of my pent-up breath. When I did, the faint scent of amber spice wafted, and I hugged Morven a little tighter. Closing my eyes, I pressed my face to his back.

"Was this what you had in mind when you wanted to go for a ride?" he called over his shoulder.

"Not exactly," I choked on a small laugh.

"Stay alert," Cade called from the velocipede beside us. "Make sure we aren't being followed."

I nodded back to him, and we continued down the dark, winding road, punctuated with a few spots of light from the glowing boulders.

After a few hours passed, we finally stopped for a brief rest near a cerecite boulder of sparkling aqua blue. My shoulder's throbbing had grown worse, and I took a few generous gulps of the green cerecite from a canteen. Circles darkened Cade's eyes, and I wondered how well he could have been holding up since he'd so recently been bedbound.

Then again, I had to remember that Cade was practically immortal after being transformed by cerecite hundreds of years ago, and although I'd only seen it happen once, he could become a Mystik dragon whenever he wanted.

Morven, on the other hand, had once told me he had a similar ability and could become a Mystik wolf. But was it true? I'd never seen it happen, and I questioned if he'd dreamed it, or if it was truth. At least he and Vevina looked healthy, their cheeks pink, with no obvious bandages.

"It doesn't look like we're being followed," I said. "I haven't seen anyone, at least."

"I agree," Cade said. "But still, we can't let our guard down."

"They'll find us eventually." Morven shook his head. "It's only a matter of time."

Vevina took a sip from her canteen as she propped against the boulder. "When we arrive at the castle, we can't waste any time. We need to create enough pharocite to initiate the time-line shift—and preferably do it before this blooming marriage happens." She cast a sidelong glance at Morven. "Why they're so determined to go through with this is a mystery to me."

"Because they're set in their ways," Morven said with a shrug. "And they want some normalcy after what happened with the miners. They think a marriage will solve their problems. It won't. I hope they'll realize that someday."

"Even if we shift the timelines," I said. "There's no guarantee the wedding won't happen."

"But some things will change," Cade offered. "Morven told me about the experiment Fernoulli brought up."

"The one in the future that was conducted on Antarctica?" I asked.

"Yes. I remember when it happened. It was all over the news. Those particles weren't just altered; they were transformed. Whenever we split the timelines, we need to be prepared for changes. How drastic? I can't say for sure."

"So, we could be living with dinosaurs or something?" I fingered the necklace's cord.

Morven crossed his arms as he sat on the velocipede's seat. "Not likely. Think subtle shifts that would result in huge changes. Altering the Earth's tilt, for example, would mean no more seasons. Increasing the size of the moon would create catastrophic tides. On Ceres, with cerecite in the balance, who knows what's possible?"

"We could be creating a doomsday world," Cade suggested.

"Or a utopia," Vevina countered. "Without mutated Mystik beasts roaming the land."

I took a sip of cerecite from my canteen. Its bitterness lingered in my mouth, and I wished I had something to wash it down. "Whatever we create, it will be better than the alternative. At least Ceres will exist in the new timeline."

"But what will happen to Earth?" Vevina questioned, placing her hands on her hips. "I've never been, you know, and I'd like to make sure it stays there so I can visit it at least once."

"Earth should be fine," Morven said. "Most of the changes will happen on Ceres."

I didn't admit it out loud, but I worried where our tampering would lead. Anna Johnson may have used tactics I didn't agree with, but she knew how dangerous it was for us to manipulate timelines.

"We should go." Morven straddled the velocipede's seat and straightened the handles. "I'd like to get to the keep before morning. We have less chance of being found in the cover of darkness. Plus, the longer we're out here, the more vulnerable we are."

Vevina replaced the cap on her canteen and got situated on her velocipede. Cade climbed behind her. Morven reached for me, and I took his hand as he helped me behind him. Under different circumstances, I would have enjoyed being out in the wilds of Ithical with Morven on the velocipede. But with the threat of death looming over our heads, my muscles had grown tense with worry.

Even so, I could still make the best of a bad situation, so I hugged Morven, reveling in the feel of his body close to mine. As he cranked the engine, and we sped down the narrow road leading through spots of brightly glowing stones, I did my best to release my worries and just enjoy the moment. Enjoy the feel of my beating heart against his back, enjoy the rigidity of his strong torso under my fingertips, enjoy the scent of wild amber that woke emotions in me too powerful to be described.

Yes, this was the man I wanted to be with for the rest of my life. Despite my feelings for him when we'd first met, I'd grown to love the person hidden behind a proud exterior. He cared deeply for this world and the people in it. All he'd ever wanted was to bring education and knowledge to a world stuck in a prior century. How much better could Ithical be if they knew the truth about their location in the universe?

His passion for the people and his thirst for knowledge was contagious. If things ever worked out the way they should, I would spend my life with him helping him bring his dreams to life. I would help him create a university, aid him in using cerecite for new innovations and inventions, and though the thought was one so distant it seemed like a fairy tale, I wanted a family with him.

Resting my cheek against the solid slab of his back, I closed my eyes, and all I could picture was Morven and me in my childhood home with a family of our own, children laughing in the sunshine and breathing in the fresh air only Earth could offer. But how could such a future ever be possible?

No. That destiny could never be ours. Even if we managed to survive, our future was cloudy at best.

When I finally dared open my eyes, my lashes were wet, and I did my best to blink through the tears and look out over the void landscape. We'd traveled to an area without any glowing boulders. The only light came from the sky, where stars twinkled like millions of multi-colored jewels, half false, yet so stunning it took my breath away.

Maybe Ceres's atmosphere held a smell of engine fumes that made me long for the open plains, but the night sky nearly made up for it.

As the sky lightened to an ashy gray, tall peaks rose on the horizon, and beyond them, I spotted the towers of a castle.

"There it is." Vevina pointed. "MacKinnon Keep. We're nearly there."

The sky transformed as we rode into the mountains. Pink tinged the clouds, making me wonder at the technology of the weather on this world—something that must have been regulated by the shield generators—a technology far beyond my comprehension. Again, I worried at the prospect of tampering with such powerful technology, and I wouldn't have considered it without the knowledge of Vincent Fernoulli.

I prayed he was still alive. If not, how would splitting the timelines be possible?

The air cooled the higher we climbed, until snow cushioned our velocipedes' long rows of glowing wheels. As the air grew thinner, and the cliffs became steeper, our engines strained and roared louder. When we reached the top of a hill, the land spread out on a flat surface. We paused to allow the engines to cool.

A brisk breeze whipped strands of hair across my face. I shielded my eyes against the rays of the rising sun, and I caught my breath at the beauty surrounding me. The mountains looked regal against the backdrop of a pink sky highlighted with wispy lavender clouds. Snow sparkled like thousands of tiny diamonds. Up here, only a trace of the mechanical odor remained, and it nearly seemed as if I were on Earth.

Imagining Ceres as a lifeless rock made my heart squeeze painfully tight. It gave me renewed purpose in our mission, and deep in my soul, I knew I would do anything to protect this world. Morven wrapped his arm around my shoulder and gave me a quick peck on the cheek.

"What are you looking at?" he whispered.

I rested my head on his shoulder. "A world that almost feels like home," I answered.

He gave me a sidelong glance. "Home?"

I shrugged, the scent of wild spruce turning my insides to fluttering butterflies. "I don't know. I could never imagine leaving Earth, not permanently anyway. Even though my dad is taking his life in a different direction, the farm is still my home. But even I have to admit, this makes a pretty close second."

So many emotions warred within me, I had trouble sorting them out. Here I stood on an alien world, with a man whose life was drastically different from my own. He was destined to become a king, to participate in politics and government. What future did I have? After what happened with Anna, I knew going back to Vortech wasn't an option.

I tried not to let the reality of my situation overwhelm me. Worrying about my future was a moot point. I wouldn't have a future unless we succeeded in saving Ceres. Still, I couldn't help wondering, if we succeeded, where did I go after this?

With Morven married to Vevina, and my dad selling the farm and moving to Denver, I would be left with no one and no place to go. Maybe I'd become a vagabond and wander the country, I laughed to myself, or I could try my hand at art and paint sunrises and make absolutely no money.

"Let's go," Vevina called. "We're nearly there. Grand will be surprised to see us on the keep's doorstep once again, I'm sure of it."

She climbed on her bike, and Cade took the seat behind her. He whispered something in her ear. She laughed quietly, and she gave him a playful jab on the shoulder. Her cheeks reddened as she looked at him through lashes that half-shuttered her emerald eyes. It was obvious the two were attracted to each other, which left us with more problems, as the date soon approached for her and Morven's wedding.

Stupid wedding.

Stupid monarchy for arranging it.

I held to Morven's waist as he pushed the handlebars foreword. We left the mountaintop behind, and it didn't take long for the mechanical scent to pervade the air—and for the magic to fade, until it became nothing but a memory.

25

The imposing walls of the tunnels surrounded us. Water dripped somewhere in the distance, and the earthy scent of mold lingered. The dank chill of the stone-lined passageway sank into my bones, and I couldn't stop the shivers racking my body.

We'd arrived at the keep several hours earlier. After a visit with Vevina's grandparents, we'd explained our situation, though we left out the more horrific details. They'd spent more than an hour gathering food, provisions, warm cloaks, and weapons, and then they'd promptly led us to the catacombs. A trapdoor beneath a rug in the dining hall concealed the entrance.

Anxiety urged me forward, although the stress of getting shot, even with the near-instant healing, coupled with spending the night traveling, was taking its toll on me. My eyes had turned to lead weights, and all I could think of was sleep. I lagged behind the others, my feet dragging. The sound of dripping water seemed to hypnotize me, and I walked as if I were in a dream, until finally we stopped at a small room with musty straw mattresses on the ground. Judging by the rusting bars across the door, I guessed at the room's purpose—it must have once been a dungeon prison.

"This should be far enough." Vevina's eyes darted as she spoke, as if she half expected Vortech guards to appear with their rifles aimed down the corridor, their lasers focused and ready to kill us. "We can rest here for a while."

"Are you sure we're safe?" Cade asked.

"Nowhere is safe," she answered. "But at least we're hidden for the time being."

"I agree," Morven said. "We should be fine for now. Everyone's exhausted. We can't keep going like this. I say we take shifts while we sleep for a few hours."

"I'll take the first shift." Vevina pointed to me and Cade. "The two of you look like you're ready to collapse."

I couldn't find the energy to argue with her. Although my arm no longer throbbed as it had, I still felt the injury taking its toll on me and sapping my strength. It would be some time before I fully recovered.

As I laid on a mattress, I felt too tired to care about the bits of straw poking through. Morven lay beside me and wrapped his arm around me, and the shivers I'd had since we'd entered suddenly disappeared, as if he'd covered me with a warm blanket.

Despite the fears of losing our world, an arranged marriage, and Vortech out to kill us, my worries faded.

"Get some rest," he whispered in my ear, and I drifted to sleep without another thought.

I woke to a room full of shadows. A little light came from the hallway outside, where a sconce filled with blue cerecite glowed. Movement in the hallway caught my attention, and panic sped my heart for half a second until I sat up, looking through blurry eyes as Vevina entered the room.

"It's just you," I breathed.

"Aye," she said softly and approached me, the blue glow highlighting the golden-red strands of her hair. Her beauty struck me, and it made me question Morven's decision to choose me over her. She was more qualified to be the queen of Ithical than I would ever be. Was he making a wise decision in not marrying her? Despite what he felt in his heart, wouldn't it be better for him to make decisions based on what was best for the survival of Ithical?

I rubbed my eyes, sleep fogging my brain. Maybe I was overthinking the situation. As usual.

"Where were you?" I asked quietly, hoping to distract myself from thinking about the impending wedding.

"I heard something in the hallway, but when I went to check, I didn't see anything." She sat on an empty mattress nearby, then motioned to my arm.

"How's your injury?" she asked.

"Better." I rubbed my shoulder. "The green cerecite seems to have healed it."

She wrapped her arms around her knees. "It must be strange to come from a world where green cerecite doesn't exist."

"Perhaps so, but Earth is home to me. Healing without cerecite is normal."

She only nodded, her gaze going to the far wall, as if she were lost in a memory. "When I first learned we weren't on Earth, it was hard for me to accept, but the more I pondered it, the more I realized it must be true."

"Why did you decide that?" I asked.

"Because none of my people have traveled beyond the shield. I've heard rumors of people trying to get through it and leave our island—at least, what we believe to be an island. They were never successful, and most everyone agreed it was impossible." She clasped her hands. "But now it makes sense why we couldn't leave. We were never on an island, never on

Earth to begin with, which makes me desperate to know more. Will you take me to Earth someday, Sabine?"

"If we survive this, then yes, though I can't guarantee what Earth will look like after we shift the timelines." Worry nagged me. Would my father still be the same? Would he even exist after we initiated the shift? I had no way to answer those questions, which only increased my anxiety.

I took a deep breath to chase away my fear, then closed my eyes and listened to the quiet sound of Morven's breathing as he slept behind me. Where had worrying ever gotten me anyway? Dad had always taken care of himself. Even so, if something drastic happened and I lost him, how would I live with myself? There were too many unknowns, and that bothered me most of all.

"You should try to get some more sleep." Vevina's voice came as a soft whisper from her spot on the mattress. "We've a long day ahead of us."

WHEN I WOKE AGAIN, VEVINA AND CADE WERE ALREADY packing up. I rose to a sitting position, and Morven approached me. He passed me a canteen of water and a few pieces of bread and cheese. Cade and Vevina spoke quietly in the far corner of the room.

"How did you sleep?" Morven asked, his dark hair tousled.

I rubbed the stiff muscles in my neck. "About as well as can be expected when you're on a straw mattress." I nibbled a bite of cheese. "How about you?"

A half-smile tugged at his lips. "The same." He took a sip from his canteen. "I'm ready to be free of these tunnels."

"I agree," I said. "I need sunlight and open spaces."

He ran a hand through his hair, managing to smooth a few of the unruly pieces. "At least we're safe here."

I swallowed a bite of bread. "When all of this is over, I'd

like a hot meal, followed by a shower, then fifteen hours of sleep in an actual bed."

He capped his canteen. "It will be easier to sleep when we're not carrying the weight of the world on our shoulders."

Cade and Vevina approached us. A few pieces of straw clung to Vevina's skirts and stuck out from her red hair. Cade plucked a piece of straw from her hair, smiling slyly as he did. Then he held the stump of his arm with his remaining hand, as if he weren't comfortable with his posture now that his arm was missing.

"We should go." Cade glanced toward the doorway. "It will be morning soon, and I'd like to get out of these tunnels as soon as possible."

We stood, slung our packs over our shoulders, and made our way out of the dungeon cell. Blue cerecite lit our way, and I suppressed the shivers coursing through my body. The dampness in the air didn't help with the chill.

Sloshing through puddles and over broken cobblestones, we only rested for a bite to eat or to drink from our canteens. A few rusted flasks and empty bottles littered the way. In one corner, we found a pile of corroded gears.

We must have trudged for hours when the tunnel widened and led to a set of crude steps cut into the stone.

"We're getting closer," Vevina called over her shoulder.

As we took the stairs, growling echoed from somewhere down the tunnels ahead.

"What was that?" I whispered to Morven who walked beside me. He shook his head, his lips pursed.

Cade hissed, drawing a knife from a sheath at his belt. We also removed our weapons from their sheaths at our belts— knives Vevina's grandfather had supplied. They were ordinary-looking daggers with unadorned hilts, yet he'd told us they'd been coated in corroded pharocite and could kill any mutated beast.

A blue glow shone brighter from the end of the tunnel,

and then disappeared, as did the growling. We stood in silence, with only the occasional water dripping to disturb the stillness.

"It must have gone away," I said in a hushed tone.

"Maybe," Vevina replied. "But I suspect it will be back at some point."

"Let's keep going," Cade replaced the knife in its casing. "We don't want to waste any time."

We continued hiking. In some places the floor sloped, and in other places it grew so steep we were forced to climb up.

Morven reached for me as I climbed to the top of a ledge. I took his hand and stood, glancing at the drop behind, steep enough to kill me if I had fallen.

"Thanks," I said, brushing the dust from my vest.

"Of course," he said offhandedly, his jaw locked as he stared into the darkness. "What creature do you think that was?"

"Something big," I suggested. "Probably mutated by the tainted water. It could be another wolf."

He knit his brows as a knowing look crossed his face. "A wolf."

I couldn't deny there might be something to the thought. After all, we had both seen Cade transform into a green dragon.

"Your wolf form," I asked tentatively, curious to know the truth. "Tell me more about it. How does transforming work?"

He tilted his head, as if surprised I'd brought up the topic. He blew out a nervous breath, then started walking. Cade and Vevina were several paces ahead of us, although we didn't rush to catch up to them.

"I try not to think of it too much," he admitted.

"Why?"

"Because I have no control over it." His gaze met mine, his eyes dark and knowing, sending a trickle of fear down my spine. "Imagine having this demon living inside you, never knowing when it might overpower your mind." He shook his head. "I have no way of controlling when it decides to make itself known. In the past, it only happened while I slept. I would fall asleep. The next thing I knew, I was outside running over the hills, my senses heightened, and my mind wild with the need to hunt. Then, I woke up in my bed drenched in sweat, my heart racing, as if I'd nearly died."

"Is it possible you could have been dreaming?"

"Anything's possible, I suppose." A half-smile tugged at one side of his mouth, but the humor didn't touch his eyes. "But… I have this feeling—although it feels more like a memory… that after I was killed in my first life as Isaac, I was reborn a Mystik wolf. It's so real, Sabine. I don't know how else to explain all the memories I have of being Isaac, and then of becoming a wolf. No. I don't believe it's a dream, although I wish that were the case."

I wasn't sure how to respond. For one, I had no way of relating to him. Reincarnation and shapeshifting? They were such farfetched ideas that I had trouble wrapping my mind around them. Then again, I was currently on Ceres; I'd gotten here through a wormhole gateway; and the final piece of cerecite had turned out to be a shapeshifting dragon. Maybe those things didn't seem so unfathomable after all.

We walked in silence until sunshine streamed from ahead. The tunnel widened to reveal an opening. I shielded my eyes against sunbeams gleaming over fresh glittering snow. A cold wind blew from the exit. We removed the fur-lined cloaks from our packs and put them on before continuing.

"We've made it to the outer rim," Cade said. "We should be close to the shield generator."

Stepping out of the cavern, I allowed myself to breathe air not tainted by the scent of mold. Icy particles brushed my cheeks, and I turned my face to the sky, allowing the sunlight to warm my skin.

Being stuck in those tunnels was enough to drive anyone crazy, and I couldn't be happier that we'd finally escaped, even if we did have the responsibility of saving an entire civilization weighing on our shoulders.

"This way." Vevina waved us forward. Glowing boulders were our only landmarks, and even so, they were so covered in snow and a layer of ice to be almost indiscernible from the sprawling white landscape.

We hiked up slopes and slipped down slanting paths. I kept my eyes on the horizon, searching for the telltale signs of the shield generator station, until finally I spotted a single spire rising into the sky, a black needle against ironclad clouds.

"There." I pointed as relief flooded my chest. We'd managed to make it this far without being attacked. I only prayed the remainder of our quest went as smoothly.

"Let's go carefully," Cade said. "You never know what's out there. Vortech's people could be waiting to ambush us."

We nodded our agreement and moved forward. At one point, we discovered the stream of orange water cutting through the frozen land. Bubbles boiled from its surface, and its stench filled the air.

We stopped to stare at the tainted water.

"I thought we fixed that," Morven said to Cade. "You repaired the pharocite generator, didn't you?"

"Yes." Cade locked his jaw, his face tense. "This is a bad sign. I repaired the pharocite generator as best as I could, but it must have failed already."

"It didn't last very long," I said as the wind gusted, and icy particles battered my cheeks.

"What happened?" Vevina chimed in, glancing at Cade. "I thought you said it would last several months?"

"I *hoped* it would." He ran his hand down his face, his blond hair blowing across his forehead in the chill wind. "Obviously, I was wrong. It was only a temporary fix, as I wasn't able to repair it properly without more pharocite, which leaves us with the same problem we had when we first found the generator."

"Not enough pharocite," I finished for him.

"So, we create more," Vevina said.

"We try to," he added. "But this won't be easy." He glanced behind us. "Even if we do manage to make more, we'll need the remaining six white cerecite stones to power the timeline shift."

"How do we get them?" I asked the question we'd all been avoiding asking.

"Someone will have to go back to the gateway and take them," Morven answered. "But once we do, we'll no longer be able to travel between the worlds."

My heart sank at the realization. If we couldn't travel between worlds, how would I see Dad again? But perhaps when everything was resolved, we would be able to put the stones back in the gateway, allowing us to cross worlds once again. Either way, now wasn't the time to worry about that. First things first, we needed to get inside that shield generator and discover the secret to creating pharocite.

We followed the stream's bank east. My boots sank into the powdery snow which nearly reached my knees. I breathed heavily as I trudged forward, following the footsteps of Cade who walked ahead of me and left his imprints in the snow.

By the time we reached the squat metallic building, my cheeks and ears had grown numb. Cade stood by the doorway, and I approached him. The building provided a little shelter from the wind, so we huddled close to the doorway.

"You remember this, right?" Cade asked, pointing to the keypad.

"Like it was yesterday," I answered, pulling the chain off my neck, then placing the triangle-shaped pendant into the keyhole. A light blinked, and the door slid open with a mechanical hissing. When we stepped inside, the warmth came as a welcome respite from the biting cold.

I removed my cloak before taking in our surroundings. Much of the room looked the same except the chamber door, which was open. Inside the room sat the machine holding the tiny particles of cerecite. The crystals sat in the glass tube, glittering orange. Hairline circuits ran around the cube-shaped machine, and each piece looked as if it had been carefully fitted so the circuits lined up with one another. Only a faint glow illuminated the circuits as the pharocite failed.

"I see why you said this was a temporary fix," I said to Cade as I approached the tube containing the pharocite. "There's hardly anything left."

"How do we create more?" Vevina asked, approaching the tube.

We stood around the pharocite chamber, watching as the glow of the material seemed to fade, as if it were dying and giving its last breaths with each pulse of light.

"I think I might have an idea," Morven said, rubbing his chin, his brows drawn together, as if he were deep in thought.

"What's your idea?" I asked.

"Pharocite is nothing more than yellow cerecite that's been manipulated through a chemical process," he stated.

I stared at him. "And you know this how?"

He took a deep breath before answering. "Because I've been remembering more about my former life as Isaac. I remember flashes of things, little pieces of a puzzle that didn't seem to fit together until now." He pointed at the pharocite. "I remember mining yellow cerecite, then soaking it in a chemical solution and boiling it down. The residue becomes pharocite."

"One part sodium dioxide and another part liquid nitrogen," Cade offered. "Yes, I'm starting to remember, too."

"But where will we find those substances here?" I questioned.

"We won't," Morven answered. "If we soak the pharocite, the particles will be released. We can then add yellow cerecite, and melt it down, hopefully leaving us with pharocite."

"So we would basically be reverse-engineering the pharocite?" I asked.

"More or less," Morven replied.

"How long will it take?" Vevina asked.

"Not long if we can gather the right supplies. We'll need a large pot or a cauldron, plus water, and yellow cerecite. We'll also need to create a fire hot enough to melt everything down. The trickiest part of this is finding enough pharocite." He nodded toward the orange crystals. "I doubt there's enough there to create the amount we'll need."

"What about the stream?" I asked.

Morven tilted his head. "What do you mean?"

"I mean that the pharocite has been leaking into the water source for a while now. Its chemical compounds have dissolved into the water, but they haven't disappeared. The pharocite is still there, just in a liquid form."

Vevina crossed her arms. "She has a point."

"I agree," Cade said. "If we could collect enough tainted water, condense it, and combine it with the yellow cerecite, theoretically, we could create more pharocite."

"It's worth a shot," Morven agreed. "Let's search the outpost for supplies—anything we could use to create a fire, any kind of vessels for transporting water, and something we can use to boil it down in."

"And be careful as we do it," Cade warned, his gaze going to the open doorway where snowy white void hid the danger beneath the landscape.

26

A s I trudged back to the gateway cave, the tainted water sloshed inside the canteen I carried. I held my breath against the odor that burned with a chemical stench. I must have taken this path a dozen times by now, back and forth. We'd managed to gut an old machine and use it as a makeshift cauldron, but getting the chemical elements right had been unsuccessful, which meant we needed more water. I didn't have much faith in our plan to create more pharocite, but it was the only plan we had.

Up ahead, I spotted the black spire of the shield generator station. It was so strange to think of the station being built far in the future, and to imagine how it must have been one of four stations powering the shield that protected Ceres. That sort of tech was beyond my comprehension. Without cerecite, I doubted such advancements would have been possible.

My feet slipped over melting snow, and I barely managed to keep my balance as I neared the station. A flash of blue caught the corner of my eye. I spun around, and my heart dropped. Three Mystik wolves stood on a hill overlooking me, although to call them wolves was a stretch. Although they weren't as large as the beast we had encountered in the cavern, their appearances were similar, with horns rimming their heads. Unlike the previous wolf, they still had patches of fur clinging to their skin, and their eyes glowed blue instead of crimson.

The trio approached me on padded paws, sniffing the air, and I couldn't mistake the hunger in their eyes. Gray skin stretched over their protruding rib cages. I took a step backward, glancing from the wolves to the shield generator. Could I make it back before they caught me?

My heart pounded. I dropped the canteen and pulled my knife from its sheath, but what good would one blade do against a pack of mutated wolves? When I took another step back, they sprang into action. Two of them circled me. The remaining wolf approached straight toward me, loping easily through the ice-crusted snow.

My throat grew dry, and adrenaline raced through my blood. I gripped my knife with stiff fingers.

"Go!" I thrust my knife at the one approaching me. "Get away!"

The wolf didn't react, as if he were laser-focused on me. If he dove at me, I would only get one chance to attack, and I would have to make it a killing blow. Even if I managed that, the rest of the pack would be on me in an instant.

I cast another glance at the shield station. Maybe running would be my best option. I took another guarded step backward when the pack descended on me. One of them knocked me to the ground. Another sank its teeth in my arm.

Screaming, I thrust my knife for anything within reach, and managed to nick a leg. Howling pierced the air. The wolf let go of my arm and hobbled away. I scrambled to my feet. The other two continued circling. I held my knife with my uninjured arm. The pain hadn't distracted me yet, but I knew the adrenaline was likely masking it.

One of the wolves leapt at me. I stabbed its throat. It yelped, then gave a gurgled scream as I ripped the knife free.

It limped away, dripping blood behind it, and only one creature remained.

Piercing eyes met mine. Their intensity reminded me weirdly of Morven, and I suppressed a shudder, imagining what it would be like to face Morven in his wolf form, not sure I ever wanted to encounter it.

The wolf dove for me, slamming me to the ground once again, and knocking the wind from my lungs. My knife flew out of my grasp. The blade spiraled over the icy ground and skated out of my reach. Fear froze me to the spot. Time seemed so much slower as the wolf aimed a bite for my neck, its wicked sharp teeth dripping with saliva.

A shot rang out. The wolf fell backward, a bloody hole gaping in the center of its chest, hot blood cascading over my face. Its lifeless body fell to the ground beside me, scattering the snow. I sat up, gasping for breath and searching the area for the shooter.

A man wearing a hood and cloak approached. He carried a long rifle plated in bronze. His cautious footfalls hardly made any sound, and I recognized his cat-like grace.

"Zen," I breathed, clutching my injured arm to my chest. "What are you doing here?"

He stopped walking and tilted his head, then he removed his hood. A twinge of fear pinched me. The last time I had encountered him, he'd nearly killed Cade. What did he plan to do with me?

He spoke, brusque and without emotion. "You are under Aeon Orion's protection now." He crossed the distance between us and held out his hand. I hesitated before taking it. He had so recently been the enemy, how could I trust him now? But if he wanted to kill me, he would have shot me instead of the wolf.

"How did you find me?" I asked, finally taking his hand and rising to stand.

"Orion told me to meet you here. When I heard scream

ing, I knew something was wrong, so I left my velocipede up there and grabbed my gun." He pointed to the top of a hill where the metallic gleam of the vehicle glistened in the sun. "You're lucky I found you in time."

I wanted to argue and tell him I would have been okay, but honestly, I was glad he had discovered me. I shifted my injured arm and flexed my fingers. The bite mark stung, although only a little blood seeped into my shirt sleeve.

"Thanks for shooting that thing." I nudged the wolf's corpse with my toe. The horns rimming its head gave it a prehistoric appearance—almost like a dinosaur, as if the mutation were doing more than just warping its appearance but reverting it to one of its ancient ancestors.

That thought sent me down a dark path. What if using the pharocite to change the timelines did more than just shift us to another reality? What if it sent it us to another place in time completely? Or even mutated our DNA?

Shaking my head, I faced Zen. I would have time to ponder later. "So, let me get this straight. You're not currently trying to kill me?"

He politely bowed his head. "That is correct." The wind blew his dark hair and tugged at the long strands growing from his goatee. He placed the butt of his rifle in the snow, his cloak billowing around him. His appearance was that of a Ninja warrior monk, with his straight posture, the burning zealot-like intensity in his eyes, and the danger I sensed in his presence.

"We must get to the shield generator." He gestured toward the hills, where the black needle of the shield generator antennae was barely visible against the sky. "I've come to help you." He opened his cloak, and six white orbs glowed from inside the fabric of his pockets.

Surprise stunned me. "You've brought the white cerecite."

"Yes." He closed his cloak. "The gateway is closed. The

timeline shift is inevitable, although I should warn you, Vortech sent a squad of its best soldiers to stop us."

"Then we should hurry." I picked up the flask filled with tainted water, then I led Zen up the hill toward the shield generator station. Zen followed behind me as I trudged up the hill. Questions nagged me. We walked in silence until we reached the top, and I turned to him.

"If Orion sent you here," I asked, wiping wolf blood from my face. "Does that mean he's alive?"

"He has ways of ensuring his survival," Zen answered stoically, his face unreadable.

I tilted my head at his response. "What do you mean? How does he ensure his survival?"

"The same way I do." A small grin curved his mouth, and he reached into his cloak, then pulled out a glass container filled with dark green liquid that looked nearly black. "Green cerecite. A very potent blend. Here." He tossed it to me. "You'll need it for that arm."

I grabbed it, then removed the stopper and took a sip. The concentrate of the green cerecite was enough to make my mouth pucker, and I barely managed to swallow it before handing the bottle back.

"Good?" he asked.

"Yes. Wonderful," I lied, and he smiled before replacing the glass in his vest. "Let's go," I said. "We're working on how to recreate pharocite, but without the white cerecite, our efforts are wasted."

"All the more reason to get this there in time," he replied, hurrying.

I marched the rest of the way to the shield generator. The snowfall had created drifts around the squat structure. Zen followed as I walked to the hatchway, then opened the door with my pyramid pendant.

"That was mine, you know." He motioned to the pendant.

I cast him a sharp look. "Yes, and you lost it in a fight with a miner."

"Hmm," he grunted. "Lucky for you."

The sealed door opened with a hiss, and I led him inside the room. Morven, Cade, and Vevina stood around the makeshift cauldron as yellow smoke rose from its bubbling surface. The stench of sulfur filled the room.

Shocked faces met mine, and I held up my hands. "Before you say anything, Zen is here to help."

No one spoke, and the silence seemed to weigh so heavily, the air in the room became thick. Vevina took a step forward. "He nearly killed Cade." She thrust an accusatory finger at Zen, her cheeks flaming red. "He attacked you and Morven. We can't trust him!"

"Vevina," I said calmly. "I understand, but please, listen." I motioned to his cloak. "He's brought the white cerecite."

Vevina traded glances with Morven and Cade. Their eyes went wide with surprise at the mention of the white cerecite. Still, I wasn't sure they were convinced of Zen's intentions to help us.

"And he saved me from a wolf attack." I held out my bloodied arm.

"Sabine." Morven frowned and crossed the distance between us, then took my arm. "I knew I should have come with you."

"I'm fine," I said. "But we should still be careful out there. I injured two, and Zen killed the other, but I doubt they're the last."

Morven looked at my arm, then to Zen. "You saved her?"

Zen gave a single nod, his face impassive and unreadable, his stance as rigid as an ice sculpture.

"He's not here to hurt us," I said.

"Then he stays," Morven said as Vevina protested, and Cade spoke up.

"Morven's right," Cade interrupted. "He had the opportunity to kill Sabine and didn't. Plus, this plan fails without the white cerecite. He stays."

Vevina didn't speak, her cheeks still red, but she didn't argue either. I took it as a sign that she was okay with allowing Zen to remain here, so I handed my canteen to Morven. Water sloshed inside as he took it from me.

"I'm assuming you'll need this?" I asked.

"Yes," he answered. "We found out how to isolate the pharocite chemical elements and break them down into individual components."

I shot him a questioning glance. "Meaning?"

He held up the canteen. "Meaning all we need to do now is add this to produce more pharocite."

"Got it."

He handed the canteen to Vevina, who brought it over to the cauldron where Cade stood.

"Let me see your arm," Morven said. "A bite from a mutated Mystik wolf can get infected easily."

I gestured toward Zen. "He already shared his green cerecite with me."

Morven gave Zen a once-over. "That's good, but you'll still need to clean and bandage it. I've got my supplies over here." He led me to the far corner of the room near a row of monitors as tall as windows. Currently the screens looked out over the snowy landscape of the outer rim, white hills punctuated with bright spots of turquoise from the cerecite boulders.

We sat in chairs near the monitors, and Morven pulled his backpack onto his lap and opened the top flap. "I know I said he could stay," he said quietly, glancing at Zen, who stood near Cade and Vevina as they poured water from my canteen into the makeshift vat. "But do you really trust him?"

"No," I answered without hesitation. "But he saved me from the wolves; he brought the white cerecite. What else was I supposed to do? Tell him no?"

Morven's eyes narrowed, and I recognized his calculating gaze. "I still don't trust him."

"Neither do I, but I would rather him be on our side than fighting as our enemy."

Morven carefully pulled up my sleeve. Bright red blood seeped from three cuts running across my arm. He used a cloth to blot the blood, then found a roll of gauze and began wrapping my arm.

"How do we know he didn't send the wolves to attack you?" Morven whispered.

"Why would he do that?" I asked.

"To prove he was on our side? Doesn't it seem odd that the wolves attacked right before he appeared?"

"Maybe, but Morven." I rested my hand on his arm. "At this point, we need all the help we can get. If we don't do something, no one else will. Of course, I don't like working with him. But I would rather do that than do nothing. If we choose to fight against him, he'll continue to do what Orion— *Fernoulli*—instructs him to do, which is to destroy this world. At least this way, we'll have a chance of saving it—in one timeline, at least."

Morven shook his head and focused on wrapping the gauze around my arm, his eyes not meeting mine. "I still don't like it."

"The feeling is mutual," I said.

When Morven finished, we stood and approached the others who stayed around the vat of bubbling liquid. Cade used a waterskin to dip into the liquid, then carried it carefully toward a table with a flat metal surface. As he poured it out, the orange-tinged liquid bubbled. Steam hissed as it rose on curling tendrils. A faint sulfuric odor wafted.

"What happens next?" Vevina asked.

"This needs to cool," Cade answered. "If it crystalizes, we'll know we were successful in creating more pharocite."

"What then?" I asked. "We've got all the materials we

need—the pharocite and white cerecite. But we'll have to divide it up and bring it separately to each shield generator station, won't we?"

"Yes," Zen answered, and we all turned to look at him. "Shifting the timelines only works if each explosion is set off at exactly the same moment in time, and in each of the cardinal locations on Ceres."

"How will we make sure that happens?" Vevina asked.

"I'm not sure," Cade answered.

We stood in silence until I glanced at the screens behind us. "What if we use those?" I asked, pointing to the monitors.

"The viewscreens?" Cade asked.

"Yes. It could work, right?" I asked. "If it allows us to look into space, surely there's a way to connect them together so we can see each other at the same time, and then initiate the explosions at the same time."

"That might work." Morven rubbed his chin.

"Yes." I crossed my arms and tapped my finger on my elbow as I pondered the situation. "But there's only one problem. The screen at the south station is busted up. Cade knows a little about that." I frowned at him.

He threw his hand in the air. "I've already apologized for that a million times. But if you must know, I didn't bust *all* the screens. I left the ones intact that link to the shield generator. We should be fine."

"Then you can go to the south station," I told him. "The last time I was there, everything looked completely broken."

"That's because you came through the station's gateway portal. There's a room in the back you wouldn't have seen. It controls the shield generator," he explained.

"Does every station have a gateway portal?" I asked.

"Yes, but they're not functional. The only way you got through the first time is because you came from Earth to here."

"And I needed the seven pieces of cerecite in order to go back to Earth and complete the gateway loop," I said.

"Yes, exactly."

Vevina spoke up. "This is all well and fine, but how are we to travel to these shield stations in any amount of reasonable time? They're on opposite sides of Ithical."

I glanced from Zen to the screens. "Is it possible to use the gateway portals to travel between the stations? Zen brought the cerecite, so we would have no trouble powering them."

We glanced at one another without speaking. "To do it," Cade finally said, "we'll have to split up the cerecite. Bring two to each station. We'll also need to each bring a few crystals of pharocite. Once we're there, we'll connect our screens. I'll walk you through how to use the pharocite and white cerecite together to create the explosives, then I'll begin the count-down to initiate explosions at each station. This will have to be done perfectly or not at all. If even one of us is a second off, all we'll manage to do is blow up the planet. If you need to abort for any reason, make sure to tell us *before* we set off the explosions. Got it?"

We nodded our agreement.

"Now we're left with deciding who goes to which station," I said, looking at each person in turn. "Cade, you've already volunteered to go to the south station."

He held up his good arm. "That's true, but I'll need help. There's no way I can set up the explosion with only one hand."

Vevina stood tall. "I'll go with him."

"Good," I answered. "That leaves me, Morven, and Zen—one person for each station, east, west, and north."

"I'll take north," Morven volunteered.

"And I can go to the west station," I offered. "Which means Zen will stay here."

The man agreed with his usual polite bowing of his head. "It will be my pleasure to serve in any way I can."

"That does it, then?" Vevina asked. "We're ready to go?"

"As ready as we'll ever be," Morven said, crossing his arms, his eyes dark and hinting at trouble as he glanced at Zen. "Let's pray we all do our part, or the consequences will be unfathomable."

I didn't say it out loud, but if we failed, it would result in exactly what Zen and Fernoulli had wanted all along—the destruction of Ceres. And us with it.

27

W e stood over the table where the liquid pharocite had dried, then hardened into crystals that shimmered in the light coming from the viewscreens. The snowy landscape outside was muted by the tinted screens, giving the interior of the shield generator a cold lifelessness. It didn't help that every surface in the room was created of stainless steel, like a hospital or lab.

Cade carefully picked up the crystals using a pair of makeshift tweezers—two thin pieces of metal tubing—and placed them into jars and containers we had repurposed from canteens and water skins we carried in our packs.

After emptying my canteen, Cade placed three crystals inside. They clinked as he dropped each of them into the aluminum-lined can. He moved on to Zen, then Morven, and finally Vevina, until we all held pieces of pharocite.

Zen placed the filled vial in his cloak, then pulled out a glowing orb of white cerecite.

Memories came to me as he cradled the object in his hands. I had worked so hard to find the seven pieces of white cerecite. I had even ventured to a remote cavern filled with the bones of the agents who had come before me to find them.

Vortech's past agents had never been successful. It was a sheer miracle that I had found all seven stones before getting killed like the others. Even so, looking at the cerecite now filled me with nostalgia.

Pearlescent colors radiated from the glowing white surface of the stone, about the size of a softball. Zen gave the first two stones to Vevina, then to Morven, and finally to me. I placed them gently in my backpack beside the canteen filled with pharocite.

Anxiety raced through my blood as I hefted my pack. I carried enough material to create a massive explosion, one capable of ripping apart the timelines. No pressure there.

Cade walked to the monitors and sat in a chair. "I'll initiate opening a doorway to the north station," he said. "Morven, you'll go first."

The nerves I had felt turned to all-out panic, and I had to take a deep breath as I watched Morven stand with his bag slung over his shoulder. He took a step toward Cade, then hesitated, and turned to look at me.

I crossed to him, and he took my hands in his. The intensity in his dark eyes caught me off-guard. I'd never seen so much strength, so much determination, and so much love.

He squeezed my hands with a firm grasp. "I'm coming back for you." He spoke with resoluteness. "We're going to survive this, and we're going to be together."

I tried to ignore the eyes of everyone around us—especially Vevina's. He leaned close and pressed his lips to mine. Every fiber in my body reacted as if electrified. We could have been standing on top of the world—just me and him together. His lips were soft and warm, molding to mine with a passionate fervor.

He pulled away much too soon, leaving me wanting more. The determination in his eyes, and the locked set of his jaw told me he intended to keep every word he said.

He leaned in close and whispered in my ear. "I love you,

Sabine Harper." He spoke with sincerity, his voice deep and unwavering.

I held his face between my hands. The slight stubble of his cheeks brushed my fingers. "I love you, too," I managed, although my voice trembled as my emotions rose up to choke me. I wrapped my arms around him, hoping to hide my tears, but when the scent of wild amber and leather surrounded me, I had to squeeze my eyes shut and press my face against his chest.

The steady beating of his heart calmed me, and I prayed this wasn't the last time I saw him alive. When he stepped away, his firm resolve stayed with me, and I tried to push away the overwhelming feeling of loneliness as he approached the monitors.

Cade pressed a few buttons. The tallest, floor-length screen shifted from a scene of the snow to the interior of the northern station. We looked at a room similar to our own, and I recognized the orange crystals glowing at the center of the room where we had tried repairing the station's power source.

A blue glow lit the screen until it encompassed the room, and a low roar hummed from the shimmering panel until the ground vibrated under our feet.

"It should be ready now," Cade called over the roar.

Morven approached the screen. My heart sank to the bottom of my chest, and my skin grew cold as I stood looking helplessly at the man I loved about to cross through the portal.

If we failed, we died.

I tried focusing on anything but that one thought, yet concentrating on anything else was impossible. Morven glanced at me one last time. I couldn't understand the expression on his face. It looked stoic, yet a flicker of emotion lit his eyes, as if he were trying hard to hold it together.

"Goodbye," I whispered before he turned away from me and stepped through.

The blue glow intensified until I was forced to shield my

eyes. When the light faded, Morven stood on the other side of the screen.

He waved and mouthed something, although his words were muted.

"Is there a way to communicate?" Zen asked.

"Should be," Cade replied, then clicked a few buttons. "Can you hear us?"

"I hear you," Morven responded.

"Good. I'll send Sabine through next. Hold on." He pressed a key, and the scene shifted to another shield generator station.

"That's the west station?" I asked.

"Yes," he answered.

"Is it safe?" Vevina asked as she stood near Cade.

"Nowhere is safe," Zen said. "We should all be wary."

Vevina pushed a wisp of hair away from her face. "But this one is closest to the original wormhole gateway. Isn't that the one used by Vortech?"

"I see your point," Cade said. "Anna Johnson and her Vortech soldiers may have gone there first to look for us. They could ambush the place."

"The truth is," I said. "They could be anywhere. Zen is right. Nowhere is safe. I'm no safer here than I would be there."

"Then you still want to go through?" Cade asked.

"I don't see that I have another choice. If I don't, we're back to where we started."

"Perhaps." Vevina cast a wary glance at Zen. "Or perhaps there's another option. One far less dangerous."

"What do you have in mind?" Cade asked.

"Zen." She raised her chin. "We demand he tell his master to call off any attacks and leave our planet unharmed."

Zen's eyes narrowed. "I have sworn an oath. I will follow through no matter what the consequences. If you fail to split the timelines as you have promised, then I will have no choice but to continue with my mission as originally planned. I *will* destroy the shield generators—that I promise."

Vevina crossed her arms over her chest, then cast a dark glance at me. "Why are we working with him again? We should just shoot him with one of your Earth weapons and be done with it."

"Choose your words carefully," Zen warned.

"Vevina, that's enough," Cade chimed in. "We've already agreed to work with him. If he agrees not to betray us, then we'll do the same."

"Even if he mangled your arm?" She pointed to Cade's bandages.

"Yes," he answered with steel in his voice. "Trust must be earned."

"Very well," Vevina said icily. "But I am watching you, Zentoku." Her voice carried as much warning as his.

Zen held completely still, unspeaking, his shadowed eyes boring into hers, as if accepting her challenge.

"Let's move forward, shall we?" Cade attempted an optimistic tone. "Sabine, I'm bringing the gateway online now." After pressing a few keys, the screen glowed blue, just as it had done before Morven had crossed to the northern station.

When the roaring increased in volume, I moved to stand in front of the screen. Perhaps I should have been nervous about crossing through the gateway, but I had worried more when Morven had stepped through.

The glow increased until I squinted my eyes against the brightness.

"It's ready when you are," Cade called.

I squared my shoulders and took a deep breath. "Here goes nothing," I whispered to myself before stepping through the gateway.

The blue void surrounded me. My lungs squeezed painfully until I took another step and entered the western station. Breathing heavily, I tried focusing, but spots danced in my vision, and the room seemed to spin around me. I grabbed the edge of a table, the metal cold and unyielding under my fingertips. When my breathing evened out, I took stock of my surroundings.

I had never visited this station, although it appeared nearly identical to the other three. I stood in a circular room surrounded by monitors. Lights blinked from various surfaces, and the air held the faint metallic scent I had come to expect. At the back, I spotted a panel in the wall which was most likely housing the pharocite power source.

"Everything all right?" Cade called from the screen behind me, and I faced him.

"All good," I answered, not sure if he could hear me.

Vevina moved into the camera's view and whispered something to Cade. He pressed a button.

"Try speaking again," he said. "We couldn't hear you."

"I said I'm good," I answered.

"We heard you that time," Vevina said.

"How was the crossing?" Cade asked. "Any dizziness?"

"A little." I rubbed my forehead. "But it's fading."

He nodded. "Vevina and I will cross next. I'm going to set up our monitors, so we'll theoretically be able to communicate in real time."

"Theoretically?" I questioned.

"Yes, a fancy word that means I'm guessing and could be totally wrong. We won't know until we're spread out at each of the stations and try communicating. Hold on." His fingers moved over the keyboard. The screen divided into four separate squares. The top left monitor focused on Morven at the northern station. The one on the top right showed Cade, Vevina, and Zen at the eastern station. The bottom left corner focused on me, and the bottom right gave me a view of the empty southern station, which looked the same way I had found it when I had first crossed into Ithical, with broken glass and busted machinery littering the floor.

"Can everyone hear me?" Cade asked, and Morven and I nodded at the same time. "Good. I've got our timing right, then."

"But what about the southern station?" I questioned. "Are you sure it's functional?"

"Should be," Cade answered. "I'm not stupid enough to bust up the power source fueling the shield. But there is one problem—"

"What is it?" Morven asked.

"Well…" Cade rubbed his shoulder. "When I destroyed the place, I was trying to make sure no more Vortech agents could get through, since they only ever came through that one station in the southern sphere. That being said, I also don't think Vevina and I will be able to get back out of the station once we cross to it. If we want to escape, we'll have to walk."

"No worries," Morven spoke up. "We'll send someone to pick you up after we've shifted the timelines."

"That would be lovely," Vevina added. "Just keep us away from MacKinnon Keep and we'll be fine."

Morven frowned. "Fat chance of that happening. We think stopping the destruction of Ithical will be the end of our problems? If we succeed, we've still got an unpleasant wedding to deal with."

"Will we deal with it?" Vevina questioned, one of her red eyebrows arched. "It seems we've only ever avoided it."

"I suppose we'll have to face reality if our world resembles anything familiar." Morven sighed and rubbed the back of his neck. "But right now, I'm more concerned about saving Ithical than making wedding plans."

Cade shifted his gaze to Vevina, jaw locked, intensity burning in his bright indigo eyes. With everything going on, I hadn't given much thought to the relationship between the two. I wasn't sure what to think of their situation. What would her family think if they found out she was falling for the palace gardener?

"I'm going to give Zen some instructions. I'll be back in a moment," Cade said, then he clicked a button and stood. After standing, Cade motioned to Zen, who crossed the room, walking with his usual cat-like grace. Cade pointed to the keys, then motioned to the gateway portal.

As the two men spoke, Vevina stood aside with her arms crossed and her eyes narrowed. After Zen sat at the keyboard, Cade waved Vevina forward. She crossed to him cautiously, her hand lingering near the knife's sheath on her belt.

"We're ready," Cade said, and Zen pressed a button on the keyboard.

I watched the monitor as a glow filled the eastern station, giving a bluish hue to Cade and Vevina's skin. They stood facing the portal, although from this angle, I could only see their profiles.

The deep roar increased in volume. My fingers ached where I balled my hands into fists as I waited for the two to cross. Would Zen allow it to happen? What if he rounded on them and cut them into ribbons as I watched helplessly?

With a deep exhale, I let go of my pent-up breath and relaxed my cramping fingers, deciding for the millionth time to stop mistrusting the man. So what if he was an assassin? I'd dealt with worse people in my life. Right?

Cade and Vevina clasped hands, then took a step to the portal.

"Ready?" he mouthed to her, his voice drowned out by the roaring.

She nodded and squared her shoulders as she faced the gateway, her face set with grim determination, yet I saw the fear flickering in her eyes. She'd spent her life as a resident of Ithical Island. While they enjoyed some technological successes, I was sure stepping through a portal held unfamiliar fear for her.

"Are you sure this is safe?" she yelled over the din.

"I'm certain. You're with me, aren't you?" A half-smile lit his face, showing his dimples, and if I hadn't been head-over-heels in love with Morven, I might have found it attractive. He leaned in and gave her a kiss, just a peck, really, but when he pulled away, her cheeks blossomed. Even with the blue glow filling the room, her skin was as red as her hair.

Vevina gripped Cade's hand, and her brow creased with worry.

"Let's get this over with, shall we?" he asked.

The two stepped forward, out of the view of the camera. The seconds ticked past. I worried that Zen had done something—could he have turned off the monitors and killed them?—but a moment later they reappeared on the adjacent monitor. Soon, the roar faded, and the bright glowing of the portal gateway dimmed, until only the pinpoints of light from the surrounding machinery gave any color to the rooms where we'd arrived.

29

"Now seal the chamber." Cade's voice came from the viewscreen as I stood in the room with the power source. The orange glow of the crystals illuminated my hands as I placed the metal lid on the glass chamber. I stood back and examined my handiwork.

Two orbs of white cerecite glowed from either end of the power conductor—a metal machine with glass tubes extending from one section to another. With Cade's guidance, I had arranged the extra pharocite crystals in the tubes, then repurposed wires from various parts of the generator to connect the white cerecite. In all, it looked like a spaghetti bowl filled with two glowing white meatballs and a tangle of wires.

"Good," Cade said. "Now, there should be a switch under the generator. Do you see it?"

I bent and inspected the area under the machine, spotting a small lever. "Yes, I see it," I called. Morven's and Zen's voices rang out from the other two stations, echoing me with a "yes."

"All right. Try turning it on and see what happens."

I pushed the lever. Humming came from above, and I

stood to inspect the generator. The pharocite chamber glowed brighter, and the crystals began to vibrate.

"Is anything happening?" Cade asked. "You should hear the generator working. Sounds like a low hum."

"Yes," Morven answered first, and Zen and I answered the same.

"Good." On screen, Cade sat back in his chair. "Now we can start the countdown. You'll need to go back to the main keyboard for that."

I crossed the room and sat in the chair in front of the keyboard. Running my fingers over the keys, I inspected each one, my ability kicking in as I touched the bumps and grooves. Most of the letters were familiar, although symbols I'd never seen ran along one side of the console and across the top row.

Only a little dust smeared my fingertips, making me realize this place must not have had a human inside it for hundreds of years. It had been sealed away, operating quietly to keep the shield functioning and the atmosphere active.

My stomach squirmed with queasiness. Was I really about to set off a bomb that would tear our timeline in two? What happened to the shield generators once we initiated the explosions?

"Stop overthinking," I whispered to myself, familiarizing myself with the foreign symbols and the unusual arrangement of the alphabet.

"We'll have to type in a code to gain access to the main systems," Cade explained.

"What's the code?" I asked.

"No clue," he answered. "I was never given access to it."

"Well…" Vevina piped up. "That's a problem now, isn't it?"

"Morven, do you remember the code?" I asked.

"A little, yes. Being at this keyboard is helping to jog my memory. But I only recall a few numbers. Seven, seven, one. Then the rest…?" he trailed off.

"Wasn't it six characters?" Cade offered.

"Yes. The next two were part of the New Atlantic code—the symbols along the top. The last symbol was a letter, I believe."

I studied each character, allowing my ability to focus on each one. Carefully, I brushed away the layer of dust and knelt until I was eye-level with the keyboard. The illumination coming from the screens gave me just enough light to see the detailed surfaces of every key.

The most-used keys would be worn—with paint missing and smoother surfaces, so I carefully examined each one.

"The letter *A*," I said. "It's worn more than the others."

"That sounds right," Morven answered. "How did you figure it out?"

"It's a gift," I answered with a hint of sarcasm in my voice.

"What about the remaining two symbols?" he asked. "Any idea what they are?"

"Give me a minute," I answered, inspecting the unfamiliar characters, until I spotted one with a chip of missing paint, and another with a shinier surface than the others. "The character like a backwards B with a line through it, and the other looks like an infinity symbol."

"Could be," Morven answered. "I don't think we'll know until we try."

"I'll punch in the code first and see if it works," I offered, typing the six characters in successive order, *seven, seven, one, backwards B, infinity, A*, until a red light blinked once, then switched off. I sat in silence waiting for something to happen without any luck. "I don't think that was it. Nothing happened."

"Try something else?" Morven offered. "Another arrangement?"

"Good idea," I answered. "Let me try reversing the New Atlantic symbols. Those are the only two unknown variables. Give me a second."

I typed *seven, seven, one, backwards B, infinity, A.*

A screen directly above the keyboard lit up, and a line of code began scrolling.

"I think that was it," I said.

"You're in?" Morven asked.

"Yes. I suspect you'll all need to type the same codes into your computers."

I repeated the code for them. Seconds ticked past until everyone confirmed they'd typed them.

"That's everyone." Zen's quiet voice came from the bottom screen. "We've all gained access. Now what?"

"Now comes the hard part," Morven said. "We need to calibrate the white cerecite to work with the generator. First, we'll need to make sure the system allows a new element into its programming."

"How do we do that?" Vevina asked, sitting beside Cade and giving him a sidelong glance. Broken glass monitors created the backdrop for the two in the southern station.

"White cerecite is similar enough to pharocite that the generators should be able to recognize the element," Cade offered. "Arrow down until you see an H with line down the middle—that's the symbol for white cerecite."

I did as he said, pushing the arrow down button until I came to the cerecite symbol.

"Push Z when you've found it," Cade said. "That will tell the system you're adding a new power source."

After pushing Z, one of the buttons on my monitor blinked blue.

"Does anyone see a blinking light?" Cade asked.

"Yes," I answered in unison with Morven and Zen.

"Good," Cade answered. "That means you've added a new power source."

Rumbling shook the room around me. Dust fell from the ceiling.

"Is anyone else's room shaking?" I asked.

"Yes," the others answered.

"It's because of the cerecite," Cade suggested. "The generators are having trouble processing the increased energy. We'll have to get through this quicker than we thought."

A deafening boom exploded. My ears ringing, I spun around, expecting to see smoke or flames, but I faced only the silent, empty room.

"What was that?" Morven called.

"It's Cade and Vevina," Zen answered in his too-cold voice.

I focused on the screen in the southern station, only to find it filled with smoke.

"Vevina," I called. "Cade, are you there? Can you hear me?"

Anxiety quickened my heartbeat as I got no response.

"Do you think the cerecite made it explode prematurely?" I asked.

"No," Zen answered. "They only took one white cerecite stone with them. I don't know why."

Morven pressed his palms to the table. "Because Cade *is* cerecite."

"Yes," I agreed. "Cade's presence could have made the explosion trigger too early."

"No," Morven answered. "Cade is too careful to let something like that happen. His cerecite remains in stasis unless he transforms. Something else must have happened."

I studied the screen filled with thick, billowing smoke, and my heart sank. "It must have been Anna. She got to them before we could finish."

"How did she find them so quickly?" Morven asked. "How did she know where they were?"

I couldn't take my eyes off the screen, my heart thudding in my chest, sweat creating a clammy sheen over my skin. "We've got to get to the southern station."

"No," Zen said sharply. "If you go, they'll kill you, too."

"What other choice do we have?" I demanded. "Cade and Vevina could still be alive. We have to save them."

"No," Zen said. "The plan is off. We won't be able to salvage the southern station or the power sources, which leaves us with only one choice."

On screen, Morven crossed his arms, and his jaw flexed with anger. "You want to destroy the planet?"

"It's our only choice." Zen spoke without emotion.

"No." I pressed my fists in my lap. "You're wrong. There's got to be another way."

"Not with the power sources destroyed."

"But we don't know if they're destroyed," I argued. "We have to go there and find out." I pointed at the screen. "It could still be salvaged. White cerecite is nearly impossible to destroy. And we already know how to create more pharocite."

"But you'd still need the interface," Zen argued. "And there are no replacements."

"Fine," I answered, my tone clipped. "We need the interface. Then I'll go to the southern station and see if anything is left, and hopefully save our friends while I'm at it."

"I'm going with you," Morven said, determination in his voice.

Zen leaned forward. "I won't allow you to do this." His words were clipped and filled with warning.

The last thing we needed was Zen fighting against us. What could I say to appease him? "Give us a chance," I begged, my tone filled with resolute determination. "One day. That's all we'll need to find Cade and Vevina, determine the status of the interface, and retrieve the power sources. If we're not back by tomorrow, you can do what you originally planned."

He gave us a severe frown. "Do you really think you can find them and the power sources in one day?"

"Yes." I crossed my arms. "I'm pretty good at finding things. It's why Vortech hired me in the first place."

He worked his jaw back and forth as he seemed to ponder my request. "Very well," he finally said. "One day. No more. If we do not separate the timelines soon, the window for changing the future will close permanently. I will have no choice but to destroy Ithical and everyone inhabiting it."

An anxious quiver ran down my spine at his admission. How could he so casually speak about destroying an entire civilization? But I sat straight and squared my shoulders. "You won't get the chance." I spoke with a firm determination that surprised even me. "We *will* find Cade and Vevina, and we'll retrieve the power sources in the process." I leaned forward, hoping he could see the resolve in my eyes. "We won't fail. That's a promise."

30

I stood with Morven and faced the blue wall of the gateway portal. He squeezed my hand, and I gave him a brief smile. He'd crossed into the western station a few minutes earlier, and he'd brought along two breathing masks, which hung loosely around our necks.

On the screen, billowing smoke had turned to a thick, blue fog. It drifted over what remained of the room where we'd last seen Cade and Vevina. Charred remnants of machinery lay haphazardly across the floor. Shattered glass had blackened, and smoking heaps of wires lay in twisted masses.

My heart squeezed painfully when I focused on the two overturned chairs sitting in smoldering piles. Cade and Vevina had sat there. If anything gave me comfort, it was in knowing that I didn't see any human remains, at least, not on screen.

"Are you ready?" Morven's voice drew my attention to him.

"I suppose I am." Nervous energy quickened my heartbeat. "I'm anxious about what we'll find once we cross."

"I feel the same way," he admitted. "Cade and I only recently started getting along. We share a bond. We were both miners, both changed by the cerecite. We've become like brothers now." He bit his lip and glanced away. "I don't know what I'll do if…" he trailed off, his gaze pensive as he stared at the gateway portal, its brightness slowly increasing. "And Vevina. She may not be the woman for me, but she's a good person all the same. Ithical needs her."

I squeezed his hand. "We'll get them back."

"Yes." Determination etched his face—I saw it in the fervor of his eyes, the rigid line of his jaw. "We will."

"Are we ready to go?" I asked.

"Ready as I'll ever be."

We stepped to the portal. The roar of the gateway engine drowned out the sound of our footsteps. I breathed deeply to keep my fear under control, then stepped with Morven through the gateway.

On the other side, the biting scent of charred metal filled the air, and I found it hard to draw in a breath, so I pulled the mask over my face, and thankfully received a lungful of air. Morven also pulled the mask to cover his nose and mouth.

When I took another step, I lifted an inch off the ground. Morven grabbed my hand and pulled me back down. "We'll have to be careful here."

"Yeah," I agreed, and we made our way through the room, searching for any signs of Vevina and Cade, praying we didn't stumble over their bodies. Yellow smoke thickened from wires, and pieces of twisted steel littered the floor.

"Look for what's left of the interface," I said, my voice muffled by the mask. "If anything."

"There'd better be something left," Morven said. "Or else Zen will follow through with his threat. I'd rather not find out if he's serious about destroying Ceres."

"Yeah, same here."

We held to bent metal and glided around the room, nearly weightless in the depressurized atmosphere. The blackened machinery made it nearly impossible to distinguish what was what, but I allowed my ability to help me discern the smallest of details. Among a pile of shattered glass, a fragment of metal glinted.

Kneeling, I inspected the object. It was only an inch long, and flecks of red paint clung to its surface. I pinched it with my pointer and thumb fingers, careful not to let the glass shards splinter my skin. As I lifted it up, I recognized it as the same style of switch I'd used recently to control the interface.

"Find something?" Morven asked as he stood behind me.

"I think so." I straightened and showed the switch to him. "This was part of the interface. The other pieces might be close."

Placing the switch in my pocket, I continued searching the room.

"If we can find all the parts," Morven said. "Maybe we can put it back together."

"Yeah," I answered without much conviction in my voice. Finding anything intact in this amount of destruction would be nearly impossible, but then again, these were machines created in the future. The materials had already lasted centuries, and they'd been designed to last even longer than that.

My toe caught on something, and I knelt. Excitement raced through my blood as I pulled out a piece of metal that resembled a circuit board, except glowing wires created a crisscrossing, basketweave pattern.

"I've seen this piece before." Although the mask muffled my voice, it couldn't hide my enthusiasm. "It's part of the interface."

He knelt beside me. "You're right. Let's check this area closely. There could be more pieces here."

I carefully laid the first piece aside as we combed through the debris. Several minutes later, we'd collected an armful of switches and metal pieces that we fit together like a jigsaw puzzle.

"It's only been dismantled," I said. "It looks like nothing is seriously broken. If we can fit this back together, we may be able to restart the interface."

I fit one of the pieces to a larger piece, and it inserted with a snap. The circuits glowed brighter.

"I found these." Morven reached into his pocket and pulled out two crystalline pieces of orange cerecite. "They should still be functional."

"Good. Once we get this fit back together, we can incorporate the pharocite. Except…" My shoulders sagged as I scanned the room. "We don't have the cerecite."

"Yeah, and we won't find it unless we find Cade."

I glanced at the ruined area around us, the glass busted to bits so small they littered the ground like sand. "And there's no way for us to get out of here. We're stuck, and we won't be able to go back through the portal to get another piece of cerecite."

"So, we have no choice but to repair the interface and find Cade," Morven added. "Or else coming here will be useless."

"Yes, but let's get this fixed first." I slid another piece into place.

Morven's eyes followed my fingers as I worked. "How do you know where to place the fragments?"

I paused as I held a section not larger than a notecard. "I guess it just comes to me instinctually. My ability helps with that, I suppose." Rotating the piece, I eyed the half-formed interface and scanned the details of the circuits. The pattern shifted from one panel to the next, the circuits running like threads through a weaving, and I used that pattern to guide me as I placed the panels into position.

The piece slid into place, and I reached for another section. Around us, the room shook. I did my best to ignore it as I continued arranging the pieces. Only a few missing sections remained to be reassembled.

"Stop." A female voice I recognized yelled behind us. Glancing over my shoulder, I shuddered at the sight of Anna

Johnson. Guards surrounded her. Two of them held Cade and Vevina. Blood smeared the two's faces, and one of Cade's eyes was purple and swollen.

Anna pointed a gun at us. "I won't let you destroy this world."

Morven stood slowly, his hands raised. "You know as well as we do, we're not destroying it. We're saving it."

"You are not," she spat. "You're working off unsound principles of science. Alternate realities don't exist. I don't care what Fernoulli told you. He's wrong. He's lying to manipulate you. All he wants is the destruction of Ceres, and you're doing exactly that."

I snapped another piece into place on the top of the interface. Only a small pile of fragments remained. I would work until she forced me to stop, which meant Anna Johnson would have to shoot me. But I would call her bluff. She may have been a shrewd businesswoman, but she was no murderer.

"Stop," one of her guards barked. "Or we kill the woman." He pushed Vevina to the ground. She bit back a scream as she landed awkwardly on a pile of broken glass. Blood streamed from cuts in her hands and down her wrists as she sat up. Her pleading eyes met mine, although I knew what she would do in my situation.

The survival of Ceres was the only thing that mattered. Not her life. Not mine. We were bound to this planet, and it to us. We would do whatever we had to in order to save it.

Still, seeing Vevina suffering as she cradled her bloody hands to her chest was enough to make me pause before placing the last piece into place.

The guard pressed a gun to the back of the woman's head.

A needle of fear pricked my heart. Maybe Anna wouldn't kill me, but her guards were trained soldiers. They wouldn't hesitate to pull the trigger.

"Anna," Morven said in his too-calm voice. "Don't do this.

Vevina is the future queen of Ithical. If you murder her, you'll be starting a war with my people."

"Fine," she snapped, her eyes narrowing, boring into his. "Then we'll kill him."

She nodded at the soldier holding Cade, and the man pointing the gun at Cade's head pushed Cade onto the ground. His knees rammed into the floor, and he winced. The soldier placed the gun at Cade's temple.

Vevina looked with panic at the man she had grown to love.

"No," she pleaded, her voice trembling. "Don't do this. Please! Kill me instead. Just don't hurt him."

"That's not my decision to make," Anna quibbled. "If Agent Harper stands down, he won't be harmed."

I held the final piece of the interface in my hands. Fear made my hands shake. I swallowed the terror rising into my throat to choke me.

But I wouldn't let the fear overcome me, because I knew something Anna and Vevina didn't.

Cade MacDougall couldn't die.

I slipped the last piece into place.

Anna cursed. "I warned you, Harper."

A deafening shot rang out. Cade fell to the floor, a stream of blood flowing from a bullet wound in his head. Vevina cried out with a sound so gut-wrenching, so heartbreaking and filled with pain, tears sprang to my eyes. She knelt by him and laid her head on his chest, her red hair fanning out to cover his shoulders.

"No, no, no..." she whispered. "Don't let this be happening. Please!" A sob racked her body. We stood in stunned silence. What could I do? What could anyone do? Vevina grabbed Cade's hand and pressed it between her fingers.

Time stretched, and I wasn't sure how long I watched Vevina sitting helplessly by Cade. But soon, she stiffened and looked up, her gaze fixed on Anna Johnson—a stare filled with pure rage. Balling her fists, Vevina stood.

"You did this," she seethed. "You'll regret ever coming to my world. All he wanted was to protect it, and you killed him!"

"We gave fair warning." Anna thrust her finger at me. "It's her fault, not mine."

"No," Vevina said through clenched teeth. "Don't try to blame someone else. You're the murderer. I'll kill you for this!"

"Vevina," I attempted a calm tone. "Don't. Or they'll kill you, too."

When Vevina took a step forward, two guards grabbed her arms. She tried to break free when a brilliant green light blinded us. Cade's glowing body floated into the air. Two massive wings sprouted and grew from Cade's shoulder blades. His head morphed into a reptilian dragon's head, followed by the body and a tail. Strands of braided DNA glowed brilliant green, replacing what might have been dragon scales. He rose to stand over us, his massive form a commanding presence.

I stared in awe. When I'd seen him last, he'd only lingered a few minutes before he'd flown through the gateway portal and completed the bridge between Ceres and Earth.

It seemed like only yesterday that I'd stood in the gateway cave as he'd transformed. But the amazement only lasted a moment as a volley of shots exploded from Anna's guards' guns, pelting the dragon's glowing hide.

The monster roared with an earsplitting scream. It rounded on the guards, knocking several to the ground with its massive tail. A few others dodged the attack, shooting wildly and screaming.

I stood over the completed interface—a gleaming silver box covered in glowing wires, about the size of a car's engine —and Morven edged toward me.

"We've got to reconnect it now," I said to him.

He searched the area. "Where?"

My mind raced as I visually searched the ruined tech littering the floor. A thin thread of circuits glowed beneath the debris, and I kicked at the dust with my toe until I revealed the line of ribbonlike routers. They cut across the floor to what was left of the main screen.

"There," I said breathlessly, cradling the interface in my hands. "We just need to find where the interface connects to it —and we've got to find the pharocite!"

"I'll work on the pharocite," Morven offered. "You figure out how to connect it."

"Okay," I agreed. Yells pierced my ears. I tried to ignore the dragon snapping one of the guards in half. The iron-scent of blood pervaded the air.

"Switch to the phage weapons," one of the men screamed.

"Phage weapons?" Morven muttered. "Where did they get those?"

"I don't know." I followed the trail of glowing cords to a recess under what may have once been a desk. The glowing cords ended at a connector, like the prongs of an extension cord, but with at least a dozen glowing, needlelike protrusions poking from the end.

"I found it," Morven called to me, holding up the glass vial containing the pharocite.

"Good. Put it in the port on the interface, and I'll locate the connector."

I searched the interface, looking for a place to connect the protrusions, but saw nothing but the smooth sides of the box with nothing indicating where to connect the cord.

Something cold pierced the back of my neck.

"Stop right there," Anna's voice seethed. She held a gun to the base of my skull. I saw her out of the corner of my eye. Blood smeared from a cut slashing across her forehead. "I don't know why you're doing this. You're going to destroy this planet!"

"No," I said calmly, though I felt nothing but terror inside me. "You're wrong, Anna. We can save this world, but not if you don't allow me."

"I don't want to shoot you, Harper. I know you have good intentions. You found the seven cerecite stones, you stopped the last flare, and you've been a loyal employee to our corporation. But if you force me to kill you, I will."

I held the cord in my hand, preparing to link the interface with the other three stations. I was so close to finishing this! How could I make Anna understand she was wrong? I could hardly hear my own thoughts, yet I felt the frantic beating of my heart, making a clammy sweat drench my skin.

Chaos reigned around us. Phage weapons blasted holes in what remained of the walls. A few of the bolts hit the dragon, and it roared with a primal scream as the weapons ripped through its hide, creating gaping holes that burned with a noxious odor.

Panic raced through me. Could those weapons kill the dragon? If so, and if Cade died, then the last piece of cerecite went with him. We had to stop this. Now. I couldn't allow Anna's guards to kill him.

"Anna, please!" I begged. "Listen to me. This is the only way to save Ceres. Once I realign the interface, we'll be able to connect to the other three stations and initiate bisecting our reality. Tell your guards to stand down."

Another bolt hit the dragon's head, and another went straight through his neck. A mangled scream choked from his throat, and the giant beast collapsed to the floor.

No! This couldn't be happening. We couldn't lose Cade!

Another scream echoed the dragon's. Vevina, who had been held back by two guards, tore from their grasp and raced to the dying beast.

"Drop the cord," Anna said in a too-calm voice. "Or I'll kill you the way we killed him."

Vevina's tangled red hair spread out over the dragon's

head. With a brief glow of blue, the dragon transformed back into the man. Cade lay gasping for breath on the floor, blood smearing his face and leaking from a gaping wound in his neck.

Vevina took Cade's fingers in his. As the blood drained from him, his skin went so pale it faded to gray, and looked out of place next to Vevina's pink flesh. Panic made my heart race, and I weighed my options. If we managed to link the four stations, we still wouldn't be able to create an explosion without Cade. But I couldn't let Anna win. If she stopped us, then Zen would fulfill his promise and destroy Ithical and everyone on this planet.

But what could I do now? With Cade dead, Anna won. Still, he couldn't possibly be killed. He'd lived so long. He couldn't die now, could he?

My shoulders slumped, and the adrenaline that had so recently been coursing through my blood tapered away, leaving me exhausted.

"Fine," I said to Anna. "You win. You've killed Cade. There's nothing more we can do to save this world. You've doomed it."

"No," she snapped. "I saved it. Guards," she called to the armored men surrounding us. "Cuff Agent Harper and escort her back to Earth for trial. Take the others back to the capital. I want them as far away from the shield generators as possible."

"You're making a mistake," Morven said as the guards grabbed his arms. Vevina protested as the guards slapped a pair of cuffs around her slender wrists.

Complete hopelessness washed over me. What were we supposed to do now? When Zen found out we'd failed, he would finish destroying the planet.

"Anna," I said, desperation bleeding through my words. "The only reason Zen isn't destroying this world right now is because we promised to realign the interface. Once he learns we failed, you know as well as I what he'll do. You've stopped us, but what will you do to stop him?"

"You worry too much, Harper," she said, her words clipped, her eyes sharp, though her gaze only lingered on me a moment before she turned to her guards. "Take them out of here," she barked at her guards, speaking as if I was nothing more than an annoyance, a blip in her plans.

I realized then that she didn't care about me, didn't care if I lived or died, didn't care if I succeeded or failed unless it was for Vortech's benefit. She'd sent me to Ceres on my first mission knowing full well there was little chance I would return. She'd known I would most likely die on Ceres. And she didn't care now, either. She was willing to defy Fernoulli because of her pride, because she believed she knew better than him, even if her miscalculation meant allowing an entire planet to be destroyed.

Vengeance replaced my fear. It welled up inside me until it turned burning hot and threatened to consume me.

No. Anna Johnson wouldn't win. I would stop her, and I would save Ceres in the process.

Only three guards remained after their fight with the dragon. Two guards tugged me toward the blasted-open doorway where icy wind blustered from outside. My hair battered my cheeks and got stuck in the tear trails streaming down my face. I jerked my arms back, surprising the guards, and one of them lost their grip on me. I used Vortech's training against the remaining man, twisting my body around until I wrenched his thumb, and broke his grasp. He gave a startled cry, and I dashed away.

I sped toward the interface, grabbed the cord, and placed it directly below the crystal chamber. Fibers reached out like tendrils and grasped the prongs. The interface glowed a brilliant azure blue mixed with hints of autumn gold, blinding and beautiful.

Since Cade and Vevina had already punched in the codes,

all I needed to do was flip the switch to reconnect the four stations. But even so, without the last piece of cerecite, we didn't have enough energy to power the explosion.

Anna rushed at me, followed by a guard, but I ignored them and flipped on the connector.

"Stop." I fumed as she and two guards approached. The remaining guard stood with Vevina and Morven held at either side of him. "It's too late," I told her. "The countdown is started." I lied, but she didn't need to know that. Without Cade, we would never have the last piece of cerecite. Even so, perhaps if I could convince Anna she'd failed, then she would leave. "There's nothing you can do to stop it. The explosion will happen. It's over."

Anna's face paled, then contorted with rage. "Kill her," she seethed. "She's committed an irredeemable crime. I can't allow her to live after this."

One of the guards lifted his phage weapon and pointed it at my chest. As he squeezed the trigger, a flash of blue pierced my vision. Pain-filled screams echoed. I thought I'd been shot, but I felt no pain. When I opened my eyes, a Mystik wolf stalked toward Anna and her guards. It struck with a powerful swipe of its massive paws, knocking them to the ground. With a ferocious growl, it pounced on Anna. It ripped at her throat until her gurgled screams quieted. One of the guards fired at the beast, but his shot went wild.

The bolt hit a towering tank, and a noxious fog spewed from it. It filled the room, thick and yellowish. Tears sprang to my eyes. The foul-smelling mist blocked my windpipe. I pulled the oxygen mask up over my face, but it did nothing to filter out the fog, so I yanked it off again and made my way blindly to where I remembered seeing the blasted-open door.

Vevina emerged from the haze. Coughing and choking, we stumbled toward the doorway just as an alarm blared. We made it outside and onto the snow. The white void and purple-tinged sky came as a welcome relief, and I breathed in a lungful of fresh air.

As we staggered away from the structure, Vevina's eyes widened, and I followed her gaze back to the building, where the giant wolf emerged from the mist. He carried the body of a limp Cade in his mouth.

My heart stopped, and I froze.

Morven.

31

"**M**orven," I whispered, my voice breathless. Cold air filled my lungs as I stood facing the creature. Calling him a mere wolf would be an understatement. He was taller than two men, glowing blue and semi-transparent, as if he were an ethereal creation of cerecite, and not something terrestrial. Still, in his eyes, I felt something of Morven there, a piece of him that even now existed, if only a small piece.

Shock rooted me to the spot as he gently placed Cade's body by our feet. He gave Vevina and me a brief glance, one of acknowledgment, possibly? Then, he turned his gaze on me, and I couldn't understand the look. It was almost as if he were pleading for something, his eyes wide and reflecting the sunlight. His stare held me with an unspoken question. But what did he want from me?

I wanted to reach out to him, to understand what he was trying to tell me, but when I stretched my hand toward him, he turned and trotted back inside the building.

Vevina stifled a gasp as she knelt by Cade's body. No longer in his dragon form, he lay limply, all the life drained from him, his face nearly as pale as the snow.

"Why…?" she said with a wail, her fingers grasping his. Her hair had tangled. An unkempt mess fell down her shoulders. I knelt by her, but too many questions pulled at me, and my gaze went instead to the structure looming before us.

"Morven went back inside," I said almost to myself, my voice drowned out by the blustering wind. "Why did he go back inside?"

The answer came to me nearly as I asked it. *Because he was transformed by cerecite just like Cade. He's the last. The explosion won't work without him.*

"Vevina." I spoke without taking my eyes off the shield generator station. "I've got to go back."

"What?" she asked. "Why?"

"Because with Cade gone, Morven is the last piece of cerecite. He's going to make sure the explosion happens. But he'll need my help. I've got to go back."

"But you'll die in there." Vevina's tone verged on panic. "Those fumes are toxic."

"But he can't initiate the explosion by himself. That's what he was trying to communicate to me." I squared my shoulders as I faced the building. I'd been afraid for so long, afraid for our relationship to end, afraid of losing the only place I called home, afraid of failing and losing an entire civilization in the process. But what was all that fear for? It was as if I'd built a wall around myself to shield me from fear. But I'd never needed to be afraid. Not really. If my next great adventure was death, then I would face it head-on, I would put the fear behind me, and I would do it with Morven at my side.

"Vevina," I said resolutely. "I have to go back. If there's any way for you to get a message to my father, please let him know I love him."

My mind was a whirlwind of racing thoughts, but that one request was the one that overpowered the rest.

"Sabine, no!" she argued. "You'll die."

"Not if we set off the explosion in time."

"And if you don't?"

I didn't want to ponder her question, so I trudged forward through the snow and toward the blasted-open doorway. I took a deep breath before entering, then I stepped inside. All I could see was a viscous wall of orange. It was most likely a gaseous form of pharocite. I had no doubt breathing it in for more than a few seconds would kill me, but I'd made my decision to keep moving forward no matter what.

I kept my hands out for balance, grabbing onto pieces of broken machinery as I went, until the fog thinned a little, and I could see a smear of glowing blue ahead. I moved toward it, still holding my breath. I found the wolf pacing by the interface. Even though I had just recently seen him, his size still took me by surprise. His head reached the top of the screen, and his intelligent eyes locked on mine as I approached him.

With so many questions swimming through my mind, coupled with the increasing lack of oxygen, I had no idea what to do. But the wolf drew near and lowered his head, then flicked it to the screen. The glass, though cracked, remained in the casing. What if the tech still worked?

Without overthinking it, I flipped the switch to turn on the screen. A second later, Zen's face appeared.

"Zen," I gasped, choking as I attempted to speak. "We've done it."

His eyes widened as he focused on the enormous wolf, and the room filled with thick, orange-tinged mist. He didn't ask any questions. He gave a formal bowing of his head, as if he understood the magnitude of the situation.

Being unable to mutter more than a few syllable words put me at a disadvantage. I wanted to tell him we'd lost Cade, but we had Morven. How would Morven make the cerecite work? Cade had flown through the gateway in his dragon form. Would Morven do something similar in his wolf form? But those thoughts were fleeting, and I could hardly grasp them as they seemed to float away with my lack of oxygen.

"Very good," Zen said solemnly. "You've done well. I'll start the countdown. While you were gone, I managed to link the remaining two stations to where I'm located, which means I'll be able to sync their explosions whenever we're ready. Be prepared to flip the switch on my mark. We'll have ten seconds. Do you understand?"

I only managed a nod. The room swam around me. Starved for oxygen, my lungs burned. I couldn't seem to focus on anything. I heard voices—one came from Mom, another resembled Mima's soft tone. Then Dad spoke, but it was too far away for me to understand his words.

"…starting the countdown now." Zen's voice overpowered the rest. "Ten seconds. Nine. Eight…"

I teetered on my feet. Grabbing the edge of the interface, I focused on the switch, preparing to flip it when Zen said zero, but my vision blurred and danced with stars. The voices returned, louder this time, overpowering my thoughts, and the world drifted. Sounds faded. My vision dimmed. I was lost in space and in time, and a grayish void surrounded me.

But something nagged me at the back of my mind. Something important.

A sound of whining broke through the fog—the whining of a wolf. I snapped awake, remembering my purpose in a rush of heated adrenaline. From the screen, Zen's voice echoed through the room.

"Two, one, zero, *now*!"

I managed to push the switch forward. The quiet unsettled me. Had I failed? Why wasn't it working, but a second later, a deafening boom punched through the air with the sound of a thousand atomic bombs—so powerful I felt my body flung backward. Searing pain engulfed me—a pain so intense, I felt as if I were being burned from the inside out.

My consciousness ebbed. A white blanket surrounded me,

comforting me, yet I felt smothered at the same time. I wanted to panic, but the world faded, and I faded with it until reality was swept away, peacefully, like the gently rolling waves on the ocean. It tugged me toward a destination so far away, I couldn't possibly fathom the distance—to a new world, perhaps—or to a new reality entirely.

32

Time passed, but I didn't know how long. It could have been seconds. Or centuries. I floated out of my body for a time, although the images were fleeting and fragmented. A voice here, a burst of sunlight there, the scent of lavender, or the memory of a rainbow. Sometimes I felt I knew the people surrounding me. Other times I wandered among strangers.

Is this what it's like to be floating between realities?

It was the most coherent idea I had while I was there.

Time slowed, and I felt my mind returning to my body. Gradually I moved my limbs. My fingers first, then my toes and legs. When I felt ready, I opened my eyes, and I stared into a startlingly blue sky.

That was my first memory in this place.

The second memory came when I took my first breath, an inhalation of air so fresh, I knew I couldn't have been on Ceres. Was I on Earth, then?

A bed of soft grass cushioned me. I ran my fingers over the dew-covered blades. I couldn't stop staring at the sky. Its blue hue reminded me of Morven while in his wolf form.

"Careful getting up," a familiar voice said. Morven. "The dizziness is no joke."

"Morven?" My voice croaked, and I laughed at the sound. It felt so good to laugh. It reminded me I was human. I turned toward the sound of Morven's voice. He sat with a crowd of people surrounding him. I recognized Vevina and Cade. Under the light of the blue sky, their skin took on a different hue—one more vibrant and full of color than I'd ever seen before. I also noted that Cade's arm was whole and healed, as if he'd never been attacked by Zen.

A person strode forward from the crowd, and I recognized Vincent Fernoulli. Or should I call him Aeon Orion? I had no idea what his real name was. Perhaps in the future, he went by a different identity entirely.

"Fernoulli," I said as he approached me, then knelt beside me.

"You had me worried," he said. "Your body wasn't realigning. I thought I'd lost you."

"Probably because of the blast." I had trouble putting my memories together, as if my brain had been rearranged and was only now coming back together—and perhaps that's exactly what had happened. I rubbed my sore temples and winced. "Everyone else made it?"

"You're the first."

"The first?" I asked, then blinked. What I'd first seen as a group of people—Morven, Vevina, and Cade—now appeared as nothing more than an empty field. My hand turned cold where I had imagined Morven holding it. Shock overrode coherent thoughts.

"What?" I spun around, searching. "What happened? Where are the others?"

"Others?" Fernoulli raised an eyebrow.

"Morven and Cade and Vevina. I saw them…" I tried to explain, but I could hardly comprehend what was happening. One minute they were here and now they were gone? "I spoke to Morven right after I woke up."

"We're the only ones here," Fernoulli clarified.

"But… no! If that's true, then who did I see?"

"It's an effect of the shift," Fernoulli explained. "Going between one reality to another may cause hallucinations."

I rubbed my forehead and winced at a tender lump under my skin. "Ouch."

He motioned to the bump on my head. "Getting a head injury could also cause you to see things."

I took a deep breath, trying to make sense of what was happening. "So, we made it, then?" I asked. "We're in the new reality? Is this Ceres?"

"From what I can tell, yes."

"But why does it look so different? The sky…?" I had trouble putting my words together, and my thoughts felt as if they were fading, like sand sinking through an hourglass.

"I don't have all the answers," Fernoulli said. "But from what I can gather, the explosion was successful in shifting the timelines. It also altered Ceres."

"How is it changed?" I asked, still glancing over my shoulder, hoping vainly that Morven would appear, that I could hold his hand just a little longer.

"It has to do with the altered timeline in this reality. It's complicated, and since you've so recently crossed into this reality, I'll try to keep this explanation as simple as possible."

"Simple is good," I said, attempting to smile, but the churning unease inside me made it hard for me to relax.

"Very well. Mind you, this is all supposition, as I haven't had time to research what actually occurred. But to my understanding, the reality we're in is an altered reality, one where Earth inhabits Ceres—and consequently discovers cerecite—much sooner than in the reality you and I come from."

"Meaning what?"

He shrugged. "That's what we'll need to find out." He glanced behind him. "I think we'll start searching to the east. I spotted an antenna down a path leading that way. We may be able to find one of this world's station generators."

Station generator. If they had station generators here, it meant they must have also built a civilization. Fernoulli held out his hand, and I took it. Dizziness made me stumble as I stood, but I breathed deeply and managed to steady myself.

"Careful there," he said, and I nodded my acknowledgment.

We started down a hill and found a narrow path covered in crushed turquoise stones that reflected the endless sky. The trail wound over hilltops and led to a silver antenna rising from the horizon. As I walked, the exercise helped me clear away the lingering fogginess. A million questions swam through my head. Did Morven and the others make the transition to the new reality? If so, where were they? And why was only Fernoulli here and no one else?

Maybe something about this new reality would help me piece together my answers. I paid attention to the landscape, and my ability allowed me to notice all the subtle changes. Not only was the sky a different shade, but there were no glowing boulders like in the former world.

"There aren't any boulders," I pointed out. "That must mean there wasn't an initial explosion like in the former timeline."

"Yes," Fernoulli acknowledged. "The implications of that are alarming, and it's what I feared. If there was never the first explosion that brought the shipwreck survivors through the portal and onto Ceres, that means this version of Ceres shouldn't exist at all."

"Yet it does," I said, confused. "And it's a more stable version. At least, it appears to be. The fresh air and the blue sky make it feel as if we're not even under a dome."

We crested a hill, and from this vantagepoint, the entirety of the shield generator station came into view—although it looked nothing like the squat, windowless structure built in the former timeline.

Here, the building was constructed as a glass dome. Modern and futuristic, it stood several stories tall. Gleaming glass walls reflected the greenery of the countryside. A single spire rose into the air from the building's apex.

"That doesn't look like any shield generator I'm familiar with," I said.

"No." Fernoulli scratched his stubbled chin. "It doesn't. Let's inspect it more closely."

I wanted to agree, but my nagging suspicions kept me from following him. "Fernoulli, wait," I said. "Why are we the only two here?"

He paused, as if considering what to say. "I wish I had answers for you, Harper. But all I can give are theories."

"Then what's your theory?" I crossed my arms. He had to know more than what he was telling me.

"You were the one who initiated the explosion," he explained. "Meaning you were the one in closest physical proximity to it. I was also close, as I managed to make it to the north generator shortly before the explosion."

"So, you're saying being close to the explosion sent us through more quickly than anyone else?"

"Perhaps." He spread his hands. "As I said, they're only theories."

"Yeah." A tingling wave of dizziness disoriented me for a half-second. Dots swam in my vision. When I regained my balance, Fernoulli had his hand on my elbow.

"You look pale," he said. "I worry your body isn't dealing well with the shift. Let's get to the shield generator. Hopefully we can find a place for you to rest there."

I managed to follow him down the hill and toward the glass structure. It towered over us by the time we reached the entrance, which was a set of glass doors that lifted as a we approached. A white void spanned inside, and nerves twisted through my stomach. What kind of place was this?

We'd shifted reality, but what had really happened? What sort of world had we stumbled upon? We'd thought we could play Gods, and now we were about to see what we had created from our tampering.

Fernoulli led the way, and I followed him into the white void of the shield generator.

33

I blinked, and we were inside the station, although I didn't remember how I'd gotten there. Dizziness made the room spin around me. I held out my hand for balance, managing to grab the edge of a table. Its surface was cold and smooth like polished marble. The solidness grounded me, and I took deep breaths as thoughts crowded my mind. *What kind of world is this? Is it even real? Could I be dreaming?*

I clenched the table's edge.

Scanning the area, I tried to get my bearings. Everything in the room gleamed white, from the floor to the furniture carved from smooth stone, all the way up to the ceiling which soared several stories overhead. A gray-blue glow surrounded the items in the space, although other than the screens ringing the room, I saw no other light sources. The benches and tables were recognizable, but other components baffled me, and I had no idea of their purpose.

"Are we sure this is a shield generator station?" I asked Fernoulli.

"It may be different than what we're used to in our reality, but I suspect its function is the same."

I shook my head in confusion, then walked to a screen

overlooking the countryside. It was similar to the stations I knew, resembling a shimmering window that I suspected could be shifted to reveal different parts of the planet. In front of the screen, a desk protruded from the wall. A white stool sat at the interface, and I stood beside it as I studied the tabletop in front of me. Nothing looked discernible on the flat, cream-colored surface. No keys or blinking lights, nothing that could have resembled a keyboard, but when I sat on the stool, the desktop lit up. Unfamiliar words written in glowing blue letters scrolled over the smooth surface.

Fernoulli stood beside me. His eyes shifted as he studied the words.

"Do you understand this language?" I asked.

"No."

I touched one of the words, and the scrolling stopped. The letters rearranged, creating different configurations, some written in odd characters. When the word MAP appeared, I touched the word. On the windowlike screen above us, the scenery transformed, showing a glowing orb.

Roads and cities dotted the globe as it slowly rotated, until I spotted a recognizable name.

"Ithical," I breathed in awe, pointing to a glowing dot where a grid of motorways crisscrossed. As I spoke the word, the image zoomed in. A tower rose at the city's center. Its flowing waterfalls and hanging gardens filled with me a sense of familiarity. Relief flooded through me. This, at least, was something I understood. "It's the palace. It looks the same. This is a good sign. If we can travel there, maybe I can find Morven."

"Yes, but we'll need to use caution. We may be stumbling into a world where we're completely underprepared."

His words struck me in a way I hadn't expected. I tried to wrap my mind around this new reality and its implications, but the overpowering feeling of being an alien in this world overrode my rational side.

What about Morven? When we'd shifted the timelines, only Fernoulli and I had transitioned from one world to the next. What did that mean?

That the Morven I knew didn't exist anymore. That if I met Morven Tremayne in this reality, he wouldn't be the person who I'd fallen in love with, who had vowed to marry me. He wouldn't even remember me.

The realization came with crushing weight. A clammy sweat coated the palms of my hands.

Maybe I'm wrong. Maybe Morven had made the transition to this world just as I had. But that queasy feeling inside wouldn't relent, and I knew—deep inside me, I knew—that the Morven I loved was gone.

"Harper," Fernoulli's words cut through my torturous thoughts. "What's the matter?"

I swallowed the lump in my throat before answering. "Did you know?" I asked, my voice quiet enough to be a whisper.

"Know what?" he asked, his brow knit with confusion.

"Know that we're the only two who made the transition. Know that everyone else who belongs to this world is here, but not the same."

He didn't answer, and his eyes lit with a flicker of measured calculation.

Yes, he knew. At least, he must have suspected it.

"Why didn't you tell me?" I asked, pleading with him to make sense of this reality.

His shoulders slumped, and he knelt to be eye-level with me. "I wasn't sure how you would take the news, Harper," he spoke softly, apologetically. "You're attached to Ceres and its people, but this was never your world, nor is it mine. Those who come from this world will have changed, as will those who come from Earth. But you and I are wanderers. Originally from Earth, but a part of it no more. We have no place in this universe, just as we had no home in the last."

That lump in my throat grew larger at his mention of

home. I'd been so focused on Morven that I'd forgotten what might have happened to my life in Kansas—and my dad. Who was he now? Would he even remember me? Was there someone on Earth who was like me but not? Maybe she was a better daughter than me. Maybe she hadn't abandoned her father like I had.

I rubbed my temples, my fingers cold against my too-warm forehead.

Fernoulli placed his hand on my shoulder, and although I didn't know him well, I was at least thankful that he was here with me. I hadn't even considered if he had a family. Since he'd said he left his home, had he left them, too? If he had indeed traveled from the future, he must have left his first family behind, and since he'd recently crossed through one reality to another with me, had he lost his family once again?

"We can make this right," he said, his voice resolute.

"How?"

He focused on the image of the capital on the screen. "We'll find our answers there. When I first crossed from what you perceive as future Earth to our current timeline, contacting other people helped to realign my reality. I was having symptoms similar to yours. Dizziness and disorientation. Hallucinations, even. But making connections with the people of the current timeline helped to cement my place in it. My symptoms stopped soon after that. I suspect you'll need to do the same. If we can connect with the people of this reality, we'll be able to make sure it's aligned."

"Aligned?" I asked. "What do you mean?"

"Think of our realities as art pieces. After you paint a beautiful picture, could you ever recreate every detail with exact precision in the next piece? Could you ensure every brushstroke were the same as in the first? Or would each attempt fail?"

"Most likely, yes," I answered. "Even if you painted the

same picture a million times, recreating every stroke would be nearly impossible. Except for a computer, maybe."

"Yes, but we're not talking computers. We're organic. When we shifted realities, we painted a different picture. Since I've crossed before, I'm able to handle the symptoms. Since the people living on this planet have always been here, they won't notice the symptoms, either. But you're different. You're originally from Earth. Ceres, in essence, was a new reality for you. But you didn't have enough experience in the previous world to make sense of a new one. That's why we need you to contact this world's original inhabitants. Once you can align their reality with yours, the more this new reality will make sense."

I rubbed my forehead. I felt like I was being asked to understand a foreign language when I only had a basic grasp of a few words. All I knew was I needed to find Morven. Everything would fall into place once that happened.

At least, I hoped.

I studied the image of the tower-like building on the screen. What if Morven was there right now?

"We need to get to the capital," I said. When the words left my mouth, the screen morphed, showing the field outside. Twin glowing lines appeared, cutting across the landscape like glowing ribbons of light. A white, bubble-shaped vehicle also appeared as if from thin air, sitting on the still rails. By speaking the words, the computer had conjured my request.

I rubbed my eyes as I stared at the screen. "Unbelievable," I muttered. "I don't know if I'll ever get used to this world."

Fernoulli only smiled. It was a look filled with familiarity, as if this world were closer to his home than mine.

34

Warm light surrounded me, helping to calm my racing heart. I sat inside the vehicle as it raced over the countryside without a bump, like we were flying. Pressing my hand to the glass, I did my best to root myself in this new reality, but all I saw was strangeness everywhere I looked. The fields—once covered in grass too green to look real—were now cultivated into rows of trees. Bunches of blue-green fruit hung from branches. Robotic creatures with four arms zipped down the strips, although I only got a brief glance as the vehicle zoomed past.

"They're growing plants here," I mused. Cade would have been over-the-moon ecstatic to see it. From the hue of the blue-green fruit, the plants must have been engineered from cerecite. In the previous reality, Ceres had a complicated system of deriving plants from cerecite; they hadn't yet learned to manipulate them into organics that could spontaneously reproduce.

It wasn't hard to imagine Cade in charge of such a project. Maybe in this world, if he hadn't spent most of his life protecting the gateway, he would have had more time to make agricultural developments. Even so, my heart gave a painful squeeze at the thought of losing the Cade I'd once known—a Cade who didn't know me.

We sped past the fields and crossed over a river, then towns dotted the landscape, and soon we passed two-and-three story buildings built of aquamarine cerecite that sparkled in the afternoon sun. The vehicle slowed, and as we crossed a bridge, the capital city of Ithical came into view. With the sky tinted such a vibrant blue, all the buildings and their facades had transformed. They had once reflected a purple-tinted sky, giving them a grayish appearance. Now, the towering structures reflected nothing but brilliant blue, which transformed the city.

At the city's center rose the capital. I caught my breath at the sight of the tower rising above all the others. Although its dimensions were the same, the reflection of the sky made the stones sparkle. The cascading waterfalls glittered with more depth than before. The flowering plants bloomed with brighter colors. It was as if the previous reality had been dimmed by the shield, and now I was seeing it for the first time as it was meant to be.

"It's breathtaking," I whispered, marveling at the scene outside, which could have been a painting.

A painting, I mused, remembering Fernoulli's words. It seemed this world could have been an elaborate painting. As the thought crossed my mind, the dizziness bent the world around me. My stomach lurched as if I were on a rollercoaster. I squeezed my eyes shut and grabbed the edge of the seat.

"Harper," Fernoulli's voice cut through the dizziness. When I opened my eyes, we stood on the steps of the capital. The portcullis overshadowed us. I allowed the sounds of passing vehicles and chatter of people to bring me back to the present.

"You were out of it for a minute there," he said.

"Yeah," I answered, rubbing my forehead. "I don't even

remember getting out of the vehicle." I leaned against one of the pillars. "How long have we been standing here? The last thing I remember, we were driving."

"We left the vehicle nearly five minutes ago. Your symptoms are getting worse," he said.

"Great," I mumbled under my breath.

"We need to get inside." He took me by the arm and guided me toward the doorway. I allowed him to lead me inside, only acknowledging in passing the elaborate tapestries and marble floors. The palace, at least, looked unchanged except for the light streaming through the windows. It was now a more brilliant shade that seemed to light up the whole palace in its glow. Only a few servants wearing palace outfits passed by, and none gave us more than a cursory glance in our direction.

The guards, which had been a constant in the previous reality, were only present in a few areas, and most didn't pay us much attention. What had happened to cause this reality to be so different? I could only surmise that problems with the miners had improved, and if there was a gateway leading to Earth, how had they kept it protected?

Perhaps there was no gateway?

My heart gave a painful thump at that thought. But there had to be a gateway. Otherwise, how had the immigrants gotten here in the first place? Dizziness made my head spin at my escalating thoughts, and I pushed away my doubts and fears to focus on the present.

Voices echoed from the banquet hall ahead, and Fernoulli and I made our way toward it. I wasn't prepared for the vast crowd when we entered the room. Every inch was packed with bodies. People were shouting and clapping. Some stood out in the hallway as there wasn't much room left inside.

I craned my neck to get a look at the dais, but only saw a sea of people.

"What's going on in here?" I asked a woman nearby. She gave a gentle smile, her eyes filled with excitement.

"We're waiting for the prince to arrive," she answered, her accent hinting at a Scottish brogue.

"Waiting for him to arrive for what?" I asked.

"For the wedding, of course." Her smile widened, and my heart sank. "Can you believe he's finally marrying Princess Vevina?"

"No," I went quiet and shook my head. "I can't believe it."

I pushed my way forward, through the sea of bodies, until I got a view of the dais. One thought nagged me more than the rest. In the previous reality, Morven and Vevina had planned to marry at MacKinnon Keep. They had said it was a symbol of uniting the people rather than enforcing the idea of the monarchy. But now, in this reality, what had changed to make them wed here?

Queen Tremayne and a few of her advisors were currently seated in thrones on the dais. From the corner of the room came the stirring melody of a viola, and the room quieted. I wasn't sure what to expect from a wedding on Ithical in this reality. One thing I knew—I wasn't prepared to watch Morven marry Vevina.

We'd been so preoccupied with saving Ithical, I'd put the wedding at the back of my mind. Honestly, it hadn't seemed real. Even Morven and Vevina hadn't taken it seriously—not really. But now? The Morven and Vevina I'd known were gone, replaced with strangers. Perhaps in this reality they'd fallen madly in love.

My heart was pounding so fast, I had to take deep breaths to keep calm. *I should leave*, I said to myself. How could I possibly stand here and watch? Torture would have been easier than this.

I turned to go, but the bodies packed behind me had become immovable. Everyone focused forward. As I tried to move my way through, a woman shot me a dark glare. I ignored her and continued my pushing until a man stopped me.

"Whatever are you doing?" he said in a thick Scottish accent. "The wedding's about to start. There's no going back."

As he spoke, the music grew louder, and I was forced to stand and face the dais.

George MacKinnon emerged from the curtain behind the dais. He wore a dark blue kilt and a plaid tartan across his shoulder. A golden scabbard hung from his belt, and the hilt of a tarnished sword peeked from the top. He stood tall, with his chest puffed out, his red beard trimmed neatly, his eyes focused forward and filled with pride.

A few more people came through a gap in the curtain and stood in a row behind him. I recognized Vevina's grandparents. When Morven walked onto the dais, I wasn't prepared for the tidal wave of emotions.

It was him!

He looked no different from the man I'd known before, the man I'd given my heart to, the man I'd promised to marry. He stood beside Vevina's father, his dark hair combed straight, his posture stiff, as if he were uncomfortable being in the spotlight. He wore black except for the green sash across one shoulder.

Morven! I wanted to yell and rush to him. But all I could do was stand and watch as Vevina emerged from behind the curtain.

She wore a silk pink dress without lace or frills. The fabric fell in loose folds around her slim frame. A wreath of delicate flowers crowned her head, and she wore her auburn-red hair in braids that encircled her head. She was lovely in every sense of the word, yet even from this distance, I could see the slant of her lips, the crease in her forehead, the sadness radiating from her. No amount of flowers and silk could mask the unhappiness on her face.

Or was I only wishing she were unhappy? Perhaps I was only hoping this was a disagreeable marriage. That maybe there was still a chance—no matter how infinitesimally small—that I still had a sliver of a chance to make Morven remember me?

When she reached Morven's side, the two clasped hands. Her father's voice boomed around the room. I couldn't pay attention to his speech, something about obligations and duty.

As I stood watching helplessly, my heart twisted in knots. It occurred to me that the timing of my arrival hadn't been an accident. When we'd shifted the timelines, I could have easily arrived after the wedding. But I hadn't. I had arrived now. Why?

Was it because this was a pivotal moment in time? The union between Morven and Vevina would mean more of the same monarchy, the same system of government, the same stifled system of education and ignorance. Yes, this world had made more progress than the last, but did they know the truth of their place in the universe? Had their technology allowed them to leave this world and explore the stars?

I didn't have the answers. All I knew was that since I'd arrived at this moment, there must have been a greater purpose in it. And if there was, then it meant Morven and Vevina weren't meant to be together.

Fisting my hands, I tried to bolster my courage, but the fear of what I was about to do caught me tight around the throat and tried to squeeze out every last ounce of my bravery.

No, I chided myself. I can't give in to fear.

I was here at this moment in time for a reason. It was no accident I'd met Morven Tremayne and fallen in love with him. We were meant to be together. I knew it more than anything. It was a truth that I knew deep in my heart and through the depths of my soul. We were meant to be together, and not just because we loved each other. It was because together, we would make sure this world became what it was meant to be. If we met our combined potential, then Ceres would do the same.

But how was I supposed to do that? Was I supposed to run up to the dais and shout my undying love for him? A person who believed me to be a stranger? I would get hauled away for sure and locked into a dungeon cell.

If running up on the platform wasn't an option, then what was? As the ceremony continued, my heartbeats quickened. Even so, I couldn't think of a single thing to do to stop the ceremony without being dragged away. My eyes roved to the corner of the dais, where guards waited with pikes held at the ready.

Even if I did make it up to the dais, what would I do? What could I possibly say that would convince Morven that we had fallen in love in a previous reality? That he was making a mistake by marrying Vevina and he needed to marry me instead?

It all sounded ludicrous. Maybe shifting realities had caused me to go insane. I couldn't help but force a nervous laugh.

I'm not insane, I chided myself. But I did need a plan. I hadn't come all this way just to fail.

A hand rested on my shoulder, and I turned to see Fernoulli standing behind me.

"Just go to him," he nudged. "He'll sense the truth in your words, even if he doesn't remember."

"How do you know?"

He only shook his head and didn't answer. A twinkle lit his eyes, and it was only now that I realized how similar he looked to my father—his eyes the same color of soft caramel brown, his wrinkles like deep furrows that hinted at his wisdom.

I took a deep, cleansing breath. On the platform, George MacKinnon was ending his speech. If I didn't act now, it would be too late. I took a step forward, and once I did, my resolve strengthened. Moving forward after taking that first step became easier. Once I reached the dais, I took the stairs to the top, reminded of that first day when I'd met Queen-regent Tremayne. My nerves had been bad on that day. Now they were unbearable.

The guards shifted their gaze to me as I approached Morven and Vevina. Their stunned faces meant I must have caught them by surprise. They weren't sure what to do as I quietly approached the prince from behind. From this angle, behind the rows of nobles lining the platform, I doubted many of the onlookers noticed me.

I took another step toward Morven, and he finally glanced in my direction. As he did, the air escaped my lungs. His eyes met mine, and he searched my face, as if he knew me, but didn't understand why.

"Morven," I said his name quietly.

"Who—" he started when rough hands grabbed me from behind. The guards tugged me backwards, but I dug my heels into the floor.

"Morven," I repeated. "It's me. It's Sabine!"

He made no reply. His eyes shifted from me and then to Vevina, as if asking her if she recognized me.

"Don't you remember me?" I asked with a laugh, as if this whole situation were somehow laughable. In a way, it was. The absurdity of it felt like a cosmic joke.

The guards tugged me more forcefully, and my chance at reclaiming Morven started slipping away. But I felt certain he recognized me, even if he'd lost his memories. What could I possibly say to make him understand?

Perhaps there was nothing I could say.

An image of Morven standing over a spaceship came to me. He had just discovered his former self, Isaac, sitting in the cockpit. He'd touched the corpse's hand, and some of his memories had returned.

"Morven," I repeated for the third time, then ripped my

arm away from one of the guards. I reached for Morven and managed to grasp his fingers. As our skin connected, my thoughts exploded in fireworks of brilliant light. Every memory I had of him came in a burst of colors and a cacophony of sounds. The touch only lasted a moment, although it could have been more than a year as each memory spiraled like lightning bolts through my head.

Morven stood with a slacked jaw as the guards pulled me away and toward the curtain.

"Stop," he called, his voice sounded as desperate as I felt. The guards held still, though they didn't release my arms.

"Sabine?" When he said my name, I knew he remembered. He'd experienced the same memories when we'd touched.

My pulse raced so fast, I wasn't sure how to answer. "It's me," I finally said.

He held out his hand. "Show me," he said in his commanding voice, and I was compelled to reach forward and take his hand in mine.

Unlike before, the room wavered around us. We stood firmly clasping each other's hand as the room shifted. The people faded, and the room around us disappeared. The light grew so intense I had to close my eyes. Wind spiraled in a tornadic wail, threatening to deafen me.

What's happening? I wanted to scream. But my thoughts got caught in the whirlwind, and all I could do was hold to Morven's hand in a death grip. He was my lifeline to reality, and I wouldn't let go.

Perhaps I had made a huge mistake in coming here to find him. Maybe by doing so, I'd ripped the fabric of reality.

But as the wind settled, I started to see patches of green around us, and above us, the brilliant blue sky, breathtaking in its simplicity.

It wasn't a mistake, I repeated to myself until we stood once again on solid ground, and the sun beat down on us.

We stood in an empty field, on top of a hill overlooking miles of lush green grass.

My eyes met Morven's, and it was at that moment I knew I'd made the right decision. His warmth surrounded me. His knowing smile gave me hope that all had been restored.

He knew me. We were meant to be together. And this was only the beginning.

35

"I want to show you something," Morven said as we drove our velocipedes up the hill. He'd been secretive the whole way here, and I couldn't guess at what he possibly intended to show me. It had been two years since I'd touched him on the dais and our world had transformed.

We'd learned that my presence had shifted reality in slight ways. For one, there was no sign that Vortech had ever existed. It came out that Morven and Vevina had never been promised to each other, and Morven and I had taken that as a sign to move forward in our relationship. We'd married a month afterwards in a small ceremony at the palace. Since that day, I'd vowed to spend my life helping Morven return Ithical to its full potential.

"What's this?" I gasped as we crested the hill. A half-built house sat on the hilltop. Robots zipped from piles of lumber to the work site, moving like ants. I still wasn't used to the sight of robots, but I'd learned that they were commonplace in this new reality, and it was something I had come to accept.

Morven flashed me his secretive smile as he got off his bike. I hobbled off my own bike, my pregnant middle throwing me off balance. Nine months of pregnancy had taught me that separating reality was a cakewalk compared to never-ending morning sickness and unbearable heartburn. Our baby boy was due to come any day now, and my anxiety at being a mother was enough to keep me awake all night.

Morven took my arm and guided me toward the half-built structure.

"I know you've been concerned about raising our son at the palace, so I've come up with a solution. This is going to be ours." He motioned to the construction site. "Do you recognize it?"

I looked from the house to the robots, then calculated the dimensions and layout. "It's my old house in Kansas, isn't it?" I asked quietly.

"Pretty close to it," he said. "I had to guess at some of the dimensions, but it will be as much like your house on Earth as you can remember."

It was hard for me to wrap my mind around everything that happened since we'd shifted realities. We'd been so concerned about saving Ceres, I hadn't put a lot of thought into my own problems. I wasn't sure I would ever again have a place to call home. It had seemed like such an insignificant thing compared to the survival of Ceres, yet it lingered at the back of my mind. An unanswered question, one that was important to me, but insignificant to anyone else. I wasn't even sure I would have a future, so I hadn't thought about anything past survival.

But being pregnant changed everything, and the only thing I truly wanted was a haven to raise our son. Standing here with Morven at my side, I stood in awe of his great scheme. "How long have you been working on this?"

He gave me that smile again—the one he reserved for me. "For a while, but I couldn't keep it a surprise much longer. I was hoping to show you when it was finished, but I think our boy is determined to come sooner rather than later." He smiled and patted my belly. "So, here it is. What do you think?"

I looked from him to the house, the woodsy perfume of new lumber hanging in the air. Sounds of pounding hammers and the hissing of robotic pistons echoed over the expanse of green fields. What sounds and scents would come from this home in the future? The scents of fresh baked bread and warm apple pies? Would our children feel the grass under their toes as they ran barefoot through the fields? Would they listen to the sound of rain on the tin roof? I could imagine Morven sitting with our family on the porch, pointing up at the stars, Earth shining brilliant blue among a billion pinpoints of lights.

Tears misted my eyes, and Morven hugged me close to him. His presence gave me a sense of comfort too difficult to describe. He kissed the top of my head. "I thought this would be a good compromise since we haven't discovered a portal back to Earth. What do you say? Should we consider this our new beginning?"

"I like the sound of that." My eyes roved up to a flock of birds soaring overhead. It was still strange to see so much life in this world. There were so many things that had changed after the realities shifted, and some things that still needed to change. Discovering a way back to Earth was one—but for now, I could wait.

"What about your life at the palace?" I asked. "Your duties…"

He shook his head. "Everything is different now, Sabine. Aunt Tremayne has given me permission to dissolve the monarchy and select a group of governors to preside over individual districts. The people will have the choice to elect their leaders. My role will be a small one. In fact, I doubt they'll need me at the palace much anymore, which gives me the chance to live the way I've always wanted. I'm building a university. Cade and Vevina have offered to help. They'll be married in just a few months, and they wanted a way to contribute."

He took my hands and stood to face me. The intensity of his presence was no different from that first day I'd met him. Some things had changed. But the important things remained the same.

"Build a life with me here," he said, his words deep and pleading.

How could I answer anything but yes? "Of course I will," I answered, those pesky tears creeping back to fill my eyes.

"You will?"

"Yes," I answered, my voice resolute, as if in this one moment, I'd finally found what I'd always been searching for. I'd hunted for the seven lies and found them. I'd helped to save Ceres from destruction. I'd discovered Morven and shifted reality once again. Now, with everything aligned the way it should be, it was time to start fresh. But until this moment, I hadn't believed true happiness would ever be mine.

Morven brushed a kiss over my lips, when he pulled away, I squeezed his hands.

"I couldn't imagine a happier future than one with you in it," I told him.

Smiling, he looped his arm around my back and pulled me to him. We watched as the sun crested over the house's half-built rooftop, the tin glinting in the light. I couldn't expect a perfect future. But I had found a world where I had a place in it, and I couldn't ask for more than that.

Morven leaned toward me. "Welcome home," he whispered.

THE END

ABOUT THE AUTHOR

Tamara Grantham is the award-winning author of more than a dozen books and novellas, including the Olive Kennedy: Fairy World MD series, the Shine novellas, and the Twisted Ever After trilogy. *Dreamthief*, the first book of her Fairy World MD series, won first place for fantasy in INDIEFAB'S Book of the Year Awards, a RONE award for best New Adult Romance of 2016, and is a #1 bestseller on Amazon with over 200 five-star reviews.

Tamara has been a featured speaker at numerous writing conferences and has been a panelist at Comic Con Wizard World. Born and raised in Texas, Tamara now lives with her husband and five children in Wichita, Kansas.

Shine

Raze

Never Say Reven

Into the Fire

Storms and Spirits